Forked Tongue

Jacob Russell Dring

www.jrdwriter.com

Contents

PREFACE

◆ ━ ━ ━ ━ ━ ◆

This book is not for everyone. While the military science-fiction genre has been a favorite of mine for so long, I've always tried to help the reader understand certain terms or things they might not.

This doesn't occur in *Forked Tongue*.

For years I've sought to write a comprehensive story that bends reality with extravagant fiction, while staying true to the tech-speak common in the world of soldiery. A book that a member of Special Forces might read without rolling their eyes, shaking their heads, or face-palming (too much). Something both grounded, and yet far-fetched. Something intense and violent, but also fun.

Forked Tongue delivers tenfold.

The lexicon implemented in this book came organically for me, over years of consuming content created by ex-SF. The purpose of this story is to entertain, while staying true to certain military practices, jargon, and exercise my reverent fascination with firearms.

Everything else a balanced journey of high-stakes action, horror, suspense, occasional humor, camaraderie, and even love.

"The difference between being a coward and a hero is not whether you're scared, it's what you do while you're scared."

Sergeant Jeff Struecker
Ranger Task Force
Somalia, 1993

"De Oppresso Liber" (To Free the Oppressed)

U.S. Special Forces motto

1

Dogs barked two blocks down. Relentlessly. A foreigner or tourist might suspect they knew something their owners didn't. Or perhaps they were just dogs being dogs. Irritable and noisy. Over-alert. But inside the teal-roofed house on the corner of Kost and Sosna, six grown men bickered about these same dogs. In their native tongue they argued whether or not the domesticated canids were privy to their own behavior, or someone else's.

Like a rival's.

Or an enemy's.

The men didn't have a long list of either. But they *did* have a list, and it was only short because of their locale. The village wasn't exactly a stone's throw from a larger population center. It was a thirty-minute drive to the nearest village, Anavgay, but a three-hour drive from Mil'kovo, the nearest urban center.

And the other 974 residents of Esso were generally well-to-do, civil, mind-your-own-business folk. They

1

hunted, worked, farmed, and contributed. They either raised families or enjoyed the single life in a way that citygoers would regard as fairytale.

Crime in Esso was virtually nonexistent.

Which was why the six men in the teal-roofed house were treading on thin ice-sheets of patience. But they wouldn't have to for long. It was almost midnight, and their buyer had insisted they meet at twelve on the dot. Their drive to the spot would take them hardly ten minutes. So, they'd leave early. Put the barking dogs behind them, and any suspicious villagers far in their rearview.

The men already knew that their closest neighbors were skeptical of their doings. Let alone their presence. They had only been in Esso for the past two years, whereas the bulk of the populace had a tenure of at least ten times that.

So long as the village itself, and its people, were unsullied by crime, the men wouldn't be harassed. Let them take their skeptical business on the backroads, in the moors well outside of Esso.

Which they had been doing, for the last fourteen months, and would again tonight.

Finally the front door clapped open with a loud, wooden *thwack*. Out stormed an annoyed hulk of a man, Hungarian by birth but raised in what his colleagues would call "the asshole of Siberia." István cursed to himself, spitting every few words, as he marched down the front porch steps and approached the two vehicles parked in the muddy gravel driveway. A waxing gibbous moon leaked argent light through thin clouds striping the night sky, almost as bright as headlamps cutting through fog.

For ten to fifteen seconds at a time, it illuminated the sparse front yard of the house, and their side of the muddy road, as if it were daybreak. And then a heavier darkness would return, scarred only by dimmer streaks of moonlight, and the streetlamp fifty feet from the end of the driveway, on Sosna.

István reached the pickup truck, tossing forty-pound duffel bags into the bed as if they were puppies. The *clang* of bulky items inside the bags ensured they were neither light nor supple. István knew that Arseni would give him shit for being so careless and rough with "the merchandise." To which István would argue that "half of it's German-made, can take abuse. Rest is Kalashnikov, never break."

No matter how sound this debate, he knew Arseni wouldn't cave. He was the leader of their pack, so to speak, and as such, even countering him wouldn't be wise.

Shaking his head, István returned to the house.

He brushed shoulders with Mikhail on his way back inside, glancing at the shorter and slimmer man with a sort of irreverent disdain. Mikhail was not small, but compared to István and the others, he was almost boyish. He waited until István had stormed back inside the house before he mumbled his disapproval. Toting two twenty-pound bags, one in each hand, he approached the back of the beat-up sedan parked diagonally from the pickup. He popped the trunk with some trouble, and then stuffed the bags into its depths. They made far less noise than what István had tossed into the truck bed.

Any idiot could glance at the bags, notice the small rectangular protrusions, and deduce that it was cash. Many, many bundles of currency. In this case, the U.S. dollar, because that was who their buyer was. It didn't shock them, either; they had sealed lucrative deals with Americans before, although by and large their most profitable transactions were with the French.

When Mikhail slammed the trunk shut, it occurred to him that the dogs had stopped barking. His brow furrowed and his head turned slightly in that direction. He mumbled, something along the lines of "vermin," and the clouds overhead glided past. Moonlight caught the intruder, splashing their shadow onto the car's back window, and his eyes widened.

Although his mouth dropped to alert his colleagues inside the house, no sound ever came out. At least, nothing of merit. The first four inches of a seven-inch Böhler steel blade had plunged into Mikhail's left carotid artery. As a crimson fan of blood sprayed the top of the trunk, the owner of the Adra knife sawed it to the right, opening Mikhail's jugular. When the serrations caught his right carotid, the knife's operator dug it to the hilt, and twisted.

The front of Mikhail's coat had been a burnt sienna. Like a pumpkin left in the sun for too long. Now it was black. Darker than the cold pines behind his house, or those from which his attacker had crept. His coat was black—not red, not burgundy, but *black*. There was so much blood; about eight-hundred milliliters, or two pints' worth. It had doused his jeans, too.

Finally the operator slid the Adra knife out of his gutted throat, and wiped it on her skintight black pantleg.

Her head turned to the right, a ten-inch-long braided black ponytail swinging to the left. She raised her right hand, clad in a fingerless glove, digits together, and darted it forward. Then she sheathed the knife in its hard polymer scabbard affixed to her torso rig. Even with a rough sheen of Mikhail's blood still on it, although she had successfully wiped off any obstructive strips of flesh.

From the darkness still swathing the opposite curb of the road behind her, two men moved forward on bent knees. Their shoulders forward, heads slightly dipped, and elbows crooked—the postures of trained gunmen, carrying automatic weapons. In this case, Special Forces operators, ex-MARSOC. Reva herself made three of them; and although they weren't Raiders anymore, it was no small feat for a Marine to receive that honor. To this day, the public knew of only two women that had ever graduated from MARSOC's elite ITC. She would've been third, except her records were expunged when Forked Tongue set their eyes on her.

Mikhail's dead eyes gazed up at her in a slack-jawed expression of confusion, pain, and terror. The fear of death. Something that his colleagues didn't possess; something that he once gravely envied.

Reva looked down at him, and tilted her head.

The automatic weapon in her hands was set to semi. Ready to deliver a fatal double-tap, if necessary. Its perforated ten-inch barrel lowered, muzzle aimed at the crook of unibrow above his nose. Waiting.

Her two teammates approached on either side of her, but slowed down.

Reva's rifle snapped up, the stock firm against her burly shoulder, and through a reflex optic she scanned the front side of the house. Silhouettes against yellowish curtains in front of square windows. A lamplight turning off in one room, then another, closer to the front door.

Behind her left shoulder, one of the two men approached. He drew her attention, and she noticed him glance at the dead body by her feet. She looked at him, shook her head. He practically sighed, his rigid posture slackening for a split-second. And then he erected again, and navigated around the backside of the pickup.

Reva's finger curled inside the trigger guard.

One down. Five to go.

The big five.

Her disappointment that the man she'd killed wasn't one of their main targets wouldn't imbalance her. She stowed it like another useless emotion—fear.

Forked Tongue didn't tolerate fear.

Reva's pinpoint gaze locked on the half-open doorway, through her zero-magnification optic, her booted feet seemed to move independently. In small, quiet steps, she moved to the right of the sedan, by its back wheel. Her knees bent to a mid-crouch, the horizontality of her rifle unchanging, but its exposure did. The barrel lowered just out of sight, below the windows. Through them, her own silhouette hopefully obscured by the passenger headrest, her eyes fixated on the doorway.

Their remaining targets were likely armed, albeit lightly. In Siberia, though, for gun-runners, 'lightly' wasn't to be taken…lightly.

This never slipped John's mind.

6

He had shifted behind the pickup truck, bending his knees a little more, reducing his robust profile behind the left taillight. John had wide, broad shoulders and a narrow tree trunk of a midsection. The snug black shirt he wore slimmed him in the night, but the BDU rig he wore, like the others, although minimalistic, made him appear bulkier. His rifle was a few inches longer than Reva's, and a little heavier, to accompany its higher caliber.

He eagerly loitered behind the truck, itching to put the 6.5 Creedmoor in his target's skull.

Nil, meanwhile, moved on swifter feet.

He could, at times, be just as nimble, if not agiler, than even Reva. He was about her height, few inches under six feet. It always made John appear as if a giant whenever Nil stood beside him; which wasn't to say that John wasn't, at 6'3" and 240. But Nil's size was often underestimated. Much like Reva was, as a woman.

Underestimating the dedication, tenacity, and lethality of a Forked Tongue operator was usually the opponent's last mistake.

John's left peripherals tracked Nil's arc without actually turning his head to watch him. Nil's naturally stark blonde hair fixed back in a quartet of braids, on either side of an otherwise bald head, and his matching goatee, became the only sign of visibility on him in the night. More so when the gibbous moon yawned its glow onto them from above, but presently cloud cover was dense, and they were cloaked.

Nil moved until he had entered a neighbor's front yard, about a hundred feet left of John. Then he slowly, quietly, approached the front porch from a perfect lateral

7

angle. Nil's expertise was close quarters, so he was inef-
fective at longer ranges. He would reach the property in
time, assuredly.

For now, the duo in front of the teal-roofed house
in Esso Village *waited*. Their patience an unrivaled vir-
tue.

The sound of bickering men and heavy footfalls inside the wooden house continued in spurts. Then came
the swinging and slamming of doors, drawers, and cabinets. Footfalls became louder; voices clearer—

Until the latter stopped altogether.

The first man exited the house, closely followed by
a second. He bumped into the first, which everyone recognized as Arseni Petropavl. His size paralleled John,
only bigger around the shoulders and hips. But that per-
manent scowl of a face was unmatched. He had stopped
abruptly on the porch to pause and look around, his nose
twitching. Had it been Mikhail that bumped into him and
not Nikolay Avacha, Arseni would've thrown the man
off the porch with a single hand.

Instead the two Russians glared at each other, their
brows almost level, and then they snorted and continued
toward the truck.

Reva and John kept their low profiles.

They breathed short and shallow.

It was a summer night, which in Siberia was still
relatively cold. But it was no colder than 48°F, just above
condensation. Their breath wasn't visible, and if it was,
their moderation and control kept it too thin to be seen.

From the shadowy doorway emerged two more
men, who they also recognized. István Balogh and Petr

Halvorson. The latter was the smallest of the four, although Reva and John were still waiting for their fifth and final target; they suspected he was still in the house.

Arseni cut a quiet whistle with his teeth against his lip, and a curt wave redirected Petr from the truck to the car. Petr nodded, almost skittishly, and headed to the sedan. He opened the driver side door and ducked in; when he shut it with a slam, and the car rocked on its chassis, Reva held her breath.

Don't do it. Don't start that engine.

When Petr did, she let out a collected breath but still held her position. If the reverse lights lit up, she was cleared to engage. And she didn't want to—not until their fifth target was visible.

István tossed another bag into the truck bed, this time far gentler than the first two. Given Arseni's lingering shadow.

John shrunk farther behind the tailgate. Had it been Arseni instead of István, John knew he'd be compromised. Arseni was sharper than a Kershaw obsidian blade fresh off the block, and didn't need the assistance of moonlight to spot suspicious shadows.

Nikolay entered the truck's passenger side, while John noticed, however faintly, Nil's approach far left of the front porch. He slowed to a stop, and knelt on the shallow, dry grass between properties.

As if mirroring him, any sign of movement in Arseni paused, too. He cut a fresh whistle from his mouth, this one a little louder.

Two seconds later, Arseni barked a name.

"Mikhail!"

Reva's lips moved to articulate the F-word, without speaking it. If this op went sideways in any fashion, she could already foresee a debriefing in which she received a strike against her record for neutralizing a target separate from the others.

It had been advised against under these circumstances. But if he *had* been one of their primary targets, it seemed like an easy kill. An unavoidable opportunity.

Just because John green-lit her to proceed, didn't mean the fault would fall on him. Forked Tongue prided themselves on individual accountability; fire-teams, especially. Three units—three points of action, operating as a team, yet capable of detached action, toward one goal.

A three-toothed cog.

Tonight, that ideology had backfired for her.

They *had* to mop it up.

When Nikolay cranked his window down and stuck his head out, he said something in half a laugh.

John's Russian was mediocre. Nil's was pretty good. Reva's was flawless.

"He went out for a smoke, eh? Maybe headed around back to help Alexei."

Even if John only picked up a few words, like "smoke" and "back," his ears perked up at the mention of Alexei. As in their fifth and final target, Alexei Zlazny.

That sneaky fuck, John thought.

He crouched to go lower, his weapon clearing the steel hitch below the pickup's back bumper. He aimed at Nil, keeping to the shadows about fifty feet to Arseni's right, John's left. With quiet taps, John communicated with Nil via Morse code and the laser sight attached to the rail of his rifle.

In the lingering darkness, Nil nodded more to himself than John, as he received the message.

Around back. Z. Move.

As furtively as he could move, while keeping low, Nil advanced between houses, slinking toward the backyard. Though moonlight remained untraceable out front, it was a little more generous behind the house. Nil paused at the back corner of the house, scarcely peering around it.

Meanwhile, Arseni seemed to accept this excuse from Nikolay in passing. He scoffed and waved, then turned around to head back toward the door.

A lot of things happened at once.

Arseni's suggested return inside was virtually unacceptable for them. Not with everyone else in one place, and Alexei soon to be accounted for. So his motion already spurred their itch to engage. And then, simultaneously, István opened the driver's side door to the truck. John's right peripheral illuminated with white lights; Petr had shifted the sedan into reverse.

Reva didn't need to see the reverse lights to realize this. She heard, in the silence marred only by the car's idling engine, its shift of gears, ensued by that distinctly higher whine of being in reverse.

The car might have moved an inch from where it was parked by the time she sprang to her feet. She erected to the car's right, enough so that her rifle would be level with Petr's head, through the passenger window.

She fired, and her unsuppressed rifle became the single loudest thing in the whole village.

Despite their approach to stealth, running a suppressor had been deemed unnecessary. They couldn't risk subsonic ammo against these targets, not because of range but muscle and bone density, and the possibility of needing to penetrate cover. So if they couldn't run subs, then a can would prove pointless—no gunshot, without subs, would be quiet enough for Arseni *not* to hear.

Still, she kept her rifle in semi-auto.

The ideal firing creed of U.S. infantry in any remotely tactical situation. Especially SF operators. Curt and accurate. Most operators could fire almost as fast in semi as in full-auto, while retaining better accuracy and clarity.

Two rounds shattered both passenger and driver-side windows. But only one caught Petr in the head, and it 'merely' grazed his face. The entire cartilaginous structure of his nose splashed the dash in a spray of blood. He screamed in pain and his feet reflexively stomped the brake. The car lurched to a stop before it got more than a few feet back.

Arseni had reached the door, but now spun to bear witness. Even for him, they moved so fast, and with such nimble violence.

John skirted left of the truck while István paused from ducking into the cab, cursing in Hungarian. Nikolay dug his hands into the truck's glovebox, as apparently he wasn't already armed.

At this range, John's 6.5mm hollow point had no

range to gather enough velocity to expand. It was un-needed, though. The bullet cut through István's lungs at almost the perfect angle, below his right armpit. The round penetrated the open truck door, and blood splashed the muddy gravel. István cried out in pain and staggered, but didn't go down.

Any man would've collapsed.

Just as Petr remained a threat inside the sedan, now fumbling for the Glock he had stuffed into the front of his jeans. Even as blood and fragments of cartilage dripped in a mucousy slop down his lips and chin.

John fired again, higher.

The silver bullion hollow point mushroomed on impact, the sheer force alone bursting István's skull. Blood, brain matter, and bone shards splattered the driver's window, inside the cab, and its roof. His body collapsed in a heap.

Nikolay screamed.

Arseni flung his coat back and drew a matte black Desert Eagle.

In this same breath, Reva dared putting her back to him, knowing John had his name written all over his next round. She leapt onto the hood of the car, and toggled her rifle to full-auto in the same instant. She squeezed the trigger for hardly a whole second; a dozen silver-cored 5.56mm bullets volleyed the windshield, riddling Petr's torso. Blood splashed the inside of the battered wind-shield and his body went limp in the driver's seat.

Arseni's burly trigger finger began its squeeze.

John's finished his own, first.

The rifle bucked against his shoulder, and a round

thundered out. The silver Creedmoor round caught Arseni's broad chest at an infinitesimal angle. The hollow point expanded beautifully, shearing tissue and splintering his sternum. Blood misted the night air, a split-second before the gibbous moon shed its light on the scene through parting clouds.

Despite the dripping red cavity in his chest, Arseni remained on his feet. He had only minutely staggered, and the heavy pistol in his hand had lowered, but not dropped.

Nikolay's right hand exited the passenger side of the truck, wielding a stainless steel revolver he'd excavated from the glovebox.

Moonlight caught it with a glimmer.

Reva's aim adjusted, like a stab. Her rifle put two quick rounds into his A-frame. Nikolay's head jerked back into the seat, the bowl of his skull a craterous slop of blood and brains.

She then crouched, boots squeaking on the hood of the car. Glass dust crunching beneath the soles. Her body swung around, aim redirecting to the front of the house. Just in time to watch John fire a second round into Arseni's body—*as* it shifted.

The imposing 'man' barely had a chance to sprout black fur from the follicles in his skin. His jeans began to rip as his leg muscles expanded, and his femurs swelled. Nails protracted into talons, and canines became fangs. Arseni's hazel irises yellowed like urine in the sun, but his metamorphosis was stalled beyond that.

So much could change in a lycanthrope as seasoned as he was, in such little time. Whereas someone like Petr, despite his smaller frame, would take as many as five seconds longer to achieve as much change.

Arseni's heart erupted in his chest when the silver 6.5 Creedmoor blossomed at a lethal angle. Half a dog-like whimper and half a man's scream stumbled out of his throat, followed by a ravine of blood.

Behind the house, Alexei shifted as he ran from an oil drum fixing to be lit up, toward the back porch. Nil bore witness, raising his submachine gun. A flash of claws and teeth achieving full length beneath the moon-light, met with the muzzle flash from Nil's compact weapon. Unfortunately, only two of his four shots landed—before Alexei's lupine form crashed through the backdoor. Glass and wood burst into the house, in his wake.

There was no hiccup to his momentum.

As he audibly tore through the house, Nil closed in on the back porch. Meanwhile, neighboring homes, though nearly a hundred feet away in both directions, lit up from windows and their residents spectated.

Out front, Reva stepped off the sedan's hood, ducked between the car and the truck, and confirmed Petr's death. Then Nikolay's. She proceeded to convene with John as they approached the front porch.

Arseni's body had fallen onto the porch steps, mid-transformation. Apart from some twitches, he was in the final throes of death. He had vomited gory bile onto the driveway, muddy gravel not absorbing the rancid odor.

John directed his rifle at Arseni's face, tics around the yellow eyes making it seem like he was winking at the operator.

Reva stepped forward, slouching her rifle in its sling with her left hand, drawing a Ruger pistol with her right, and in the same breath dumping two 5.7mm silver hollow points into Arseni's skull. It opened up on the porch, and he twitched no more.

"You always have to take from my fun," John said blandly, staring at her.

She failed to hide a dark smirk, and shrugged, before holstering the Ruger.

Inside the house, a loud crash followed by a painful howl. Then a huffing and puffing sound, which told John and Reva all they needed to know.

Nil had wounded Alexei, who had shifted. Nil's silver ammo was now burning Alexei's blood, possibly his marrow, depending on where the bullets struck. Knowing that Nil ran hollow points in his SMG, unless he switched to the shotgun, this likely meant expansion and deep cavitation. Resulting in far grander a pain for the lycanthrope than if a silver bullet or pellet had merely passed through.

Creeping inside the house probably wasn't Nil's wisest idea, but he pursued Alexei regardless.

He felt it his responsibility, anyway, for having missed half his shots at such a range.

The house's interior was mostly dark. And Nil wasn't about to go around flipping switches with the muzzle of his weapon, or risking removing a hand to do it. Then fumbling with a crap switchplate, or faulty wiring—

Besides, most of the furniture and lamps inside the house had been knocked over in the wake of Alexei's agonizing, frantic warpath.

The second Nil spotted the beast buck its way past a front window, sparse moonlight dappling its dark brown fur, he squeezed the trigger. A series of rapid single shots tracked Alexei through what was otherwise complete darkness. This time, despite the poor illumination, and the tension of being inside a house with a lycanthrope, Nil hit his marks. Each 9mm round opened up inside Alexei's body, the bulk of them center-mass. Two tore through and shattered the window, ten feet to Reva's right. Through it, then, Alexei's lupine body crashed, taking a chunk of the wall with him, too. He landed poorly, as even more silver stung his insides, including a ruptured lung and penetrated spleen; a wooden shard impaled his aorta from behind, spearing his broad torso.

Alexei choked on his own blood, clawed fingers curling in like dead spiders, as the life secreted from his organs.

"Exiting," Nil announced, and his two comrades relaxed in front of the door.

Nil emerged, the SMG slackening in his hands, its sling assisting.

"Well done," John said. He glanced over at Alexei, and then eyed the hole in the wall, then looked back at Nil and shrugged. "Not exactly clandestine, but well done."

"Job's done, ain't it?" Nil said, and puckered his lips. He even made a smooching sound, before trotting down the steps—giving Arseni's corpse a wide berth.

The two previously lupine bodies, Arseni only partially shifted when John executed him, were now completely human. No indication otherwise would be found by coroners.

Only the peculiar realization that everyone had been slain by military-grade pure silver ammunition.

"That it is," John said, sighing and following Nil down the driveway.

"I see you two lovebirds made a mess of things," he said, observing the bloodshed.

Down the street, the dogs started barking again.

"Cut that shit," John said. Reva walked beside him, and puckered her lips at him. He smiled briefly, but shook his head. He stared at the back of Nil's head as they crossed the road, and John's tone was a little aggressive. Sincerely. "If the higher-ups have any proof, beyond rumor, we'll get canned. And Forked Tongue is my life."

"It's all our lives," Reva pressed, staring at Nil as they continued to nonchalantly walk past houses on the opposite side of Sosna.

"Jesus, relax, nobody's here. What, you think one of these Serbs is a plant?" Nil shook his head. "Fuck's sake. Take a breather. I won't say anything if y'all wanna run around back and take a load off."

Nil glanced back at them and winked, clicking his tongue.

John shook his head. "Funny guy."

"I mean…" Reva said, shrugging.

A rare, big grin graced John's stubbly face, beneath his thick black mustache.

"Don't start, bitch."

"We could be quick, yeah?" Reva teased him.

They reached the dark treeline sixty paces behind the yellow-roofed house they had just passed. The stretch of woods was thinner than it looked from this angle, pines spacing apart the closer they got to the moors behind them.

It was a long walk to a pair of Linhai ATVs they would ride for about three minutes before reaching the makeshift airstrip where their private plane had touched down. The Eclipse 550, operated by a Ukrainian pilot and contact of Forked Tongue, was a four-passenger jet that would fly them to an airport in Tigil fifty-two miles north of Esso. Their flight time was a mere eleven minutes, and wouldn't be spent relaxing. But from Tigil, John, Reva, and Nil would find a far more comfortable flight back home. And home eagerly awaited them, in North Carolina.

"Listen," Reva said, after several minutes of walking in silence. Relatively speaking—their boots sloshing through the damp heath as they trekked across the moors. "I didn't realize that guy was a familiar. Had I known, I wouldn't have popped him separate from the others."

A few seconds passed.

"Doesn't matter," John said. "We mopped it up. Together. Nobody got hurt. Well…nobody that mattered."

Reva nodded.

"*I* wanted to stick somebody," Nil mumbled.

They kept walking. The quads were coming into view, parked by a copse of pines. Moonlight out this far was generous even when scant. No objects to steal the light. At their angle, the trees didn't deflect or absorb any of the moon's glow. The ATVs waited for them.

Fortunately, they didn't have to worry about the American buyers that Arseni's crew was going to meet with. There *were* no buyers.

Forked Tongue had feigned the whole deal.

2

Moyock, North Carolina
July 27, 2024
4:40 PM

Chatter was minimal. Even the smallest voice carried in the small auditorium as if on the swift wings of wind, a vortex of noise. And that would be disrespectful. Everyone in the room had nothing but reverence for the man standing on the stage, and the two people on either side of him, each about twenty feet away, by the exits. They stood with their hands clasped behind them, as if bodyguards. Their faces generally emotionless, unless the man on the stage decided to play some sarcasm, or try a joke.

John Aguirre wasn't the most humorous man.

But sometimes he tried.

That was more often Nil's role; it hadn't been assigned to him, it just came naturally.

Diarmid Nilsson currently stood to John's far left, or the audience's right.

Of the twelve people scattered in their seats, mostly toward the front of the auditorium, only three were women. Forked Tongue strictly recruited from upper echelon infantry, favoring those with experience in Special Operations Groups, like Rangers and Raiders—although some SWAT members with high commendations were occasionally selected. Even a few ex-SEALs occupied their roster. Women were simply too rare in these branches, which was one of the reasons why Reva was so revered by female trainees. And so intimidated by the men.

Among the present audience, and they had been sitting here listening to John for the past forty minutes, these three women periodically glanced at Nil. Ogling him, and he would sometimes humor their gazes. But he knew better than to entertain them more often than not.

The bulk of the audience had eyes for Reva, however, they wouldn't dare look at her for longer than a glimpse. Not for any other reason than John; it was no secret at the Forked Tongue facility in Moyock that they were a *thing*. Purely hearsay, of course, for the sake of their job safety and the company's rules against romantic relations between members. This didn't keep John from being an imposing menace, and Reva herself wasn't exactly a harmless butterfly either.

Standing to John's far right, the audience's left, Arevalous Bakhara never humored their gazes for even a nanosecond. She stared forward, blankly, during his presentation. Whenever he chanced some humor, she might crack the tiniest of smiles.

Unlike Nil, Reva had to ardently defend the respect she was given by trainees and fellow active members. She was almost inherently intimidating, thanks to her dark traits and angular features. She had her Armenian and Azerbaijan roots to thank for those. Rigorous fitness regimens honed her physique into something that most men hungered for, but also feared. She regularly exhibited her combat capacity on the mat in the CQB room, to trainees, once a week. More regularly, she sparred with other active members, women and men, as part of her routine.

John and Nil frequented the CQB room as well, albeit far less habitually as Reva.

Her defensiveness about her name was only secondary to her physical self-respect. Last November she had broken the arm of a trainee whose attempt to flirt with her became egregious, and just two months prior had gotten in a physical altercation with an active female member who taunted her with *"Arevalous"* while sparring. It wasn't until after their session, in the locker room, that Reva retaliated, after the woman threw it around some more.

Thanks to her tenure and a Forked Tongue's zero-tolerance rule of harassment, she wasn't penalized for either incident. If anything, Forked Tongue lauded her actions and used them as examples in their facility SOP.

Arevalous meant "the light of my life" in Armenian. Naturally, it was the polar opposite of Reva's personality and nature. Even in her softer moments with John, privately, the name never came up. It was a relic of her past, and much like people's respect for Nil's moniker, it was largely unused.

Nil's abbreviated nickname came about during his time as a Marine, before his graduation from

MARSOC's ITC. Despite his tendency to be comedic, he was a nihilist and often preached about the absence of an afterlife. He used this as self-motivation, resulting in the name "Nil." During his tenure as a Raider, although far from religious conversion, Nil became less grim about his beliefs, and more receptive of others. Though his credo remained, he wasn't pompous about it, but the moniker stuck in part thanks to his surname.

Nil had no qualms with it.

"John's just John," Nil had shrugged once, introducing their team to a group of trainees one day. "Boring ol' John. Half-white, half-Mexican, but one-hundred-percent Tom Selleck on steroids."

"Except he *doesn't* juice," Reva had insisted.

"Yet," Nil had muttered.

The group had a small laugh.

Outside of the auditorium, CQB room, armory, and gun range, the members of Viper Three could almost pass as regular people. But inside those rooms, during those hours, they were by and large some of the most esteemed, envied members of Forked Tongue.

At least here.

The Moyock-based facility was one of two in the whole world, the other stationed in Salem, Oregon. While the Salem facility oversaw ops along the West Coast, with their Headquarters in Portland, the one here had domain over the East Coast. Everything in between, and internationally, was dealt with on a proximity basis.

Teams at each facility were never compared to the other, as they often faced different threats.

In the six years of their active duty, Viper Three

had the highest number of ops and a superior record of eliminations. Or, colloquially, kills. These were not tallied by individual, but as a squad. Viper Three deployed, on average, twice a month. Most active fire-teams went on ops no more than once a month, and operators in training might see field action four times a year if lucky, after a required ten months strictly at the facility.

All the more reason for the trainees in the auditorium to heed every syllable that came out of John's mouth.

"For new operators, depending on your op, the Cage Trolls will provide reccs for your loadout. Right down to which optic you should have, if you should run a can, supers or subs, *everything*. You entrust them with these decisions, the same as you'd respect the words coming out of the Founder's mouth."

A few people in the audience smirked at the mention of 'Cage Trolls.' It was the casual nickname for the armorers at the facility, who pretty much *lived* in the gun-cage. Of the five people, two were women, and only two of the men were inarguably homely. They, unfortunately for the others, had prompted the cave troll wordplay.

"Now, for trainees, these aren't *just* recommendations. They're required. Once you've seen a few ops and have no strikes against your record, you can be more flexible with your gear."

A young man center of row four raised his hand. John pointed at him.

"How long was it before *you* were able to customize your loadout?"

"Three months. Five ops. But hey…I'm an exception, haven't you heard?"

A fleeting chuckle swept the room.

John cleared his throat. "Now. Who can tell me, which of the Dreaded Five are the *most* well-organized, armed, and funded?"

A few seconds passed.

A man with a snug blonde ponytail, far left of the second row, tentatively raised his hand. John pointed.

"Uh…w-what are the Dreaded Five?"

John rolled his eyes. "I went over that last week, didn't I? You should all know this by now."

He had even suggested they put up informative posters regarding their various enemies and advised tactics, around the facility, to help drive the point home for trainees. Unfortunately, this would be far too risky in the event of surprise visits by State Department officials to ensure that their compound was legally operated.

Only the higher-ups in the Department of Defense knew about Forked Tongue's true purpose. Certain immunities could be issued, but as any other PMC, the company was still subject to scrutiny from lower-level government eyes.

"I…I think I know 'em." A woman with a dark complexion said, half-raising her hand. She sat center of the fifth row. When John gestured at her and nodded, then held his hands behind his back, she cleared her throat and threw her voice a little. "Skinwalkers, vampires, reavers, lycanthropes, and imps."

John was wearing black cargo pants and a fitted olive green T-shirt that accentuated the burly niches in his chest and shoulders. When his hands moved forward to clap, there was a slight relaxation in his carriage that only the women in the room might've noticed, or in this case Reva. She tried not to ogle his backside.

"Bravo, Mitchell, bravo. Only one mistake, however. Technically two, but I'll let the 'imps' slide. Better that you didn't say *demons*." He stopped clapping, and his posture became stern again. "The other mistake may seem small, but with us, it's a big one. Forked Tongue is *very* specific about what we *call* these things. Our enemies."

John's gaze studiously swept the faces of those listening, and then noticed a sort of shameful acknowledgement on Mitchell's face.

"Care to amend your error?" John asked her, the tonality of his naturally deep voice lifting slightly.

"Um, yes, it's…it's vam-*peer*, correct?"

John nodded. "That's right. Vampyr. Singular and plural. But hey, rookie mistake. At least you didn't say *draculi*."

The audience chuckled.

"Seriously. I've been hit with that one before." John said, stiffly and unsmiling, but wide-eyed. "Like they're fucking cactuses."

Just when the trainees had started to stop laughing, they burst out again.

John turned to pace across the stage, and glimpsed a fleeting smile from Nil. When he turned around to pace toward the other end of the stage, he glanced at Reva. A telescope would be needed to spot the little smirk that had crept onto her face; or just John. He let his own crack

27

beneath the heavy black mustache, and then his expression went solemn again.

"Unlike reavers, their mutant feral brethren," he elaborated, "vampyr are highly organized, gregarious, disturbingly well-funded, and often have military-grade equipment at their estates."

He paused and looked in Nil's direction.

"Give us some stats, Nil."

Without hesitation, from where he stood off to the side, Nil spoke up.

"Vampyr are believed to compose at least twenty-five percent of the criminal underground in the United States, and as much as *forty percent* in the U.K. and Europe."

"Correct," John said.

Some of the trainees muttered amongst themselves in disbelief.

"Just because they're nocturnal doesn't mean they're any less dangerous or capable. They also have a high degree of influence on weak-minded humans, especially those who have criminal aspirations, or even want to be turned. These of course are called *familiars*—errand boys for vampyr, and sometimes lycans. Although strictly human and usually nothing more than a hassle, they can be instrumental in expanding their master's domain, often serving as daytime envoys. Which makes them all the more important to *us*, especially from a strategic standpoint.

"On that note, *never* underestimate a vamp stronghold. And if you ever see a mansion that doesn't look as old or archaic as most vamp estates, but it has gargoyle statues outside, it's *definitely* vampyr. Can anyone tell me why?"

Three raised their hands, but Mitchell did so with gusto. John pointed.

"They're known for using gargoyles like watch-dogs. A common misperception—apart from them being just ornamentation, or as run-offs for rainwater—is that gargoyles are strictly nocturnal. But really they can 'come alive' anytime, as long as the property is under attack."

"Abso...lutely...correct." John said slowly. And then he kicked into high-gear again, while still sustaining his audience's attention. "Although not themselves in the Dreaded Five, gargoyles are not to be trifled with. They're loyal to the death, not to their masters or owners, but the *building* they belong to. Vampyr take advantage of this, breeding them as pups inside a certain abode, so that when they're mature—a terrifyingly fast process, mind you—they assimilate, like next-level chameleons, to whatever their post is...stone, marble, brick, even adobe...and pass as mere statues to anyone else.

"But the second the property faces a threat, and it has to be graver than just a B-and-E, these gargoyles 'come alive,' as Mitchell said, or *animate*, and attack. Since they retain some of their assimilated material even after animation, killing them is no small matter. They're bullet sponges, but with the right penetrative caliber, even the biggest gargoyle can be neutralized in two shots."

John collected his breath, clapped his hands, and then opened them.

"Vampyr, on the other hand, lack the brute strength and ferocity of reavers—much less gargoyles, or the other Dreaded Five—*but*, don't let that fool you. They can still be a massive pain in the ass."

A few smirks in the audience.

"And how does one go about neutralizing a vampyr?"

Three people raised their hands simultaneously.

"Say it together," John shrugged.

"Decapitate," they said.

"Correct. Preferably, after piercing the heart; this tends to slow them down dramatically. Any other wounds are null and void, unless by fire. Enough bullets to the head is comparable. Garlic and crosses are a joke to vampyr. Harnessed daylight is a myth, and UV gadgets are a fantasy. Only the sun's true beauty can melt a vampyr, so we at Forked Tongue like to use bullets to the head and heart, then a blade to the neck.

"The only exception to this rule are reavers, that is, a reaver can kill a vampyr without severing the head. Something to do with a viral toxicity in their DNA, when their blood crosses. Seeing as how reavers typically have bleeding gums, especially when they feed."

Some of his audience squirmed uncomfortably in their seats. It certainly wasn't a pleasant image.

Then a trainee raised his hand, a bit too eagerly.

John sighed. "Yes, Pickett?"

"Are vampyr ops less common for trainees for this reason? Carrying a sword, I mean."

"Per se," John said, half-assed. "There are far more serious conditions that make vampyr a less-than-ideal enemy for trainees. *But*, graduating from the CEC first *is* required before anyone can tackle a vampyr op."

Forked Tongue's training program for bladed weapons was called the Cutting Edge Course, or CEC. While kodachis were frequently used by female operators due to their size and grace, men typically carried a xiphos or falcata. Still, in order to graduate from the CEC, one had to train with all three, and master at least two.

Although Nil occasionally enjoyed the machete-like falcata, he preferred the kodachi, same as Reva. Whereas the Greek xiphos was John's unsurprising favorite. To which gladiator jokes would abound.

"And the difference between skinwalkers and lycanthropes, anyone?" John asked.

A few hands raised. This was always a good sign.

"This isn't high school," he said, tired of feeling like a teacher, or even a professor. "Sound off."

"Skinwalkers can shift into any animal," one of them said, "whereas lycans can only do wolves."

"Yes and no," John said quickly, simply. "Anyone?"

Another trainee rolled her eyes at the guy who had said what he did, and so confidently to boot. She went on to correct him.

"They can't shift into *any* animal, only predators. And only whatever they've interacted with before."

"More or less," John said. "Not so much *interacted with*, but…had a *calling* for. Hard to explain. Sociologists at the Headquarters in Raleigh still scratch their heads over this one. There *is*, however, one more thing to correct what Lee said."

A few seconds.

Mitchell raised her hand again, but immediately took it down and spoke up.

"They don't shift into *just* wolves," she said. "They're capable of both bipedal and quadrupedal mobility, but not quite like bears. They're more humanoid, and they're *big*. Even smaller men or women still have bigger-than-themselves wolf forms."

"Goddamn, give this woman a medal or something," John said, and clapped twice.

Mitchell appeared particularly proud of herself.

John glanced at the clock on the wall. It was five to five, but nobody in the room appeared itching to leave. And he still had a few points he wanted to run through, knowing he wouldn't see this lot of trainees until next week.

"If you guys don't mind sticking around for a few more minutes," he said, "I'd like to hit the nail on the head some more, far as the cage goes. Ideal builds for certain ops, and the like. Things that you won't have control over for some time; but it's not just about accepting what the Cage Trolls give you, it's about *understanding* your loadout. Knowledge is a weapon, remember. That's not just some tacky fortune cookie shit, it's legit."

John clapped his hands.

"So. It's about five. If you wanna call it a day, won't hold it against you. If you wanna kick it for a few more minutes and let me talk *at* you, stay put."

While John held his big hands clasped, a few trainees gathered their notes and got up. Ultimately four of the twelve made it to the exit by Nil. Among them one of the women, who all but fleetingly flirted with him before leaving. Opposite side of the room, Reva rolled her eyes.

The door at the end of the ramp from the exit, unseen from inside the auditorium, opened and shut with a reverberant clang.

John nodded and lightened up some before pacing again.

"Awesome. Glad most of you stayed. Now…no more questions, I'm just gonna lay it on you."

Reva didn't have to turn her head to know that Nil smirked at that, despite John's steadfast austerity.

"So let's get right to it," he continued. "Whatever the Cage Trolls issue you, as a trainee, that's that. Don't grill 'em about it. Two reasons; one, they're busy. Two—if you've gotten that far, it means you're about to deploy, and you're above second-guessing anything of that nature.
But that's why I'm here, to beat this info into you. Sure, you'll learn more about it from Kelley and Laszlo when you hit the range. But *I'm* the frontline, and it's best you don't volley them with stupid questions, as by then it's assumed that I've done my job well enough to weed out the morons."

A few smirks in the audience.

"Okay, so let's focus on your build, and understanding *why* a Cage Troll has made certain selections, based on the info they've received about your op. It all boils down to your enemy. Thankfully, the Dreaded Five don't comingle, apart from vampyr and reavers, which makes the cage's job really easy, and less of a mind-fuck on your part.

"We'll start with lycanthropes. As some of you may know, just last week my team went to Siberia for some sight-seeing. And let's just say those puppies weren't thrilled to see us. Fortunately, we were prepared. As *all* of you should know by now, the only fatal enemy of a lycan is silver. Not only is their blood allergic to it, but it hinders their cellular healing. This makes silver bullets lethal where lead or copper would not be; say you blast a lycan, in his human or wolf form, right in the heart with a nasty .50-cal—he's gonna go down, and probably take a minute to get up, but he *will* get up. Shy of obliterating the brain, or decapitating him, a lycan is invulnerable to non-silver rounds.

"Hollow point ammo is ideal when engaging lycanthropes, as the expansion effect creates tremendous cavitation, and since silver is less dense than lead, bits of it stick into the flesh like splinters. *However*, since no op is performed solo, it's ideal to recognize variables you're bound to face in the field. You don't want every member of your team running hollow points; say the enemy is behind cover—then they have the upper hand. Your HPs won't penetrate most materials.

"Now, I know I said no questions, but fuck it. Let's see how bright this lot is. Can anyone tell me how an operator would go about *killing* a lycan behind substantial cover? Without the use of explosives or fire. Sound off."

Two people seemed to have the answer.

They exchanged glances before one of them took

the initiative. To John's surprise, it was Pickett again, but this time nothing about his answer would have to be corrected.

"Silver plating," he said. "They would have to be running silver-plated ammo, ideally a non-pistol cartridge, like five-five-six or seven-sixty-two, whatever."

John nodded repeatedly.

"Precisely. Well said, Pickett. See. Silver-plated ammo would get the job done through cover, but of course only fatal if the bullets penetrated the heart or brain. Otherwise, they'd still inflict a great deal of pain, supposing the rounds passed through cover *and* the lycan's body. As a round would do without cover, but this doesn't nullify their potential, or make them comparable to non-silver rounds, just because they don't stick around like an HP.

"Last week, Nil and I ran HPs. But Reva's five-five-six mags had silver-plated M855s. Worked like a charm, penetrated a windshield and neutralized a lycan on the other side. Beautiful work.

"However, keep in mind, these specialist rounds aren't just spray-painted or dipped in silver nitrate. They're electrolytically refined silver-plated to avoid tarnishing and retain efficacy even after penetrating other surfaces."

John collected a few breaths as he paced a bit.

When he stopped again, he moved on.

"We talked vampyr and lycans. Let's touch on reavers real quick. As they are technically vampyr, the same rule applies with decapitations and natural sunlight. *However*, they can be far deadlier than vampyr given their feral state—no dialect, no sociality, and no motor functions. Their inability to carry firearms, much like cambions, doesn't make them any less dangerous. As evident in lycans and skinwalkers in their bestial forms."

John turned around and looked at the huge projector screen behind him.

"Now, I could very well load up some unpleasant images of reaver anatomy for you, including their abysmal mandible system and feeding patterns. But I'll spare you that reminder. Just try to remember—reavers have a much simpler internal structure than humans, or vampyr. Heart, lung, aorta. The big three. When they feed, the blood irrigates their system. Anything else ingested gets vomited. No other digestion. Which, frankly, is a *little* comforting, no? I for one would never want to even *think* about a reaver taking a shit."

Some chuckles.

"And you heard me. *Lung.* Singular. See, inside a reaver, behind a reinforced sternum, is the key to the city. Heart, lung, aorta. Penetrate that bone plate, destroy that fusion of organs, and you get a dead reaver. Considering that reavers don't travel rogue, and are typically found in packs of six or more, this is momentous."

Mitchell coyly raised her hand.

John nodded. "Yes, ma'am?"

"Is that plate of bone, the reaver sternum…does it take anything special to puncture?"

"Solid question. The vague answer? Yes and no. Yes in that a nine-mil or forty-five wouldn't do the trick; not even a few. That chunk isn't going to split apart with repeated pressure; it doesn't splinter. Not even the tip of my xiphos, with *me* behind it no less, will penetrate that fucking *rock*."

The trainees weren't completely foreign to how a reaver operated, but the detailed approach to neutralizing one was new info.

"Instead, the right AP ammo would suffice. The cage usually recommends Lapua. Ideally in .308 or 6.5 Creedmoor. Now, some people might call it overkill, but a black-tip .50 BMG never doesn't get the job done. Just good luck carrying one in the field before you've been active for at least three years."

After a couple of seconds, as John gathered his thoughts, Mitchell spoke up.

"Um, you *did* say yes *and* no, though."

"Right. I sure did. Because penetrating that sternum with the correct round isn't as easy as a trigger pull. You have to hit it at a great angle, head-on; sometimes even a follow-up shot is needed, to truly decommission that blood-hub beneath. And if your whole team is running .308s when you walk into a reaver nest, you're *fucked*. They're fast, like monkeys, and frenzied. Basically, even if you're able to manage a .308 or Creedmoor in full-auto, it'd likely be hectic and unideal. So one or two of your team will have regular rifles, probably SBRs since reaver engagements are never farther than mid-range, maybe even an SMG. These won't be running hollow points, but probably steel-core bullets or solid copper, for some added penetration, but at that point the idea is to *circumvent* that sternum, and bleed the trifecta of organs beneath it 'indirectly.' This would take one of two things—insanely good aim, or sheer fucking luck.

"Nil here could tell you, if his ego wasn't so god-damn big, that most of his own reaver eliminations were from dumb luck."

John turned to look at Nil.

He shrugged where he stood. "No idea what you're on about, John. My aim is *impeccable*."

John smirked. He faced the smiling trainees, and his face sobered.

"As I said. *Dumb* luck."

This got a smirk from Reva, too, however brief.

"Skinwalkers I won't rant about, because they're straightforward. Brain, brain, brain. Heart ain't shit. Sup-posedly, a skinwalker shifts because of some mental, subconscious, astral plane connection to the animal. Alt-hough blasting a heart with a .308 would falter a grizzly-walker's step, it won't put the fucker down for good. But a couple nines to the brainpan? Out like a light."

A few of the trainees were actually taking notes.

He appreciated this, too.

"Last of the Dreaded Five, and then I'll call it a day," John said, glancing at the clock. Fifteen after. "Cambions. For the uneducated, *demons*. Not a phrase Forked Tongue likes, given the discrepancies with scrip-ture and the general misperception of that term. Ironically, if you've ever dabbled in demonology—and I suspect none of you have—a cambion is a term for the offspring of a demon and a human. Gross, right?"

A few scattered smirks.

"While that isn't the case here, the name was as-signed because these creatures are almost like a hybridization of the demons we 'know' from the Bible, and even media, but also from interactions that only Forked Tongue…and its predecessors…can attest to."

A pause for his lungs.

"So, in a way, they *are* offspring of humans and demons. Or at least, human perception and the twisted reality that they belong to."

"I wish I'd just said that, Mitchell, I swear," John said, shaking his head.

She smiled.

"Generally speaking, though," he continued in a voice fit for the auditorium, "you'll rarely hear the word *cambion*. Although there is a known hierarchy of these creatures, including Centurions, Barons, and Dukes, *imps* are the main pawns. To our understanding, they are the lowest rank in the caste of evil-on-the-other-side. And just to clarify, if I haven't already—*no*. These things aren't from 'hell.' At least, not traditionally speaking. Which is another reason why we stray from the term *demons*. Because the ones *we* worry about, the proven ilk, exist on a parallel plane; imps can influence weak minds, much like biblical demons, but they're much fiercer, and very corporeal.

"This ain't *Constantine*. Not only can imps cross over onto our plane, they do it all the damn time. Typically only to engage *us*, though. They don't like exposing themselves to humans, or maybe it goes against some sort of rulebook we've never read. Aramaic isn't exactly part of the curriculum. But whenever Forked Tongue shows up to investigate a possession or the like, they won't hesitate to pop out and show those ugly half-skulls. While they *can* be very lethal, with behavior akin to reavers, they're not exactly bullet sponges, and go down easy. Imps, anyway; Centurions wear armor, and Barons are the size of polar bears. Fortunately, those rarely cross over. To my knowledge, we only know about them from the founders of Forked Tongue, illustrations and texts dating back to the late 1800s."

That was a tangent John had actually been instructed not to entertain. It was someone else's job to divulge the history of Forked Tongue to trainees. Someone far more well-spoken and educated on the matter.

"But *imps*. They're gaunt, ugly, and very mortal. Proof that good and evil exists, and that goodness *will* prevail, especially if it's a 55-grain M193 five-five-six."

Reva nodded proudly.

John wasn't grinning, but the sort of disgusted-yet-angry expression he wore, what the kids called "stank face," was his equivalent to a big, vigorous smile.

It almost unnerved the trainees, producing a stillness in the auditorium. And then his face nonchalantly relaxed and he asked if anyone had any questions.

A young woman in the third row reluctantly raised her hand. John looked her way, and then she lowered it before speaking up.

"What is *cab*?" She asked. "I…I've heard it thrown around the facility, mostly by active operators."

"Ah, yes. C-A-B, probably our favorite acronym at Forked Tongue. CAB stands for checks-and-balances. It's like a motto that acts as the antonym for Murphy's Law. It's probably Nil's least favorite concept, but for the rest of us who don't fester in a shell of cynicism—"

Nil smirked and shook his head, off to the side.

"—it's not just a phrase, but a belief system," John continued. "A sort of creed among experienced operators, those who have dealt with the Dreaded Five, but especially imps. And what does it all boil down to?"

John opened his arms and half-turned toward Reva.

She sighed and raised her voice.

"Balance," she said, rather commandingly. Facing forward, retaining her statuesque poise. "The reassurance that even the foulest, most violent and merciless enemy still has a weakness. A fault. A reminder that this world remains ours, and even the so-called immortal can be vanquished."

John nodded, lowering his arms. He puckered his lips briefly and shook his head.

"Beautifully put. You see…" He clapped his hands. The resulting sound was high and low simultaneously. The trainees still in their seats proceeded to lean forward. They were hooked; had he started to lose them toward the end there, moments ago, John had them again.

"Imps can 'peer into' our realm whenever they want. They don't *have to* expose themselves to cast influence, but it helps get their fucked-up point across. Or to taunt *us*. But…as soon as they physically interact with something on our plane, be it a human or as simple as touching an object, they're pulled from their realm, and anchored in ours."

"CAB," Reva declared, dragging out the A.

"Precisely."

Following a three-second pause of silence, some

41

clapping built from the trainees. Others stood and collected their notes with what John would like to believe was a hint of enlightenment on their faces.

"Thank you everybody for staying, and I look forward to seeing you next week," he said, backpedaling from the edge of the stage. "Remember, the facility locks up at six. Have a good evening."

They funneled out of the room, some giving John small nods or waves, others muttering casual farewells to Nil as they took his exit.

One woman, Mitchell, took the *other* exit.

She tentatively paused by Reva, to talk to her, but then resumed her pace, choosing not to. An uncertain relief came over her when she heard Reva say "wait up" and follow her onto the secluded ramp.

"Paula, correct?" Reva asked.

Mitchell nodded, her eyebrows raising briefly. Trainees weren't used to being called by their first names, especially by tenured operators—despite themselves favoring first-name bases. Only higher-ups in the company, older men and women who didn't go on ops, adhered to military tradition and went by their surnames.

For a trainee, especially in Mitchell's mind, it was a nice change of pace. And usually an immediate indication that the operator regarded them with more respect than deemed standard.

"Listen, you were great today," Reva said. "I don't normally volunteer compliments, but you killed it. I've heard, too, that you're an absolute beast behind a scope. Hitting sub-MOA at two-hundred yards."

Mitchell pursed her lips and nodded.

"Trying to do that at three."

"Keep trying. You hit sub-MOA at three-hundred yards with the .338 and you won't be a trainee for long."

Mitchell broke a full grin, but quickly wrapped it up. She thanked Reva for her vote of confidence, but then scratched an itch of a question.

"Um, I've been wondering, since John hasn't addressed it at all these past three weeks…"

Reva nodded once. She hoped Mitchell wasn't about to sully this nice back-and-forth with a personal inquisition.

"How common *are* long-range engagements in the field?" Mitchell asked, almost with a frustrated tone. Not with John, or Reva, but in general.

Reva relaxed some, and found herself even fonder of Paula. That dedication to the job, and the brazen pursuit of knowledge, was definitely a key to success with Forked Tongue. She hoped to hear Paula's name come off the trainee list in the coming months.

"Great question, and I might have to talk to John a little myself, urge him to discuss this next week, because it really is important. But I *will* give you a quick answer."

"Thank you so much," she said, clutching her note-taking tablet as if an attentive student. Essentially, she was. She just happened to be 29 years old with six years of commendable experience with Baltimore SWAT.

"Basically, the cut-and-dry answer is *rare*," Reva said. She took a breath, noted Mitchell's eager attentiveness, and decided to open herself up a bit, to John's role. "Of the Dreaded Five, which ones do you think would *benefit*—us, of course—engaging at a distance?"

Mitchell deliberated for all of three seconds.

"Well, the only ones that we'd be *able* to engage at a distance, successfully, are vampyr. And I guess lycans and skinwalkers, in their human form."

"Correct. Imps are never visible to us unless we're right there with them, and reavers…well, John already covered that today. Vampyr could be executed at range, but given their lack of physical prowess in closer quarters, and our CQB training, it isn't really necessary. Plus, they're usually not strolling out in the open. It typically comes down to the *benefit* of eliminating a known lycanthrope or skinwalker, at a safe distance. Keep them from shifting, eliminate the threat prematurely."

Mitchell nodded fervently.

A knock on the padded wall behind Mitchell startled her. She touched her chest and shook her head when she realized it was John. He'd peered around the corner, only his head and right arm visible, to the shoulder. He withdrew his knuckles from the wall.

"Sorry. Everything good?"

"Yeah, just going over some final thoughts," Reva said.

John nodded. He began to withdraw, while Mitchell glanced back at him, and then noticed a shift in Reva's face. Her brows raised and her dark eyes darted at Mitchell. John paused and cleared his throat.

"Mitchell. Uh, you were great today. Real sharp. Keep it up."

Mitchell lit up. "Thank you. It was a great lecture. A lot of information. None of it taken for granted."

"Excellent. Appreciate that." John nodded once

more. He glanced at Reva and gestured over his shoulder.

"I'll be out in a few," she said, then shook her head. "But don't wait up. Gonna hit the pads 'til seven or eight. Tell Nil."

John appeared mildly disappointed, but found it understandable. He nodded.

"Alright. Have a good one."

"Likewise," Reva said, almost insistently.

Mitchell stood there like an awkward third-wheel witness.

John left. Reva took a deep breath, the heave of her chest barely visible in the black fitted long-sleeve shirt.

"That man can be dense, I swear," Reva mumbled.

Mitchel snickered.

"Anyway," Reva said, and Mitchell perked up again. "Engaging lycans and skinwalkers from afar, in their human form—while ideal, is unfortunately seldom an opportunity. Lycans rarely socialize in the open; they're too paranoid for that. Skinwalkers, however— they do, as they're generally more free-willed than the other Dreaded Five."

"Wow. Thank you so much, Reva."

"Of course. I guess I kind of pulled a *John* and rattled off more than I intended."

"Color me grateful."

Reva smirked. Then she pursed her lips and put her hands on her lower back.

"Anything else?"

Mitchell glanced at her wristwatch.

"Um, I feel silly for saying it out loud, partly because it's just crazy they *actually* exist, but also because I've noticed they're very hush-hush around the facility."

Reva already had it in her mind, what she assumed Mitchell was talking about, but waited for the reveal. She also expected her to say the D-word, and not their actual name.

She wasn't disappointed in this.

"Dragons," Mitchell finally said, wincing as she did. "What's their deal? How are they not in the Dreaded Five, big as they can get?"

Reva took a deep breath.

"It's a thing of reverence, and yes, CAB." She smirked briefly. "Just remember—*wyverns*, not 'dragons.' Don't let anyone who isn't another trainee hear that word. Much like the classic vampire slip, much less 'demons' and 'werewolves.' Especially if you hope to excel here."

"Never again, I assure you," Mitchell said, sounding wholeheartedly committed to that.

Reva nodded. She didn't mean to sound like such a hard-ass about simple words, but was just looking out for Mitchell's best interest. Because, as John had pointed out, Forked Tongue was very thorough about the terms used for their enemies. It contributed to the strict organization and efficiency of such a program.

"Although a *type* of dragon, technically, the wyvern is the only known species still alive to this day." As she spoke, Reva subconsciously feared she was sounding too much like John-the-lecturer. "Whether others were ever active as far as Forked Tongue knows, is anybody's guess. But wyverns are so hush-hush because, as immense and dangerous as they can be, they're simply never the latter. Not to humans, anyway. They keep to themselves, and you'd expect something the size of an airliner to be noticed at some point over the last century, but they don't go flocking around. They're extremely reclusive, supposedly abhorring human civilization and avoiding contact with us at all costs. Instead they favor mountainous regions and expansive caves as their dens. While more common in Europe, there have been occasional sightings by operators along the Appalachians, Rockies, and Sierra Nevada."

"Wow, I…I truly had no idea about them. There really is so very little info available on real-life wyverns. I mean, you know, Forked Tongue has that big list of *all* the confirmed cryptids and myths that actually exist out there today, wyverns being on it…that unmistakable dragon-like figure impossible not to notice at first glance, even if they're more serpentine than what most people imagine…"

Reva nodded. "They're beautiful, in person. I mean, captivating but absolutely horrifying, too. If you could imagine being in a situation where one was threatened."

Mitchell's eyes widened.

"Have…Have you actually—?"

"No, no, no," Reva chuckled, shaking her head. "John and I, two years ago. We were part of a flyover in the Rockies, northern Montana, investigating a possible wendigo nest. We spotted a red one lumbering back into a cave carved into the side of a cliff, where the trees of the forest didn't quite reach. Didn't even see the head, just the wings attached to the arms, you know, tucked along its thorax. The haunches, and that tail. If you've ever seen a blood moon, like a true blood moon, it was *that* color. Shades darker along the joints; wing membranes like a burnt sienna. Gorgeous."

Mitchell's eyes were dazzled with intrigue.

"I bet."

"So…" Reva cleared her throat, fearing she was getting too lost in a nice memory. "Anything else? No pressure, one way or the other. Regardless, I really do appreciate your curiosity."

"Thank you," she chuckled a bit nervously. And then: "Actually, if I may…is it crazy to say that skinwalkers *shouldn't* be in the Dreaded Five? Everything I've learned about them pales compared to the other four."

Reva nodded. "Good point, actually. I probably shouldn't openly say this, because Forked Tongue is steadfast with that list, but yes…I wholeheartedly agree. While the guys and I *have* encountered some vicious skinwalkers in our time, they're usually reclusive and until threatened, civil. It's more the rogue ones that you have to worry about; most ops that tallied skinwalker deaths involved small rogue factions trying to stir up shit, often with lycans. Apart from vampyr and reavers, they're the only ones that comingle, and even then it's rare."

Mitchell nodded repeatedly.

"Is it true that lycans look down on skinwalkers, like they're inferior?"

"Oh, yes. Ironically, that's a two-way street. Most skinwalkers perceive lycans as vermin. Think about it; say you can turn into a bear, a jaguar, a wolf, and even a croc. But a lycanthrope can *only* turn into a wolf? It's also an inherently painful process, even if it doesn't seem like it to the more seasoned lycans. Whereas skinwalkers supposedly feel a form of ecstasy when they shift. Also, lycans are deathly allergic to *silver*—a natural metal. Sure, skinwalkers can be killed like any other human or animal, but that's the way of life."

"Yeah, wow, I…I'd never thought of it like that. So they're basically rivals, even when they *do* socialize. It's only business, then."

"Correct."

"Thank you. I really do appreciate it. I honestly wasn't expecting to get an addendum to John's lecture. You really should be up there, too."

Reva chuckled briefly, shaking her head.

"Spotlight ain't for me. Hell, even John hates it half the time. Or pretends to, anyway."

"Well, regardless. We're grateful."

Reva nodded, and offered her hand. Mitchell eagerly shook it.

"Shit," she said with a laugh, retracting her hand after, and shaking it.

"Sorry," Reva smirked.

"No, no. It's wild. You're an inspiration, in so many ways. Sometimes I think I'm focusing too much on my marksmanship, I know I could be better on the mat. Like, much better."

"Acknowledgement and awareness are the first

steps to change. Evolve in steps, you'll surprise yourself over time. In the end, I think most trainees have one true calling, and, frankly, they often lose a lot of progress because they try to do-it-all, as opposed to focusing on what they're naturally good at. For you, I think that's downrange. Achieve a sub-MOA at three-hundo, *then* sweat the mat."

"Wiser words," Mitchell said, clicking her tongue and shaking her head. "Thanks so much. Oh! Um, one more question, if I may."

"Shoot."

"You told John you'd be here 'til seven or eight. I…I thought the building shut down at six."

"Doors lock and programs end at six. This place almost never truly sleeps, though. Some of us, with tenure privileges, stay as late as nine sometimes. Hitting the pads, even the range. But only indoors. Outdoor range is closed for safety reasons. Some of the guys will even sit at a workbench and routinely clean their weapons with their earbuds in. Meditative, ya know?"

"Sounds almost like a dream. Maybe someday."

"You're young, healthy, sharp, ambitious." Reva shrugged. "Someday sooner than you may think. We've got active operators who have only been active for less than a year that exercise some of these privileges based solely on their clean record and consideration. These are rare exceptions, of course, but Forked Tongue lauds ambition and a respect for others."

"I…honestly don't think I knew that."

"Yeah." Reva sighed. "Sometimes the company,

and people like John, focus on sternness and even intimidation, over shedding light on what really makes Forked Tongue a family above all else."

"Well, I can't thank you enough for this talk. Like I said to John, I really don't take any of it for granted. I should run, now, before I get locked in here and become a laughing stock like Anders last week."

Reva smirked. "Good deal. Talk to you later."

Mitchell flashed one last smile before jogging down the ramp. The exit door clanged in her wake.

Reva had not been so talkative, even if it was solely about "business," with a trainee before. Not in years, anyway. It felt good, and some levity had been injected into her after standing there like a statue while John did his thing.

Now, she looked forward to hitting the facility's gym for an hour or so.

3

Having decided to skip showering at the facility—which wasn't to say she always did; Forked Tongue did offer great areas for that—Reva made a beeline home. She had changed into black fitness shorts and a white sports bra for her time in the gym. They were both now soaked with sweat, especially the shorts. She looked forward to bathing. She had given the equipment a run for its money, staying longer than expected.

The hanging punching bag was her favorite. Occasionally she'd take a hiatus from jabs and leg checks to flip forward, hug it with her thighs, and perform inverted sit-ups.

Reva left the facility around 8:50, although she stopped her routines in the empty gym fifteen to twenty minutes prior. Following that, she cooled down, drank some electrolytes, and used the restroom.

One of three late-night security personnel let her out. Reva's drive home in her Jag was usually a twenty-minute ride. Tonight, she hit more traffic than expected thanks to some road construction. When she reached the end of her driveway, she cruised down it and began to preemptively relax.

Headlights cut across the lightly wooded area her house had been built in. The driveway was long and straight, until it wove around a large oak that she had demanded the landscapers not cut down.

"I'll slalom if I need to, to park," she had said. "Nobody's cutting down any fucking trees for me to live."

Those that did surround the relatively modest home were like a scattered copse. Canopy coverage was scant, which meant less of an insect problem, and less danger from falling limbs during a storm.

Her home, and her car, were still somewhat low-end considering her pay. Nil, and a handful of other veteran active members of Forked Tongue fed their ego. A big house, at least one luxury sports car—spare no expense.

"I'm grateful, what can I say?" Nil had defended himself.

She and John were on the opposite end of the spectrum, within reason. Fact was, Forked Tongue paid well; *very* well. While trainees were essentially interns with minimal pay, active members received a handsome salary, and became eligible for bonuses. There were annual good-behavior bonuses, further encouraging operators to handle themselves and those around them with high esteem. Then there were bonuses per op, as a sort of acknowledgment that their jobs were far more dangerous than most PMC contracts.

John's place was similar to Reva's, only a slightly different style—traditional modern to her contemporary—and with a tad more personality inside. Ironic, she'd jest, considering his lack of one. Which of course was purely a joke.

What wasn't so much a joke was the aesthetic of Reva's house.

"Brooding," Nil had said, grimly, when he first saw it, about four years ago. "It's very…dark, and brooding."

Then he shrugged, grinned, and theatrically shook Reva's hand.

"Congrats!" He beamed. "Very, very you."

She would take the compliment, even if it was made in jest. Nobody could detract her appreciation for the house, and although it had a slew of modern amenities, it was generally minimalistic. It had a very low profile, its highest point twelve feet. This was the stacked-stone chimney, flush with one end of the rectangular house, facing the similarly shaped pool. Apart from that, all ceilings were eight feet.

The garage was a separate housing.

Excluding that, the house itself occupied a space of only 990 square feet, comparable of a tiny home. Inside the ebony and glass exterior was one bedroom, a standing shower space in the compact bathroom, and a kitchen shared with the den. Above-ground utilities were stored in a space attached to the garage.

Reva parked in it, which was essentially a large cubby fit for as many as two vehicles. Her matte charcoal '21 Jaguar F-Type was a hard-top convertible, although she had not taken it down in months. Reva rarely "went cruising," but adored the red and black interior exclusive to the convertible. It was "only" $88k when she got it three years ago, which paled compared to the usual triple digits that operators like Nil would put down. *Per* car.

John was true to form and drove either a massive pickup or a '68 Mustang GT Fastback by Revology. His truck was barely fifty thousand, but the restored Fastback was nearly $290k.

He seemed dedicated on convincing Reva to buy a '67 Shelby GT350 from Revology. Even if it cost her $305k.

Her appreciation of American muscle made it tempting. The price tag wasn't an issue, especially with how much she saved on living minimally. Still, she wouldn't tire of being 'persuaded' by John.

Thinking about him brought a light smile to her otherwise tired face, as she killed the Jag's supercharged V8 and climbed out of the car. A thumbprint reader on the front door handle provided keyless entry. The foyer automatically illuminated, and porchlights turned on. The foyer light was dimmed per a timer, but as the door automatically locked behind her, the light deactivated.

Reva's brow furrowed, as she stepped out of her shoes, now barefoot.

Odd. I don't remember setting that to—

She detected movement in the dark. It was subtle, suggesting the intruder was either small and nimble, or adeptly trained. Possibly both. Her pulse quickened. The curtains were shut, all around the house, so exterior porchlights didn't offer any assistance.

Reva shifted her footing, prepared to make a bee-line to her bedroom. And the sidearm she literally kept under her pillow. A Kimber Raptor that John had gifted her when 2023 became '24. She looked forward to putting its textured grip into her palm, and legally pumping the intruder with at least three rounds of .45 ACP.

The dark wasn't a disadvantage.

She could navigate her home blindfolded, better than most could in stark light.

Reva reached her bedroom, never needing to open a door. Because there were none. Which also meant no barrier against her enemy. Her fingertips grazed the corner of her mattress, inches from the pillow, when the intruder became an attacker. They grabbed her long, braided ponytail and gave a firm tug. Reva's teeth gnashed and her body jerked back.

Her shoulder blades struck a firm chest, like a fucking wall. Her breath would've jarred from her lungs had she been any other woman. But Reva was not.

She stomped her left heel down, hoping to get the man's toe. But his foot withdrew. Then her right elbow jabbed back, and his bulk shifted left; she missed his ribs.

A burly arm slipped under her chin, and the flexing bicep grinded against her throat.

Reva's eyelids fluttered.

Her nostrils flared.

Her—

Very slowly, almost devilishly, the semblance of a smile appeared on her face in the dark bedroom.

Creed Aventus. A dab behind the ears, and on the wrist. No more.

Reva opened her mouth and let a sound come out. It was a fragment of a moan, barely audible. Then she brought her teeth down, and gnawed his forearm. He grunted and released her—momentarily. She bounded forward, leaping onto the bed. When she pirouetted to face him, Reva snapped "lights!"

Voice-activated.

The bedside light-globe washed the room in a supple yellow glow. By which time John had mounted the bed, too. She felt the mattress shift toward his feet.

"Clever girl," he said through a wicked, toothless grin. It was a kind of wickedness she knew so very well.

Then he lunged forward, and she leapt back, the arches of her feet perching on the ledge of the bed's taupe velvet headboard. It was narrow but sustainable. Her palms pressed against the vertical mahogany slats that composed the wall behind her, as she towered over John. The only way she ever could, unless of course she was riding...

"I didn't see your truck," she said plainly.

"Did you slink around back?" He raised an eyebrow, and took a lumbering step forward. "Slip on your NODs?"

Reva scoffed.

Her infinitesimal smirk didn't waver.

"You *drove* on my *lawn*?"

"Right. Like you care about the grass."

"Maybe I should invest in a moat."

"You wanna make me *swim*?" John crept forward another step. "And get all wet?"

She shrugged, now leering down into his piercing

brown eyes.

"Someone has to be," she said, and her smirk burgeoned.

John lunged forward, his big mitts grabbing her calves. He pulled. Her legs shot forward, but his hands transferred to her wide hips, and kept pulling. Reva's arms extended, her palms pushing off the wall; guiding herself into his motion. She fell, supine, gliding between his legs. Those big knees dropped, and squeezed her hips, savoring both fat and muscle through the skintight black fitness shorts. Thinned with sweat, still moist.

In runner's shorts and a fitted black tee, John descended upon her. His right hand shot to her throat, and squeezed as his mouth met hers. She leaned into it, her fingers cinching fistfuls of fabric from his abdomen. Pulling him, or at least lifting herself, too. Their mouths clashed so hard it almost hurt.

Whoever delivered the kiss was debatable.

They shared the action in the moment, like a mutual execution.

When John pulled away to catch his breath, it seemed as though she might possess a third lung. She dug him out of his own shorts, and before he could perform basic math, he was inside of her. Respiration wasn't one of her concerns.

He loved her braided ponytail, and knew how long it took her to do, when she performed it herself. However, in this moment, he pined to run his weathered fingers through her lush, seemingly endless, cascade of black hair.

Her mouth distracted him from this desire.

Suffice it to say, he managed.

The second she raked in a fresh, viscous breath, however, John recuperated. He seized her strong shoulders and hoisted her to her feet. But was surprised when she rebounded off of him, and dismounted the bed. He lashed out, reaching for the back of her sports bra, but his hook-like fingers missed it by centimeters.

As if reading his mind, en route to the attached bathroom left of the bed, Reva shed the sports bra. The sweat enrobing her C-cup breasts cooled, and the skin beneath them tingled pleasantly. Her areolae were already horripilated, and each nipple rigid, as if reaching for something.

The motion-activated LED ceiling trim in the bathroom illuminated. It was perhaps the only room in the house that wasn't quilted in dark earth-tones, but traditionally white and cream-colored.

She began to step out of her fitness shorts, in the threshold of the open glass shower door. But suddenly his *hands* were upon her. Squeezing like vice grips, her narrow waist. Thumbs kneading the dimples above her ass. Almost digging into her.

Reva gnawed her thick bottom lip and let her body loosen some. Her backside wobbled toward him. John's nose buried itself in the crevice between her ass and upper thighs. His head tilted back, black bangs disheveling from his head, matting against his brow, gleaming with perspiration. His tongue lunged forward, before hooking high, and dragging back. Through the sweat-thinned, clingy black fabric Reva felt him taste her.

The F-word never felt more at home in her throat.

How it rose, and slithered between her teeth.

Then the knuckles of his fingers burrowed against her hips, as each digit slinked between skin and fabric. He pulled down, violently, and the material made an audible sound of stress. Without ripping them, but just shy of doing so, John wrenched the shorts down past her knees. A scant black thong followed them.

His densely mustached face returned for seconds.

A famished snout buried itself into her from below. As he fed, Reva moaned and worked her nipples with a free hand. The other clutched at the shower door for stability. Keeping herself afoot; mental balance, and composure, were completely forfeit by now.

When John jolted to his feet, he was bottomless. He peeled his shirt off while his lower body seemed to act independent of everything else. Their bodies fit like pieces destined to do so, even when imperfectly. The ampleness of her ass embraced him before he was ever properly inside of her.

Once his shirt was on the heated tile floor behind him, the vigor of his lust propelled them both forward. She almost slipped on the shower floor, though the tile was not damp in any way.

John caught her, only to pin Reva to a wall.

His left hand snaked under her arm, and shot up to her throat. He gave a gentle enough squeeze, simultaneously pushing her head back. It tilted, and her dark brown eyes, slick with hunger, leered up at him.

"Can you…can you believe?" She moaned. "We're only a rumor to them."

John smirked. "Let's give them…"

Where's his right hand? She briefly mused. *Where's his—*

A moist gasp lilted from her mouth.

"Something to talk about," he growled.

As John's hips pumped, Reva's body jolted. They were like two machines linked up and working in unison.

"Need you," she moaned, in a fractured statement. The words continued to fumble past her lips as John firmly held her against him, and worked her insides.

Meanwhile, in a chasm somehow telepathically shared in their minds, *Something To Talk About* by Bonnie Raitt played, as if from a PA speaker.

Before Reva climaxed, she heard Bonnie sing "how about love?" As if on cue, John came seconds later, while Reva's thighs were still quivering, little tics making her prominent quads shudder.

The idea arrived first in her mind, to speak "water" and trigger the showerhead. But she could hardly formulate syllables at the moment. Besides, John had something he wanted to say first, and in hindsight she cherished that he did.

As he kissed the space behind her left ear, his immensely deep, hoarse voice transferred as if satin. And the words came, once more like a display of clairvoyance—

"How about love?"

4

Convening right before the facility's opening hours meant an emergency op had been drawn up by Forked Tongue strategists in Raleigh. Viper Three was contacted individually at nine in the morning to be at the facility ten-sharp. Which was just when the doors opened to everyone else. Mainly eager trainees and veterans who didn't know anything different than waking at the crack of dawn to work.

Whereas the members of Viper Three weren't thrilled about their wake-up call, the team nonetheless responded soberly and without a hitch.

In Nil's case, there was some literal sobering-up to perform, and a few cups of joe helped.

Although it wasn't obscene for either Reva or John to *not* sleep over at one another's house every night—they didn't yesterday—this morning, they were. Reva was at John's place in Barco, an eight-minute drive from hers, and about thirty from the facility.

They made good time, better than Nil.

Regardless, he arrived short of ten, and together they loitered outside the conference room in an empty hallway that gave what Nil called "ghost town vibes." Even when the facility was open and bustling with activity, this could be said about the particular wing of the building they occupied. Replete with conference rooms and small offices. The rest of the facility teemed with opening personnel, including the preemptive readying of gun ranges and cleaning of gym equipment. In about twenty minutes the building would be bustling with early-bird-gets-the-worm activity.

"If this is a major vamp op, I'm gonna be none too pleased," Nil said, kneading his brow.

He had always maintained that vampyr were a "waste" of their efforts, and more befitting of other squads, especially less experienced ones. Regardless of their organization and armaments.

"But you'll nut up and shut up, won't you?" John said, rigidly.

"Golly, sir, I sure will," Nil said blandly.

Reva shook her head. John rolled his eyes. And the door opened—

The three of them straightened their postures and faces. They weren't as stiff as soldiers reporting to a higher rank, and there was no saluting. This wasn't the military, despite some striking parallels.

Coincidentally, the man in the doorway had been a Sergeant Major with the SAS when he was recruited by Forked Tongue five years ago. Even at his age of 58 at the time, he'd gone on three high-risk ops in his first year before accepting a higher role. Often regarded as the British SEALS, the SAS was no joke. And if anyone was proof that age could be just a number, it was Seamus Price.

He nodded at Viper Three and beckoned them into the room. The stark LED ceiling fixture was almost blinding, and immediately Nil struggled to find a seat without appearing hungover. It was so bright that, as Reva passed Price, she swore she could see a microcosm of conditioner in the man's impressively thick, grizzled beard.

Even John took a moment to adjust to the brightness. But once seated, opposite Nil and left of Reva, he had acclimated.

Reva as well.

Price shut the door, and stood by it like a bouncer. At the opposite end of the room, at the head of the rectangular table, stood an androgynous woman carrying a tablet. The blonde pixie cut suited her frame, and her face almost never exhibited anything less than a let's-get-down-to-business attitude.

That was Sara Calder in a nutshell.

Four years with Forked Tongue, including one of active duty, during which she saw six ops. Recruited from her tenured role as a Combat Engineer in the USMC, she swiftly became one of the company's most treasured assets behind-the-scenes.

Much like Price, she wore very blasé attire, like military fatigues but without any name-tags or branch insignia. Just the Forked Tongue logo stitched to the left breast—a Y-shaped snake's tongue with an F and T on either side.

"Good morning, Viper Three," Calder said. "I know this is all very short-notice, but you know the drill. I'll keep things concise, but won't skimp on need-to-know."

The three operators sat up even more, had they been slouching any. Even Nil straightened. The key words there were "you know the drill." Although generally vague, for an experienced Forked Tongue squad it only alluded to one thing: an urgent op.

"Now, I've opted out of a standard presentation," Calder half-turned, gesturing at the rolled-up projector screen behind her, "for sake of urgency, and believing you're all well-versed in what I'm about to present."

Still obscure, but they had faith in her assumptions.

"Nonetheless," she added, and her steel blue eyes lifted from them to link with Price. She nodded at him, and he reached out, adjusted a dimmer switch on the wall. The LED ceiling fixture hushed to a mid-level glow.

Thank Christ, Nil mouthed to himself.

"Naturally, you aren't the only ones at Forked Tongue who are privy to the kavū's existence."

Nil's head bowed.

Reva's teeth grinded a little.

And John…John tried not to smile.

"Your fascination with the kavū is…unsettling," Reva had told him the last time the creature came up in a discussion.

"Still, it remains an immensely rare species of cryptid, what we'd consider endangered. Two sightings a year, rare. To my understanding, in your six years as a fire-team with Forked Tongue, you've deployed on three kavū ops."

John nodded. "Correct, ma'am. The last one was two summers ago. A trio in Cairo. Beautiful creatures; a shame they had to be put down."

Calder sighed. "As I've heard, Aguirre, you are…unusually infatuated with the kavū. Is *that* correct?"

John's head tilted. "I'd argue the word is *fascinated*, ma'am. As one might be fascinated with sharks; doesn't mean they aren't terrified of them."

She nodded. Her eyes squinted slightly. Then she leaned forward, tablet still cradled against her.

"Would you hesitate to kill one?"

"If it was posing no immediate threat, yes ma'am."

She seemed to appreciate the blatant honesty, but wasn't thrilled about the answer.

"And if it was?"

"If it so much as *looked* at a human in a displeasing way, I'd not breathe until the life had left its eyes."

She smiled slightly, and then stood again.

"Splendid. So, we're all on the same page?" She looked at Nil and Reva, who each nodded sternly. "Good. As you all know, the kavū originated in India. But now, sightings stretch as far as western Africa and even East Asia."

Believed to have crawled out of massive banyan trees in sacred groves in India, the kavū were quadrupedal beasts of intriguing nature. They featured brown, furry bodies but had rhinoceros-like armored skulls and limbs. Their mobility was comparable to big cats, only with the heft of a grizzly bear. As such, they were often misperceived as any variety of predators in different cultures over the centuries: bears, wolves, hyenas, and jaguars.

Among known cryptids, the kavū had been misattributed as the *kerit*, an elusive bear-like creature in Kenya, by the Nandi people. Often described as bipedal and having a tendency to scalp people. Although kavū were incapable of walking on their hind legs, like bears they do sometimes stand upright as an act of intimidation. The latter trait was somewhat accurate; kavū have been documented, especially by Forked Tongue, as prioritizing a human's brain.

Theories were, unfortunately, only theories.

A leading one was that the kavū relished certain nutrients that the human brain was rich in, such as niacin, thiamin, and vitamin K. Another theory was that the kavū *required* hormones specific to the hypothalamus in order to function.

Regardless of the reason, that the creatures fixated on the brain of their prey was inarguably unsettling.

"In *this* case," Calder continued, "we find them all the way up in Romania. At seven-AM EST, which was four-PM in Romania, a group of hikers lost on their way back to the trail saw, and reported, what HQ has established to be kavū. Fortunately, the hikers were not attacked, and nobody in their village believes them.

"The sightings occurred in the woodlands just north of a commune called Stejaru. Which is about…thirty klicks southeast of Babadag, the nearest town. A population of nine-thousand. Mind you, villages are scattered all over this region. Most are no more than a few hundred residents, and some communes go as high as a thousand. As you all know, despite how dangerous kavū are, they don't typically raid settlements. *But*, given their unusual presence this far north to begin with, we can't be too sure of their behavior."

Calder took a breath.

Nil seemed puzzled. He tentatively half-raised his hand. Calder sighed and pointed.

"How in the hell did kavū get all the way up to Romania?"

"The question shouldn't be *how*, but *why*. And not just the distance, but the region. This area of Romania is composed of scattered forests, flatlands, and fields. It seems that the kavū have not, yet anyway, migrated farther west, into the more mountainous and densely wooded highlands of Romania. Which is, as you know, more akin to their usual habitat."

"Which makes me fear," John thought out loud, his voice grim, "that more and more sightings will be made in the coming days."

Calder nodded. "Hence the urgency. Now, folks in Raleigh believe that maybe something spooked them, or drove them out of their original habitats—and have them skeptical of their usual terrain."

Nil's brow furrowed. "What other cryptids would even be capable of repelling kavū?"

Calder shrugged, and scanned their faces.

"The mighty Viper Three…stumped?" She scoffed. "No ideas?"

"A big enough faction of skinwalkers fixated on a specific biosphere might be compelled to push them away." Reva shrugged. "If even able."

"Improbable, but possible," Calder said. "Anyone else? I'm sure HQ could use some spit-balling."

They were drawing blanks.

And then John spoke up, even though he knew he was reaching. It showed, too, in his expression and tone.

"There *have* been wendigo sightings as far as Portugal, Spain, and Algeria." He shrugged. "If anything could scatter kavū, it's them. Similar habitats, too."

Calder nodded, considering this.

Despite belonging to Native American folklore, John was right about the wendigo. Experts believed that ancestors of the Algonquians—who originated tales of the wendigo, and were most prevalent in Quebec—once inhabited neighboring land masses, now overseas, during Pangea. This would certainly account for the verified reports of them as far as Spain and Algeria.

"Bit of a reach, but possibly the most likely theory we have at the moment," Calder said, and John was surprised she was genuinely considering it.

He would never express it, except to Reva in private, but an excitement bubbled inside of him at the prospect of his own idea reaching Forked Tongue HQ.

"At any rate," she said, with a shake of her head, refocusing her attention, "they are where they are, and that's that. Right now we are to believe there may be as many as *four* kavū in the Stejaru region, your AO.

"The details of the witness reports have been compiled into a dossier that I've shared with the armorers.

Once you're down there, they'll hand over the dossier.

"Your bird will be wheels-down momentarily. It'll take you to the airfield in Fentress, VA. From there you'll board a Learjet and fly to Tulcea, Romania. Estimated flight time is nine hours. That's about as fast as we can get you there, shy of teleporting. During this time, Romania will see nightfall. Supposing the kavū act accordingly, since they typically aren't nocturnal hunters, they'll be asleep while you're in the air. It'll be just past three in the afternoon when you arrive. Romanian sunsets in the summer are at five-thirty, so work fast. Best-case scenario, you'll RTB just as night reclaims the country."

"Ma'am?" John asked, two seconds after she stopped speaking. "Have there been any casualties yet?"

"Fortunately, no. A hiking party filed the report, which we successfully intercepted and, presently, everything is being handled on that end quite well."

Forked Tongue wouldn't be as successful as it was without its superior oversight committee, and their dedication to the subdual of leaked information from witnesses around the world. For this, the HQs in Raleigh and Portland worked in tandem, around the clock.

"Good," John said, relieved nobody had been attacked. Kavū didn't tend to leave survivors.

"From Tulcea, a Bulgarian contact will pick you up in a Bell 206, and take you to the last known sighting. Tulcea's fifty klicks north of Stejaru, so expect a ten-minute helo ride. By then, hopefully—and I only mean that for the sake of an update, of course, not an attack—

there'll be fresh reports, and you'll be notified immediately of any changes. Keep your sat-phones charged on the plane."

Everyone nodded. John was impatiently bouncing his leg.

"If there are no further questions," Calder said, "I'll wish you good hunting."

The three scooted their chairs out, Calder nodded with finality, and they motioned toward the door. Price opened it for them, stepping into the hall and holding it with his heel.

"Godspeed," he said. "Good luck, happy hunting, the whole nine yards."

"Appreciate it, Price," John said, shaking the man's hand, firmly, before urgently striding down the hall with his teammates.

John, and he knew he wasn't alone, almost always had to fight the impulse to call Price 'sir.' His age and tenure in the military alone had this reaction.

Viper Three reached the armory room three minutes later. Impressive, considering it was usually about a five minute brisk walk between those locations in the facility. Since the doors had just opened minutes ago, crowds were still too thin to be bumping into people. The occasional trainee that felt bold enough to attempt conversing with any of them got either nudged aside or ignored outright.

Viper Three was on a mission, both figuratively and literally. Their urgency was top priority.

Only two of the usual five Cage Trolls were active at present. The other three were set to arrive at noon.

The dossier was initially handled by John, but shared to the other two operators while the armorers readied their gear. The cage itself was a large cube-shaped chamber composed of steel mesh painted off-white. This, by intention, made it feel less grim to those that spent their entire shifts inside. Whether it actually worked was up to debate; most armorers found their job meditative if anything, not depressing.

And no Cage Troll had claustrophobia.

Presently, until Viper Three left, the armory was barred to anyone else. This allowed them to be vocal about their op, although conversation would be minimal as they focused on ensuring the readiness of their equipment.

While Nil sat at a workbench off to the side and studied the dossier, John and Reva stood on either side of the cage receiving their gear from the two armorers.

"Got a Trijicon MRO red-dot," Pike Schumann said, pointing at the optic mounted on John's rifle, a lever-action Marlin Trapper. "Since you'll likely be in mid- to close-range engagements, only 1.5 magnification. Sucker's zeroed-in for 2-MOA, but I trust you could hit an elephant's tail at fifty yards in the open on iron sights, you sick fuck."

John smirked, shaking his head.

He cocked the black nitride steel lever—which had some nylon rope coiled around it for added grip—a few times for the feel of it. He had not run the Marlin in over three ops. It was usually overkill for most enemies, except bigger lycanthropes in their wolf form.

"Your vote of confidence is duly noted, Pike.

What've you got in the bag for me? Steel-core?"

Pike glanced over his shoulder, in the direction of the female armorer currently conversing with Reva.

"Not you, buddy. Reva's getting steel-core five-five-sixes, *you've* got Barnes VOR-TX." Pike slid forward a mostly-empty carton of standing cartridges. Six total—five for the tubular magazine, one in the chamber. As John loaded the weapon without inspecting the rounds, Pike continued. "Talkin' 300-grain bad boys, Triple-Shock. Just got 'em in last month."

"No shit. Put to shame my last Marlin load? What was it, Steinel 500s?"

"Those suckers would dead a charging rhino," Pike said. "Or cut through two kavū, side-by-side. But penetration isn't really an issue with 45-70, and only parts of a kavū are armored. You and I both know the best way to put one down is center-mass. Chest or shoulder. So some expansion would do better than going straight through."

Pike handed him a bandolier of the Barnes 45-70 Gov't ammo, as well as a Velcro caddy to mount on the rifle's buttstock. The buffalo leather caddy held five rounds in firm loops.

John secured it with a distinct Velcro sound, and then tossed the cowhide bandolier of fifty rounds over a shoulder. He was not only hoping, but expecting, to fire no more than twenty rounds on this op. But it helped to have too much than too little.

He plucked one twenty-gram cartridge free from a loop and kneaded the concave 'tip' with a thumb.

"Solid copper hollow points," Pike said. "Opens up

like a flower of death, without sacrificing velocity. Recent ballistics tests prove that they usually retain one-hundred-percent their original weight. Effective as fuck."

Pike articulated those last three words slowly, emphatically.

"Brutal, though," John shook his head.

"Look," Pike sighed, leaning forward and lowering his voice. "I know you're fascinated with kavū. Hey, it's how I feel about wolf spiders. Doesn't mean they don't need to be exterminated, though. And with extreme prejudice, too."

John smirked dryly. "Yeah."

He slid the round back into the loop.

"HPs normally inflict immense pain, I get it," Pike said, leaning back. "But those suckers, from a Marlin no less—hit it right, and that kavū won't feel much. Just death. A kind of peace, if you ask me."

"Shit," John clicked his tongue. "Pike the philosopher. Never thought I'd see the day."

"Then you'll love this, smart-ass," Pike said, gingerly sliding a heavy stainless steel revolver across the smooth counter.

John had already secured his torso rig, which had less magazine pouches than usual, since the Marlin was individually loaded. The revolver, too.

After slinging the eight-pound rifle, he picked up the handgun. It felt at home in his palm, thumb massaging the outer grooves of the stainless steel cylinder, and then the textured surface of the hammer. He only opted for this over a .45 1911 when the enemy rivaled big game.

"Your favorite lycan-killer," Pike said. While he talked, John ejected the cylinder to inspect the loaded chambers. "Only I've swapped the silver hollow points with fluted copper penetrators. Underwood, 250-grain."

"Might do well against the armored parts," John said, no longer hung up on the allure of kavū. He reminded himself that human lives were at stake, and that kavū driven from their original territory would likely be more dangerous than if they had stayed.

Which was a terrifying thought.

"Bet your ass," Pike said.

John nodded, and closed the cylinder with a click. The five-pound Smith & Wesson 460 XVR Magnum was a monster in its own league, especially loaded with .454 Casull.

"Happy hunting, brother," Pike said, and John thanked him before turning.

He reached where Nil sat, who slapped down the dossier on the workbench. He stood, to go to Pike for his own gear. Nil being Nil, though, had to run his mouth a little.

"Four kavū, two the size of Kodiaks, and two like Bengals. Absolutely splendid."

"Better than all four as big as Kodiaks," John said. "You goddamn cynic."

Nil scoffed, and strode up to the cage.

Pike was delivering his loadout from a counter behind him, to the one flush with the window in the mesh.

"…hardly any changes, namely the ammo," Bailey Evans was telling Reva, as she received her Noveske N4 assault rifle from the armorer. "Winchester M855, 62-grain steel-core, an operator favorite against kavū."

"I recall. Thanks, Bay."

"And for your beloved Ruger-57, mags have been loaded with 40-grain V-Max for ultimate penetration. Not much stopping power against a healthy kavū, but some well-placed rounds might cripple it. If your N4 doesn't do the trick, a few five-sevens could distract it while John cuts it down. Pike said he was giving him the 45-70."

Reva whistled.

"Beautiful. Appreciate it. Look forward to coming back and praising the underrated work you all do in this mesh-prison."

Bailey's smirk was short-lived.

"And you better get your ass back, Rev," she pressed. Reva nodded sternly, and extended an arm. They bumped fists, briefly interlocking knuckles, then Reva withdrew. There lingered a grim weight to Bailey's stare, even after Reva left. It held respect, but that came naturally among them. There was something else, there, in her hazel eyes. Something dangerously close to dread.

It wouldn't shock them if anyone in Forked Tongue felt that this op was 'cursed.' If Viper Three had been assigned to neutralize kavū rampant in territories they were known to occasionally surface, that would be one thing. But as far as Romania? This meant the creatures had to have trekked through Iran, up the Caucasus Mountains, and across Ukraine, before finding enough solace in Romania to expose themselves, likely to hunt.

Something had driven them away.

That was what unnerved everyone about this op. The inherent danger of engaging kavū was secondary to the reason they had ventured so far north to begin with. Unfortunately, Viper Three could do nothing about that, and brainstorming theories only served as an unnecessary distraction outside the conference room.

So they had to banish those thoughts and focus on what *was* within their purview.

Eliminating threats.

Reva saw John leaning against a workbench as he secured his gear—from rig to holster to sling.

Six workbenches surrounded the armory, in pairs. Each resembled a single-sided picnic table, with an ample brushed-nickel anti-reflective stainless steel workplace. Operators would sit at them and arrange their gear, fine-tune their builds, load magazines, or clean the weapons. The armorers did all of this for them by default, but sometimes adjustments were made.

Not today.

Viper Three's trust in the Cage Trolls doing their job to a T ran parallel with their urgency.

"A hiking group, right?" John said, knowing Nil could hear him, while Pike arrayed the counter with the same weapons Nil had carried in Siberia. "Middle-aged Romanians, four men and two women, probably already on foot for an hour. Early fatigue, plus heat. Low to mid-eighties, this time of year."

Nil glanced back at John. There was a tiredness in his eyes; not necessarily fatigue, but an expression of "this might be a clusterfuck." It was a classic Nil look.

"Hot, tired, distracted old people." He clicked his

tongue. "Great."

John cut off a laugh. "I didn't say *old*. For fuck's sake, Nil. *I'm* forty."

Nil scoffed. "You're definitely getting there, brother. I'll be nipping at your heels soon enough."

"You already are. That's not how aging works."

"And I'm 54, numb-nuts," Pike said gruffly.

Nil shrugged nonchalantly. He was 35, but more often than not felt half that. John would agree; if he truly *felt* 40, he wouldn't be as good as he was at the job.

"Point is," John said, "it's possible they didn't see what they think they saw. The kavū could be smaller, or bigger; quantity alone is uncertain. They normally flock in packs of six; them venturing as far north as Romania suggests no less than that, I'd argue."

"Well, shit." Nil glanced back again. "Aren't you just bursting with good news?"

John shrugged coldly, and then ran over his gear again, periodically glimpsing Reva in his peripheral. The three of them wore drab green attire, knowing their destination would be grasslands and forests. Although kavū saw in color and had panoramic sightlines, their vision was desaturated. Akin to how felines viewed the world, only a little sharper. The muted tones, however, made any attempt at camouflage go a long way.

"Don't worry, I didn't fuck with your Scorpion. Just the can and ammo." Pike tapped the Richmond Tactical Stinger suppressor, and then the transparent magazine. It was loaded into the all-black CZ Scorpion, an upgrade kit from Nexus Firearms called the EVO Gen 1.

"Can's sexy, I fuck with it," Nil nodded, running a hand over the sectioned, hexagonal, black anodized six-inch aluminum suppressor. "Tell me about the ammo, though. Just make it snappy."

Pike had no qualms with that.

As much of a narcissistic chatterbox as Nil *could* be, sometimes he settled into a state of sheer focus and his quality as a tenured operator shined through.

Pike revered this.

.   John Aguirre being the poster child of that mold.

"Here we go," Pike said, sliding across the counter a quartet of transparent mags. Nil didn't hesitate to secure them into pouches on his rig, while Pike explained. "Thirty-five rounds each. Federal HST, jacketed hollow points. Nine-mil, 147-grain."

"Copy that," Nil said, satisfied. He ensured the polymer sling was secure before setting the EVO submachine gun onto his back.

"FNX45," Pike said, handing Nil his preferred sidearm, a match-grade .45-caliber pistol from FN, along with three spare magazines. "Fifteen rounds each, 200-grain Lehigh penetrators, monolithic copper."

"Hello, luv," Nil said, eyeing the pistol. He racked the slide, spotted a chambered round, confirmed the safety was on, and holstered it at his right hip.

"Last but not least," Pike said, tapping the long and slightly curved magazine loaded into his Derya Mk-12. His other hand slid a thirty-shell bandolier across the counter. "Swapped out your buckshot with slugs. Salt Creek five-petal Twisters. Brutal wound cavity, segments like shrapnel and maintains velocity, comparable to .30-caliber rounds. Figure they'd do better against a kavū, hell even a lycan, than those Federal Sluggers you last ran. Tremendous as those can be."

Nil nodded repeatedly. He slung the bandolier, secured his sling on the semi-automatic shotgun, and then hoisted it as well.

"Much appreciated," he said, and slapped the counter. Pike slapped it in return, and Nil spun on his heel to head back to the nearest workbenches.

The pair of handguns Reva already had holstered dangled from their harness, one below each armpit. She unslung her rifle, and with it set both magazines onto the workbench that John leaned against.

"We've got six kavū that probably didn't all come from the same region, and one biosphere." Her tone was rigid, tarnished only by an inflection of intrigue. "The woods. Which is both good and bad, for us."

"Why don't you enlighten us, Your Highness?" Nil said, sarcastically.

"Kavū are predominantly brown and black," she said. "Some might prefer the woods, but they don't camouflage very well in predominantly green environments. Which means they'll likely be sticking to the ground, navigating trunks, where they blend in the most. *But*…if they didn't all come from the same region, it means they're forcing themselves into a pack, because they're spooked."

John nodded. He appeared finished with his gear, wearing it all like a second skin. Nil was moments away himself.

"Good for us 'cause they'll be more visible, and

less at home," John said. "But bad for us be-cause…they'll be less predictable."

"And a fickle kavū ain't a kavū I wanna fuck with," Reva said. Then she slung her N4.

"Fair," Nil said. He approached Reva, and they finally stood together, a mere two feet apart from each other. "But what if the reports are bogus, and we're out there facing *more* than six?"

"Then somebody will be carving our names into the lobby floor," Reva said simply.

"Cut that shit," John snapped. He emphatically tightened the strap on his bandolier of 45-70. "Not today."

Reva nodded once, her dark brown eyes locked with John's in an instant of tacit, intimate trust. In faith, and the confidence that came with it.

"Cage!" John hollered, marching past Reva and toward one of two exits from the large room. "We'll be seeing you!"

"Looking forward to it!" Pike responded.

"Go get 'em!" Bailey shouted.

Nil followed Reva, and as a single column Viper Three exited the armory.

Through corridors teeming with more and more people, they made a beeline for the helipad out the south wing. It wasn't on the roof, but a large space of clear tarmac. Before they even opened the metallic double-doors, the thumping sound of helicopter rotors was audible.

A Sikorsky UH-60 Black Hawk awaited them on the helipad. Price was out there, shouting at the copilot. Not aggressively, but just to be heard over the roar of rotors and the hum of twin T700 turboshaft engines.

They reached the helo and Price turned away to look at them. He beckoned them toward the open cargo doors.

"Here to bid you off," Price shouted. He exchanged passing looks of goodwill to Reva and Nil as they boarded the helo behind John. Then he shook John's hand again. "Wish I could go with, frankly. But I trust it won't be necessary."

"We'd be honored," John hollered back. "Maybe some other time. An op with you in the ranks would be one hell of a ride."

"Likewise. Fly safe!"

They nodded in unison, and then John boarded the Black Hawk. He slung the door shut in his wake, and joined the others. A row of floor-to-ceiling mounted nylon seats accompanied them, complete with harnesses nobody used for this ride. Each operator secured a headset, allowing them to speak to each other, and the pilots, without having to shout.

"Fentress airfield," the copilot announced. "ETA six mikes!"

"Copy," John said, and thrusted a thumbs-up for the head-turned copilot to see.

Nil watched through a window in the cargo door as Price backed up to the edge of the raised tarmac. He brought a flat hand to his brow as a makeshift visor, as the helo's skids cleared the pavement. Once a few hundred feet in the air, the aircraft pitched forward slightly and accelerated. The Black Hawk's cruising speed was 175mph, but the pilot would eventually achieve just above that. If he could get his passengers to Fentress sooner than six minutes, he would try.

Although only the armory, outside of higher-ups like Calder and Price, knew the details of their op, the pilots didn't need to. That it was an urgent matter was probably all Price had relayed to them, and that was more than enough.

"From here on out," John said, looking at Reva and Nil, who sat across from him, "I don't wanna hear anything outside of the op. No theories, guesses, or deductions on the how-or-why. Only what directly pertains to our situation, and our enemy. Understand?"

They nodded. No verbal confirmation needed; their eyes spoke volumes. Even, if not especially, the silence from Nil. Sometimes his gaze was louder and clearer.

John's demands weren't out of the norm. That he was voicing it was, however. Every op they went on, a similar credo was assigned the second they left Moyock. It was implicit, a given. No quips or jokes until after the enemy was neutralized. Depending on the circumstance, a dry one might slip from any of them, particularly Nil. This could be excused.

Today was a little different.

The spit-balling they'd done in the office with Calder had been cathartic. And what few words on the matter they shared in the armory. Outside of that, their focus was narrower. Better they keep it that way, wheels-up or on-site. At least until they were heading back.

With a nine-hour flight on the private Learjet ahead of them, the team predicted at least four or five hours of sleep. Nil might tack on as many as six or seven. The remainder of their flight would be spent going over their kits—minus their weapons, for safety reasons—discussing op details or strategies, and of course the necessities. Getting some protein, water, and using the lavatory.

The last thing they wanted to do was wake up an hour before arrival, and transfer to their contact's small helo, groggy.

They had to be keen.

As sharp as the combat knives they carried.

Because kavū were sharper.

5

Three klicks northwest of Stejaru, fresh reports of "large wolves" and "strange bears" had been intercepted by Forked Tongue, given by passersby driving from Vasile, a local village. Informed of this, Viper Three's Bulgarian contact and helicopter pilot, Boyan, rerouted to the national forest of Kavaculla. Had the team been tourists, the helo wouldn't feel so claustrophobic. But with their gear in tow, it was clearly not an aircraft made for military transport. They made do, though, in knowing it was a short trip from Tulcea to Stejaru.

News of fresh reports was on par with what Sara Calder had hopes for upon their arrival. No attacks or casualties, just an updated eyewitness account. The vagueness alone suggested they didn't receive a clear view of the animals, either, which meant the kavū had not ventured out of the foliage.

Open, unoccupied grasslands stretched between Kavaculla and Stejaru. A few kilometers northwest of the forest was the small village of Vasile, separated by more pasture.

"Best-case scenario," John said, before Boyan landed in a field a few hundred feet outside of Kavaculla, "we eliminate the enemy before they decide to hop-skip-and-jump to Vasile. Or Stejaru, for that matter."

After disembarking from the helo, Reva tried out, for the second time today, her rough grasp of the Bulgarian dialect. It was passable, according to Boyan, who did speak English as well. She thanked him in his native tongue and he bid goodbye, but would await their call via sat-phone to pick them up. Hopefully, in an hour or two.

Once the helo was airborne, John addressed the team again. The Romanian sky was a watercolor canvas of thin, gray clouds. Sunlight penetrated them sparsely, dappling the green terrain below in muted tones.

"We've got ninety mikes before sundown," he said, shouldering his Marlin, the 16-inch barrel pointed at the ground. "So we work fast, but vigilant. Nil, take point. Reva, stagger ten paces. I'll hang back, navigate closer to trees and try to stay concealed."

He pointed at his collar mic.

"Acknowledge anything suspicious, and call-out your shots."

They nodded.

The headband-shaped device affixed to the collar of an operator's shirt was intrinsic to communicating between team members. In addition to sporting a sensitive touch-activated microphone, it wirelessly connected to a pair of Peltor inner ear-protection plugs. The device acted as an extended battery for the ear-pro, and audible connectivity. As a standalone, the Peltor ear-pro auto-matically suppressed high-end frequencies, such as gunfire, while permitting lower-end, like voices and environmental sounds.

Standard for Forked Tongue operators.

Bulkier headsets with the same function were used around the world by men and women in the field, too.

Some ops prohibited the use of inter-team comms, though. Viper Three forewent them in Siberia, knowing that even a whisper could be picked up by most acute lycanthropes. Sometimes a twitch of white noise from a collar mic would suffice, too.

Fortunately, there was no animal on this Earth as keen as a sober, attentive lycanthrope.

"Let's *move*," John waved a single finger in the air.

The team disseminated toward Kavaculla, crossing the latter quarter of a grassy field. The nearest treeline was neither dense nor scarce. Deciduous trees with dark, thin trunks and low, broadly arching canopies were rife with lush vegetation. Underbrush was copious, but manageable. When Nil reached what appeared to be the most welcoming gap in the treeline, his knees bent slightly and he navigated into the forest. His semi-auto shotgun preceded him with its 16-inch barrel. He used it to push light branches and thin brush away from his face.

Ten paces behind him, Reva followed.

Their heads on a consistent swivel in the realm of green.

Some twenty paces behind her, and staggered to her four o'clock, was John. His angled, distant approach offered a potential strategic advantage, especially with the Marlin.

There were very few cryptids under Forked Tongue's scrutiny that could be handled like regular wild animals. And the kavū were not among them. Which meant they couldn't be lured or baited, unless by a human.

And no human wanted that job.

In a manner of speaking, and John knew Nil might very well make this argument, he and Reva were presently the bait. John hung back, ready to make it count. This wasn't explicitly part of their plan, but the formation suggested it.

And made it possible, but only by happenstance.

In less than a minute, the undergrowth in Kavaculla had dispersed. It was only thick along the perimeter, where sunlight was ample. Beneath the dense canopies, only verdant grass, cloves, and ivies grew as high as the ankles. European beech and black locust trees populated the woodland, mitigating Viper Three's navigation and visibility.

They just hoped they didn't stick out like sore thumbs themselves.

Their weapons and gear had not been wrapped with vinyl camouflage, nor painted. Only their torso rigs wore the PL Woodland pattern.

After traversing the dimly verdant innards of Kavaculla for about four minutes, something occurred to John. He depressed his collar mic button, as one would a walkie-talkie, and spoke quietly.

"Y'all notice anything unusual?"

A pause as the other two deliberated.

"Care to elaborate?" Nil asked.

"Quiet," John said. "And I hate to be that guy, but…it's *too* quiet."

"Well…" Reva said. "Given the circumstances, it isn't necessarily strange. Introduce the kavū to a new habitat, and the local fauna are bound to either scram, or—"

"Be eaten," Nil interrupted.

"Exactly."

"True," John said. "I hope it's the latter."

"A bit cruel," Nil said.

Their discussion remained quiet. The collar mics were effective, and their Peltor plugs made it seem like everyone was whispering in each other's ears.

Meanwhile, their spaced-apart formation continued to advance through the scattered trees. Cloud-obfuscated sunlight slowly became sparser and dimmer through the dense canopies.

"Think about it," John said. "If the kavū have a menu *here*, they won't have to pay Stejaru or Vasile a visit. At least not until tomorrow, or the next day."

"True," Nil said. "Then again, they won't have a tomorrow."

John sighed and didn't press his collar mic to make any further contributions on the matter. Reva, on the other hand…

"John has a point, though," she said. Her optic eye remained fixated downrange. "As long as they're satiated with the wildlife, they won't leave this little safe haven. And it's quite possible they'll be less aggressive with us, too."

It was a hopeful thought that they would all cling to. Or at least John and Reva. Nil was Nil for a reason; his pessimism ran thick in his blood.

At least he wasn't always spewing it.

Regardless, none of them were skeptical about their ability to handle aggressive kavū. Especially as a team. It helped, in a debatable way, that their enemy had no firepower. While not projectile weapons, the claws or teeth of a kavū weren't to be underestimated. They could just as well nullify any form of infantry protection, meaning that the operators had foregone vests, plate carriers, and helmets. In theory, steel plates would stop the claws of a kavū, but the pressure of a bite or step from one would easily crush anything beneath that armor.

"Let's face the facts, people," Nil finally said. "The kavū are an invasive species. But they're also nomadic. I doubt they have any intention of staying here, especially after such a long trip. This is probably just a pit-stop for them. But because of us, it'll be—"

The absence of helmets provided improved perception and awareness. Had he been wearing one, Nil didn't think he would've spotted the shudder of a giant leaf near the base of a beech trunk, at his three o'clock, fifteen feet away. His voice fell short and his finger relinquished the collar mic button to return to his shotgun.

Besides, it grew tiring to hold that thing up with just one arm.

Although he didn't address the movement on their comms before putting both hands on his weapon, the sudden drop-off of his voice in their ears was caution enough.

The large, frilly leaf's movement appeared independent of surrounding foliage.

Nil's boots planted like anchors in the grassy earth about twelve feet from it. Ten strides behind him stood Reva, also pausing. She directed the barrel of her shouldered N4 at this hint of motion, which she just barely caught from her angle and range, at the edge of a light brown European beech.

Some thirty feet behind her, John sidled to the right, trying to slink around trees and clusters of underbrush to get a better—

The small bush whose leaf had been moving suddenly exploded. Leaves and branches flurried around the kavū, which was about the size of an adult male lion. The sound emitting from its black jaws, though, was like that of a dying deer. It would never not send chills down Nil's spine. He leapt back, rotating on his left heel, and the choked muzzle of his shotgun lit up in the shady green environment.

The quadrupedal beast with thick orange-brown fur everywhere except its skull and limbs had pounced at Nil. Four five-inch talons on its right paw missed him by a foot or two. He literally felt a gust of air against his face before he tumbled to the left, popping up and shouldering the shotgun again.

Nil saw a streak of red behind the creature's right shoulder before it landed in the grass and rolled. When it sprang up again, a clawed paw caught a tree trunk for purchase, and it swung around the beech to face Nil.

A trainee would've been startled by its nimbleness despite the wound it had sustained. Blood pouring through the savage cavity behind its rocky, naturally armored shoulder had matted large tufts of amber-brown fur. It even audibly dappled the ground where it now stalked, in a crescent maneuver to face Nil.

Years beyond a trainee, Nil's experience made him a stern and almost fearless combatant.

His Derya had not yet lowered a single inch.

Nonetheless, the injured kavū stared him down.

"Firing," Reva breathed into her mic, and released the button to lock her hand onto the angled foregrip beneath the N4's fluted barrel.

Bullets ripped out of it with a sound that didn't faze a single one of them thanks to their ear-pro; the kavū was another story. It flinched on impulse, first from the sound and then the assault. Four-gram steel-core bullets volleyed the kavū's left side, peppering its fur-coated ribs and penetrating the flesh.

The kavū would've charged Nil head-on, had Reva not engaged it. Now it seemed puzzled on how to proceed. It began to retreat.

Nil stepped forward, as one might, boldly, to intimidate a single wolf that was already showing signs of hesitation. Only this act, with a kavū, went above and beyond "bold." It could be argued as reckless.

Except that Nil wasn't alone.

When he stepped forward, the kavū seemed to call his bluff and suddenly lunged toward him. Its piercing yellow eyes flared with enthusiasm, black jaws gaping and fangs the shade of raw charcoal dripping saliva—

Nil squeezed the trigger. His semi-automatic shotgun roared, another 12-gauge slug nearly three inches around exiting with a fury. Once more segmenting upon impact, this time the slug caught the kavū right below its oblong skull. In the throat. An exit wound that misted the air with more than just blood but also chunks of flesh splashing foliage left the kavū faltered.

Nil glimpsed the light flicker from its eyes.

It wobbled as if drunk, John witnessing the latter part of their engagement through his optic thirty-some feet away. Reva herself had navigated to Nil's two o'clock, ready to bury a few more rounds into its furred rump if need be.

Instead the kavū asphyxiated on its own blood, and then collapsed with a defeated heap. It was almost a splash, given the gore it had shed before death.

Nil gathered a breath and touched his mic.

"Target down. Target is…dead."

"Copy," John said, but didn't relax. He averted his aim from the slain kavū corpse, scanning nearby trees for signs of movement. With as many as six, possibly more, of the creatures in the area, it was highly improbable one would be roving alone.

Then again…

The odds were already stacked against them.

Kavū shouldn't have traveled this far to begin with. This simple fact complicated the op to no end. These kavū could be acting on entirely unprecedented whims.

"You hear that?" Reva asked, brow furrowed.

Nobody replied, as they held their breaths to listen to the silence. John's aim returned to the direction of Reva and Nil, though she had moved like a clock hand well away from him. She was now only about twenty feet from John. Through his red-dot scope, he watched Reva pluck one plug from her ear.

And then Reva's head tilted back.

She looked up.

John couldn't see her face, but Nil could. First he noticed Reva's already inherently big brown eyes suddenly get bigger. They widened, their surrounding whites almost blinding. An expression of shock and disbelief, even fear, had bleached her typically stern face.

"Nil, *move!*" She bellowed, not even touching the mic button. He was within earshot, anyway. Reva bounded away from where she'd been standing, coincidentally in John's direction, opposite of Nil. He scrambled, too, and only glimpsed movement above them before the impact followed.

Something big and heavy—but with the give of an animal and not a rock or tree branch—struck the ground where Reva had been standing moments ago, with an incredible wallop.

Blood even splashed nearby tree trunks and leaves. Some leaves billowed in its wake.

"Talk, report," John pressed. He very cautiously approached the scene, still swivel-headed.

"Jesus H," Reva panted. Then she pressed her mic. "It's a *kavū*, John. Size of a fuckin' tiger. It's *dead*."

"How far did it jump from?" Nil asked, gazing up at the canopies. He wasn't engaging his mic.

"It didn't," Reva said, almost as if offended. She shot Nil a bewildered look, as he and she tentatively approached the corpse. Two of its limbs were compound fractured, and its head was twisted in the wrong direction.

More than that…

"What do you mean, it didn't jump!?" Nil scoffed. He gestured at the treetops, while glaring at Reva on the other side of the 400-pound dead kavū. "It dropped like a fucking rock!"

"Exactly," she snapped. "It *fell*."

Nil recoiled in disbelief. But it quickly set in. And then he noticed what Reva already had, but was slow to process.

"Report," John in their ears. Except he had stopped about twenty feet behind Reva, at her five o'clock. He had detected movement, and was now scanning the trees to their far right.

"John," Nil said, now activating his mic. "This kavū *fell* to its death. It didn't jump. It was *attacked*."

"Come again?"

"It's clawed up real bad," Reva said. "Mauled. I think it may have been dead before it hit the ground."

"How? What could've—"

John's voice vanished.

And then started up again, with a roar of urgency.

"Contacts, at your two and three o'clock," he said. "Reva."

"Copy," she said, and immediately snapped to attention. She swung her body and weapon to her right. Peering downrange through her optic, she scanned the trees for movement. Catching blurs of quadrupedal creatures weaving through the forest in bursts. The closer they got, the surer she was that they were kavū. Coloration and the inconsistency of their physiques were dead giveaways.

"Tracking kavū at your one o'clock, Rev," Nil said.

She had planted her ear-pro back in, but it still filtered select frequencies. She managed to catch the sound of breaking tree branches, again, this time without having to remove one. When she looked up, it was just in time—

A kavū was leaping down toward them, bounding from one dense branch to another. She cursed through her teeth and backpedaled, firing the N4 so fast in semi-auto one might mistake it as automatic.

Rounds drilled into the kavū just as it reached the lowest bough, which suddenly split like a crack of thunder. The black locust tree trunk shuddered, and the lion-sized creature's body tumbled to the green ground below, taking a moment to right itself. Unlike the one that had fallen earlier, this kavū was a little lither.

Had it landed properly, Reva would've been in far graver danger.

Nil noticed it had claw gashes along its right flank, *in* the coarse black hide of its hindquarters. Only certain ammunition could penetrate those parts of a kavū's body; or, other kavū claws.

The beast snarled at Reva, who kept firing.

Despite her pounding heart, she stayed her ground and not one shot went awry. A few bullets did catch the creature's rigid brow, glancing off the natural black armor shrouding its elongated skull.

And then it shrunk back onto its haunches, preparing to launch itself at her—

John's Marlin thundered from twenty feet away.

A 45-70 Gov't round drilled it in the left flank, with enough pressure to fracture its hip but not penetrate that tough outer husk. The kavū whimpered in pain and staggered, bumping into a tree.

Clenching her jaw, Reva took one brash step forward—and rolled her shoulder against the N4's buttstock. Her aim fixated. She squeezed the trigger. A single 5.56mm barreled into the kavū's left eye socket. Steel-core lead penetrated the hub of nerves in the socket and sustained velocity expanded that side of the creature's skull. The left half of the kavū's head split open, chunks of black cranium and mauve brain matter spilling to the forest floor. Its body went limp.

John cocked the Marlin lever, ejecting a brass casing that trailed a tail of smoke.

Then he swung the barrel away from Reva and Nil, his peripheral vision tracking movement through the trees far right of them. Out ahead of himself. Enclosing.

The second he had an opening, he took it. And the Marlin roared again. His shot clipped the rump of a kavū, the round flowering and inflicting a grave amount of pain that he wished he could undo. Then the creature barreled into another, and the two beats rolled into a small clearing about twenty feet from where he stood.

John lowered his rifle, and in awe, pressed the mic button.

"Regroup, on me," he said. "Maintain aim, but hold your fire."

It wasn't difficult for them to locate John amid the trees. He had approached a point of interest that was impossible to miss. The cacophony alone—
Two kavū quarreling. Except it was more than just pack rivalry. This was something else, an undocumented savagery. In all the decades of kavū knowledge, there simply were no accounts of infighting among them. They were beyond it, in a beautiful and admirable sort of way. Not even the most benevolent skinwalkers were above to clashing within a clan.

Viper Three congregated at the edge of the small clearing, to bear witness.

One of the kavū was the general size of a brown bear, except in the shape of a cougar, only with no tail. The other was a little bulkier, almost shaped like a boar. This added mass of muscle might have led it to a winning side of the fight, except that its opponent was agiler. Grizzly-like claws tore at armored shoulders and flanks, scoring the dense hide and drawing shrieks of pain.

Every swipe of a paw that missed actual meat was too close a call that was bound to become less and less common.

Finally, the bulkier kavū, which had endured more lacerations, slammed its right shoulder into the other's chest. It recoiled into a tree, disorienting the beast. Viper Three witnessed its furry gullet receive a swipe from the other's giant black claws, opening troughs in the flesh. Cascades of dense, dark red blood poured through the gashes, preceding the kavū's collapse.

John shook his head, raised the rifle, and then noticed something. He was grateful that all three of them recognized it.

An actual *look* on the kavū's animalistic face.

There was *fear* there—panic, even.

A pang of empathy struck a chord deep inside John, and he liked to imagine the others felt something similar. Then, abruptly, the kavū jerked toward John, saliva frothing from its widening jaws.

The brunt of the Marlin's recoil into his shoulder pressed the heel of one boot a few inches into the grassy earth. Twenty grams of copper hollow point mushroomed in the back of the kavū's throat, and the reinforced nature of its skull was nullified. The back of its head burst open in a messy plume, the heft of its body hitting the ground a few feet from John's toes with an impact that made his tibiae tremble.

He didn't realize his teeth were grinding until Reva squeezed his shoulder. Then he relaxed, without completely letting his guard down of course, and looked at his comrades.

"Hell of a shot, holy shit," Nil said.

Reva rolled her eyes. "What's the game plan, John? That's five. Should we—"

"Cut through," he said. And then cleared his throat. His voice returned without an iota of waver to it. "We cut through, until we reach a treeline. However long that takes. Kavaculla is ninety acres, but with our approach, if we keep straight, we should only have to cross about two before the other side."

"Two acres?" Nil said. It was half a question.

"Let's say," Reva's eyes darted in thought, "half a klick."

She looked at John and shrugged. He nodded.

"That's fair."

"I can do that," Nil said.

"Goddamn right you can." John's voice was un-yielding. "Because as soon as we're in the open, we make a call. Reva—you phone Boyan, get us airborne. I raise Calder, and report this whole shit-show.

"You got it," Reva nodded.

"Then let's get it done. Same formation, but closer. I'll still be hanging back, just not as far, and always at an angle. Nil…I know, things happen. But try to call-out movement and contact."

"Wilco," he said, and, tucking the Derya firmly against his shoulder, advanced. Reva followed suit, about seven strides behind him, and John trailed accordingly. As he did, he routinely loaded three more cartridges from his bandolier into the Marlin.

Not forty seconds later, Nil's pace slowed, but didn't stop. He activated his mic.

"Got a dead one," he said. "One kavū, badly muti-lated. Its, uh…"

Nil released the mic button, returned his hand to the shotgun, and dared getting within arm's reach of the kavū corpse. The mauling it had endured was alone proof of death, and the immediate area was further evidence. Pools of blood formed a rough ring around the dead cryp-tid, even chunks of flesh and tufts of red-tinged fur laid about.

Nil touched his mic button again, but only once Reva had her weapon trained on the creature. Regardless of its obvious death. The stench alone was a little nause-ating.

"Its skull has been *excavated*," Nil said, sourly.

"They're eating each other," John said. His own voice sounded hollow.

This was almost as bad a sign as the kavū attacking people. In a strange way they wouldn't want to admit, it was worse. Unprecedented and disconcerting.

It didn't occur to them at first, but there *was* an upside to this. Which was, simply, that it meant less threats for them to deal with themselves.

"I want to ask *why*," Reva said. "But I don't think I want to know."

"We'll find out, regardless," John said. A shift of movement in Reva's peripheral drew her eyes to him, sidling a tree. His voice in her ear, vaguely comforting. "Let's just focus. Nil, proceed."

"Copy. Moving."

Reva let out an even breath and followed Nil, still about six or seven strides behind him. Her barrel discipline was flawless. She aimed in a slow, vigilant fanning motion just right of him. Whereas his aim navigated the trees and light underbrush straight ahead, and to his left.

John's advancement never led him as close to the dead kavū as his teammates had been, but he didn't doubt their findings. And certainly didn't need to smell the full brunt of the fetor himself. Even as he gave it a wide berth, he caught a faint wind of it that sufficed to wrinkle his nose.

Coincidentally, about half a minute later, Nil was struck with another wave of something rancid. This time, though, the odor was slightly different. He was experienced enough to discern why it might be.

"The live ones smell worse than the dead ones," he had remembered Reva remarking after their first ever encounter with a kavū. It had been a trio of them a few miles from the Tibetan border, just outside a small Indian town called Nako. That was when John's fascination with them truly began. Apart from their notorious bad breath, the kavū *could* be a beautiful sight. In the same manner a Siberian tiger might be, or a Great White so long as its jaws weren't agape. It had helped, too, that Nako was a beautiful milieu in rural India.

"Might have a live one ahead," Nil said, releasing his collar mic as soon as he finished speaking. His knees bent slightly and he pressed forward with greater caution.

"Coming to you, four o'clock," Reva whispered.

"Fanning right, at your three real soon," John added.

The staggered operators enclosed on what was not only a hub of stenches, but a small commotion, too. Discernible given what was otherwise a pall of absolute silence in the forest.

Sunlight was beginning to diminish more noticeably, and none of Viper Three wanted to acknowledge that in forty minutes it would be dark here.

For now, their integrally illuminated red-dot sights sufficed. And their eyes were sharper than ever.

"I've got motion," John whispered into his mic. He could see the hindquarters of a kavū, limp like a ragdoll, making strange movements. Tugging back and forth. His brow furrowed. The rest of it was obscured by a small copse of European beech.

"Eyes on," Nil said. His heart sunk as he cleared an overhanging branch for better visibility. "Shit, we've got a live one."

"Hold," John said. "I'm taking the shot."

"I don't have visibility. Fucking trees."

"Hold, Reva. Soon as I shoot, you will."

"Copy."

Collecting his breath and steadying his finger as it curled around the aluminum trigger, John used a tree trunk to assist his aim. Through the enclosed red-dot optic he had a clear shot, as if provided by a deity, bracketed by the perfect arrangement of trees and branches.

A kavū with blood and entrails smearing its black, jagged snout was devouring the contents of a dead one's skull. Occasionally its jaws with catch bone and jerk the corpse's body, hence the movement John had seen earlier.

He would have never, not in a hundred years, anticipate seeing cannibalistic kavū. It just wasn't in their genetics to kill each other, for any reason. They would sooner go extinct than feed on another, let alone quarrel.

It left a really bad taste in John's mouth.

This went beyond the defamation of kavū as a species in John's mind. It was a violation of nature itself.

Something was terribly wrong here.

Livid and in dire need of answers he knew he wouldn't get anytime soon, John narrowed his focus.

The sat-phone in a back pouch on his belt rang. It

was a jarring sound that startled himself, and the kavū. Its fierce head lifted, gore dripping from its snout.

"Shit," John cursed, reaching back for the phone.

The call dropped before he could grab it.

His target made eye contact with Nil, and snarled before retracting onto its haunches. Preparing to pounce—

John squeezed the trigger.

The Marlin boomed, and the sound didn't catch up to the kavū until a flowering hollow-point tore into its left rib cage. The brutal round ripped through fur, skin, muscle and flesh—then its shrapnel-like petals sheared into organs. A lung deluged with blood, and the kavū faltered to its right.

That distinct yelp of pain scarred John's soul.

He angrily cocked the lever, his red-dot leaving the kavū only for half a second. Apparently, it was enough time for the beast to redirect. It growled anew, blood and saliva frothing from its jaws, before its fiery orange eyes locked onto Nil once more.

An uneasy feeling plighted his blood.

He wouldn't dare admit it was fear, though.

Nil side-skirted around a tree and fired his shotgun. The slug grazed the wounded kavū's shoulder, one of the shavings from the slug ripping a trough of blood through its back. The creature howled a terrifying sound and galloped toward him.

Reva had swung around a thick bush of wild strawberries, and punched three rapid shots into the kavū's preexisting wound. From a slightly posterior angle, her bullets cut into the kavū's innards. One round must have ruptured its aorta, and the beast's gait broke down as if a vehicle with a blowout. It struck a tree and came to a dead stop. The trunk was just thin enough for the lion-sized beast's momentum to shake it, loose leaves showering Nil and Reva as they chanced getting closer to the kavū.

John approached, swiftly.

He vaulted a log en route to Reva's side.

"It's down," she said, not pressing her mic. Within earshot of Nil, too.

"Permission to confirm?" Nil angled the muzzle of his shotgun.

"Negative," John said. He saw subtle motion in the kavū's left eye, and let the sling carry the weight of his rifle. He drew the Smith & Wesson from its holster, cocked the heavy hammer, and squeezed the trigger without any further delay or warning. The report was thunderous, and had there been any birds left in their nests, they would've deserted Kavaculla in that instant.

A thin smokescreen billowed between the operators. The kavū moved no more, and John holstered the revolver.

Reva squeezed his shoulder.

"Let's make that call," she said.

There was an anger in her voice, too. It sounded subdued and composed, even, but present nonetheless. John appreciated it. When his gaze lifted and locked onto Nil, there was some solidarity in his eyes. They exchanged nods, and John returned the full weight of the Marlin to his hands.

This time, *he* took point.

The rest of their trek was uneventful.

When they reached the nearest treeline, about eight minutes later, relief came over them the second they were in the open. The sun was faintly visible in the distance, about a quarter mile away it seemed, and yet endlessly farther. That amber eye, its cyclopean stare hindered by swollen gray clouds, had already begun its sluggish descent.

Reva didn't hesitate to pull out her sat-phone and hail Boyan. While Nil took a moment to check his gear and ensure everything was optimal, John stepped aside to phone Calder. He raised the long, stiff antenna and dialed.

As soon as the line connected, her voice came through.

"Viper Three, this is Calder," she said, and her use of a name instead of a call-sign immediately notified John that it was a secure line. As he suspected. Calder's voice, though, was tinged with the onset of bad news. *"My call dropped. Are you still in Kavaculla?"*

"Negative. We just made it out."

"How much did you cover?"

"Less than ten acres," John sighed. "But we believe the AO is clear. *Eight* kavū are confirmed dead."

"Eight? Jesus. Copy."

"It gets worse, but I fear you called out of urgency."

"Correct. I'll lead."

John's pause of silence was enough confirmation that she had his full attention.

"As we speak, Cobra Five is being briefed for an

op in Atlanta. Apparently, the Hemic Syndicate is experiencing a...climactic event. Reavers, they're attacking the vampyr."

John shook his head. He looked over at Nil, who caught the motion and lifted his attention from the Derya to John. Reading the bemusement in John's eyes was disconcerting.

At the same time, Reva bid farewell to Boyan over her own sat-phone, in Bulgarian, and hung up. She faced John, discerned something was off, and stepped closer.

John put the phone on speaker.

Calder seemed to acknowledge John's silence as him taking in that bit of unusual info, and processing it slowly. This was logical. Reavers didn't attack vampyr, they were like pets to them. Occasionally one would bite the hand that feeds, but not an outright mutiny.

"I'm sorry, can you confirm that?" John finally said. "The reavers are *feeding* on Hemic?"

Those words were for Reva and Nil. Immediately they went from staring at his satellite phone to looking at John with the same befuddlement previously on his face.

The Hemic Syndicate was the biggest criminal organization in the southern United States, with vampyr connections that went back as far as the 1920s. If there was any clan of vampyr that had their shit together 24/7 it was Hemic and Sanguine, the latter being a syndicate that dominated the west coast.

All the more reason for concern.

"Negative," came Calder's firm response. *"Not* feeding, *Aguirre. Just* attacking. *The Hemic's own reavers have turned on them. Inexplicably. It's a frenzy*

down there. Factors can't be accounted for, but in about an hour Cobra Five will be on-site to provide a better sit-rep. And to neutralize the reavers."

Cobra Five was one of Forked Tongue's star full-force squads. Composed of five operators, four tenured and one rookie that had in recent months shown exceptional talent in the field.

"What about Hemic?" John asked.

"The Syndicate won't be touched, apart from whatever Cobra deems necessary. We can't risk destabilizing the entire Georgia underworld over this. Now, I'm sharing this because it's pertinent to your current op. Or so the brainiacs in Raleigh believe."

Not only was this a secure line, it was an isolated one. John would've smirked at any other time. Not even Nil's face showed a crack of humor. They were all invested in a way that struck, and moved, them to the core.

"Understand?" Calder said. *"HQ wants Viper Three back in Moyock ASAP. They've already dispatched a cleanup crew to Kavaculla, from a safe house in Bucharest. ETA is eighty minutes. How are you on evac?"*

John looked at Reva. She flashed five fingers on one hand and three on the other. Having deduced the time that had already passed since Reva got off the phone with Boyan, he said—

"Six minutes, we'll be wheels-up."

"Copy. Anything else I should know? You were saying earlier..."

"Are you sitting down, ma'am?"

Calder chuckled dryly over the line.

"Skating a fine line, Aguirre. What's going on?"

John sighed. "The kavū, ma'am. They're attacking each other. Eating, even."

Silence. Calder was processing. Maybe even sitting down.

"I read you, Viper Three. Will inform the cleanup crew, and Raleigh. Just get your asses back to Tulcea, and board that jet. I'll be informed the second you're stateside again. Once you land at Fentress, you'll RTB via helo."

"Copy. Looking forward to it."

"Likewise. Price, too. He's even talking about suiting up himself."

John's head recoiled. He looked at the others. Reva's eyebrows raised. It was a surprise, alright. A bittersweet one.

"Hopefully it doesn't come to that, for *their* sake," John said.

"Can confirm. Have a safe flight, Viper Three. Out."

The call terminated. John sighed and retracted the antenna. He then stuffed the phone back into his pouch.

"Boyan said he was in Casimcea," Reva said. "Didn't want to wait in Stejaru, for fear of alarming them any further."

"That's a good call," John said. A few seconds later, they heard the distinct thump of approaching rotors. Soon thereafter, the shape of the Bell 206 approaching as dusk inched closer to the region. John took a deep, haggard breath. "We need more of those."

"More of what, boss?" Nil asked.

"Good calls. Good anything, for fuck's sake."

6

Aboard their Learjet, John was stirred first. The copilot had left the cabin to personally wake him, and the second that John's groggy eyelids peeled open, the man gently woke Reva. Nil required a more rigorous approach, but eventually he came out of his abyssal slumber. Once realizing the time—a little over an hour ahead of their arrival—Nil even hit the copilot with a dramatic "what's the meaning of this?"

The answer was brisk, and concise.

"Calder made contact an hour ago," he said.

That alone alerted Viper Three and helped them shake off any relics of fatigue.

"She delivered a briefing package," the copilot said, whose name eluded John, but he recalled that he was valid Forked Tongue personnel and not just some international contact.

More to the point—

A briefing package was only disclosed when operators were abroad, and couldn't make it back to the facility before their next op. This suggested they were being rerouted elsewhere, and something far more urgent needed Viper Three's attention.

"But insisted we wait until the Virginia coast was visible to wake you."

The copilot directed their attention to the TV screen built into the wall just right of the cockpit door. John was already sitting in the nearest seat; Nil behind him, and Reva in a seat over his left shoulder, across the aisle. Nil got up to loom over his right shoulder, while Reva stood in the aisle. Then the copilot spoke again, garnering their attention.

"We're still over the Atlantic, approaching Chesapeake Bay," he said, already retreading back into the cockpit. "We'll land at Fentress within the hour."

John nodded kindly at him, and then the man closed the door behind him. After a deep breath, John looked down at his armrest and pressed a raised button on the built-in remote. The play icon triggered the TV to play a prepared video file.

Calder appeared, sitting at a desk.

It was evident that she was neither comfortable nor content.

"I regret to inform you that your RTB has been delayed. Due to recent developments, which indicate that something bigger is afoot, you'll be taking a Black Hawk in Fentress to a new destination."

Calder kneaded her brow before putting her hand

down and sighing. They could tell that her voice was getting hoarse, likely from being on calls in and out of the facility for the past day and a half.

"Upon landing, you'll resupply for a new op in Long Island. Unfortunately, given the time crunch and limited manpower, you won't have a chance to modify your gear or rearm. Price, however, *will* be accompanying you to the Hamptons.

"Additionally, you'll *hopefully* be joining Boa Five in New York. Your AO will be a large estate called the Skyline Villa, owned by big-money vampyr, which has become overrun with reavers *and* gargoyles. As of 1800 hours, Boa Five has confirmed that all resident vampyr—both inside the villa and the subterranean compound—have been neutralized. Familiars, the main staff operating the villa during daylight, however, are still scattered. The sheer number of reavers and 'goyles, paired with the fear that vampyr will be sending their own cleanup crew at nightfall, demands backup.

"That is where your team comes in. You will infil with Price, and until your RTB, accept the call-sign Viper Four. Your flight from Fentress to Southampton should take just under two hours. We can all pray that Boa Five will have reduced the threat by then, and the lot of you can have a breeze mopping up."

Calder feigned a weak smile.

It vanished as soon as it had appeared.

"Make no mistake, Viper Three. Something far greater than we might have feared, or suspected, is at work. HQ is still brainstorming, but the early theories are much worse than even our wildest thoughts."

"Fuck me," Nil said under his breath.

"The hell could that mean?" Reva asked, exchanging grim looks with John.

The prerecorded video continued.

"Thank you for your commitment and tenacity, Viper. We look forward to welcoming you, Price, and Boa back at the facility once Skyline is clear."

She nodded, more like bowed her head with a hint of finality, and the video ended.

John sat back and his leather chair made a sound.

His stare was blank and aimless.

"Reavers *and* gargoyles?" Nil said, scowling. "Sounds like a clusterfuck."

"We've known about Skyline for two years, now. We just haven't been given the green-light to raid it, because…" John shrugged. "Semantics. Bureaucracy."

"The 'goyles are just doing what comes natural," Reva said. "Protecting their post. That villa. But this reaver problem. First Atlanta, now New York. What the hell has gotten them all riled up?"

"Whatever pushed the kavū so far north, I'm guessing," John said. He stood, and Reva stepped aside. She and Nil followed him aft. Their gear was secured in a low compartment outside the lavatory.

"Approaching the Fentress airstrip. Landing in two minutes." The copilot's voice. "Please sit down and put your seatbelts on."

Nil cursed under his breath and spun around to head back to his seat. He paused a few feet down the aisle to look back. John was hunched over the open compartment, rifling through the contents for his gear.

"Hey, John, just wait 'til we land," Nil said.

Reva was torn between following suit or returning to her seat.

"Beginning descent," the pilot announced, his voice slightly different from his colleague's.

With a rugged sigh, Reva grabbed John's shirt and tugged. He stood, turned, and gave her an inexorable look. She showed her palms, and beelined back to her seat. Nil, buckled in his, just shook his head.

The Learjet's altitude changed. It was a slight adjustment at first, for those seated. For John, even the brute of a man he was, he had to grip a seat to stay upright. He made his way back to his seat, wearing his torso rig, 45-70 bandolier, and holster—with the revolver secured in it. Pouches were still empty and he had not retrieved the Marlin, thankfully.

As he passed Reva on the left, he gripped the top of her seat and bowed his head. He kissed her, hard, and she lifted her hands to hold his face. The Learjet's descent took its final dip, and Nil looked out the window to his right. Past the wing and its beady indicator lights, Fentress Airbase was sufficiently illuminated. It was early nightfall, just past eight.

The slight shift in elevation within the plane almost made John fall into Reva. He channeled this into his kiss, and for a split-second their teeth made contact. When their mouths parted, Reva held hers but a smile crept through her fingers.

John smirked beneath his dense mustache and strode across the way to plant himself in his seat. He buckled seconds before the plane's wheels touched down. It was a pretty smooth landing, considering the size of the private jet, and minutes later they had taxied to a viable spot on the tarmac. The pilot announced his gratitude and wished them Godspeed in their endeavors.

Somehow a simple "have a good evening" didn't suit the occasion. The operators were glad the jet crew were professional and aware of their situation, at least to some degree.

While Nil and Reva stood, John ironically staying seated, the copilot emerged from the cabin. He turned right and disengaged the passenger door, then extended the attached staircase.

Nil and Reva headed aft to gather their equipment. John finally unbuckled and stood, approaching the copilot who waited by the open hatch. He personally thanked him for exhibiting competence, and put in a good word for the pilot, too.

Once Nil and Reva appeared to his left, loaded up, John stepped aside and returned to retrieve the rest of his equipment. As they descended the three blocky steps, Nil and Reva were alerted to an approaching vehicle. The UTV's headlights washed over them when they were boots-down. Tires screeched to a halt, the driver parking it parallel with the Learjet. The two operators recognized a familiar face sitting shotgun.

Not just familiar, but comforting—even invigorating. Seeing him outside the Moyock facility was a rarity, one to relish. Of course, it wasn't without an indication of emergency.

Seamus Price exited the Can-Am Defender, a two-seater UTV with an extended bed behind the canopied cab. The driver, wearing a Navy uniform with Ensign insignia and a Fentress patch, stayed seated.

"I'll be damned," Reva said, unable to resist a big grin. She firmly shook Price's hand, and Nil followed suit.

"That I'm here," Price said, "should constitute otherwise."

Reva's smile had begun to fade when they shook hands, but now she practically laughed.

"Touché," she added, milliseconds before John arrived behind her.

"The man, the legend, the…poet?" John smirked, and shook Price's hand.

"When dire circumstances are all we have to face," Price's rugged no-nonsense voice returned in full effect, "sometimes poetry is the whiskey down the hatch."

Viper Three exchanged dumbstruck looks all around, as if to say "who is this guy?" And then Price gave the Learjet pilot a gesture of goodwill and farewell. He looked at the operators and nodded back toward the UTV. They followed him to the bed, where all four climbed in and sat down. Price seated himself with his back to the cab, and slapped the roof.

"Get us there, Pruitt," he declared.

"Yes, sir," the Ensign said, and turned the UTV around.

Price looked at the three operators sitting before him, and shook his head. He leaned forward, and believed he addressed them privately, although he knew the driver could probably hear him, too.

"Can't seem to shake the *sir* with these uniformed

guys," Price said.

"You're former SAS, a Sergeant Major no less," John said. "Can you blame 'em?"

Unlike most of the active members of Forked Tongue, no matter how esteemed they were in their fields, nobody outside of the organization knew their names. Price was different; he was a legend in some circles, even here in the States.

"I reckon," Price said, and kneaded his gruff, grizzled beard while gazing out at Fentress Airbase. Both stadium-style lights and grounded floodlights illuminated the 32-acre Naval asphalt.

"Where's the Hawk?" Nil asked, looking around.

"Lima Two-Six-Six had a slight hiccup," Price said. "She had to taxi one of our fire-teams to Richmond. Few klicks out of the city, got some full-mooners raising hell."

"Jesus. Amidst all this other shit?" Nil shook his head. "Can't be coincidence."

"Doubtful," Price said. "It's all connected, HQ says. How, we don't know yet."

"Who got the full-mooner op?" Reva asked.

A colloquial term at Forked Tongue for lycanthropes that preferred their wolf form, adopting a feral lifestyle. They were usually very quarrelsome and exhibited no signs of civility. Packs were rare for full-mooners, they tended to favor running rogue. And very seldom ventured anywhere close to cities.

"Asp Three. Plus a trainee tacked-on for extra firepower. Promising lad, so hopefully it won't be regretted."

"Asp is elite, I'm sure they'll take him in well, and vice versa," John said. "What about us? Lima gonna be back soon?"

Price looked away from Viper Three to stare out past the cab, squinting against a glare of floodlights they approached.

"Helipad's just ahead," he said, facing them again, and then looking at his wristwatch. He tapped it twice. "She should be back in three to five mikes, max. We'll make good time, don't worry. Boa's holding down the fort, last I heard. Skyline's still a mess, though. Anticipating a vamp cleanup crew any minute, unfortunately."

Nil shook his head in disbelief, and disappointment.

"Speaking of which," Reva said. "Calder mentioned a resupply, but that's it. So…no blades?"

Price clicked his tongue. A small smirk broke through that dense beard.

"You really thought I'd cut you lot out of the fun?"

"Cut. Nice." Nil said.

Price's smile vanished.

Nil looked away and shrugged.

Reva and John exchanged fleeting grins, just as the UTV came to a lurching stop that almost tossed Nil overboard. The helipad was twenty feet away, but between them and the platform was parked another UTV. Same Can-Am model with the extended bed. Except that nobody else was around, chocks were by the wheels, and a large chest occupied the bed. A five-foot worklight stood a few feet away.

"Here we are," Price said, and hopped over the

edge of the bed as if a limber teenager.

Meanwhile Nil took his sweet time, even groaning as he did. His excuse would be the nine-hour flight, except that it had been aboard a luxury private jet.

"Appreciate it, Pruitt," Price said to the driver. Who proceeded to salute, adding "a pleasure, sir," and then drove off.

Price sighed and convened with the others behind the other parked vehicle. He mounted the back right wheel and threw open the lid of the chest, then retrieved two items before anyone else. His rig was already loaded with magazines, a sat-phone, and even light provisions. But apparently he had left his actual weapons in the chest.

"What're you running tonight?" John asked, while he and the others gathered strictly ammunition from the chest. The mags even had white-out initials on them, for Viper Three. J, R, N. After asking his question, though, it occurred to John that there *was* a single firearm in the chest, which matched the magazines with a 'J' on them.

"Hold up, I see a light in your eyes," Price said, smirking a little. "Go on."

John hoisted the weapon from the chest, and secured a mag. He racked the firing lever on the SBR, and nodded a few times.

"I guess Calder wasn't a hundred-percent truthful," he said.

"She was, but that was last-minute. At my behest. Figured the Marlin wasn't perfectly suitable for raiding a villa. Hence no ammo in there for ya, but I can see your belt's still loaded, so oughtta be fine."

"Very fine," Reva said. Then she looked at Price, and shrugged. "The rifle."

"Right," Nil said.

She elbowed him.

"DDM4," John said, still relishing the short-barreled rifle. "Probably my favorite SBR. Three-hundred Blackout?"

"Copy," Price said. "Surefire SOCOM can, six-inch barrel. Will make the rest of us wishing we were running subs, too."

John shrugged, and pointed at his ear.

"Peltors are solid. Doesn't matter much, but I can't say I don't appreciate the smooth action."

"If we ever split up, or it gets that way," John said, "you could still sneak up on a familiar. Less likely a 'goyle or vamp, but hey."

"I'll take what I can get. Speaking of which. Calder said all the vampyr on-site were KIA."

"Likely, but stragglers may still be in hiding. Then there's that cleanup crew."

"True."

They had finished resupplying. It wasn't like Viper Three had expended large amounts of ammo in Romania. They had been lucky, in a way, that the kavū proved cannibalistic.

Price then noticed Nil and Reva pick up laser-sight devices and flashlight mounts from the chest. Nil didn't question this or say anything, he just affixed them to his weapons. Two of each for his shotgun and SMG.

Reva clicked her tongue at John, catching his attention. She activated the Holosun LS117 laser-sight in her hand, and a bright green bead appeared on his chest. Then she turned it off and mounted it to the left rail of her rifle.

John glanced at the chest and peered in, retrieving his own devices. The remaining laser-sight had a white 'J' drawn on it. Whereas the Modlite PLH flashlights could be mounted worry-free, the lasers had to be zeroed-in, weapon specific. He thought of the Cage Trolls, and how damn good they were at their jobs.

"The only other additions," Price said. "Necessary given the low-light. To our understanding, the power's still on at Skyline, which is why we didn't pack NODs. That *could* change by the time we arrive, we'll just have to deal with it.

"Flashlights should be last resort, *if* it is dark. Don't want to give away our positions. Not that reavers are that attentive, but 'goyles can be too predictable, and vamps are sneaky little fuckers."

"I hear that," Reva said, pointing her rifle's barrel skyward, and thumbing the flashlight to confirm its healthy battery.

"Considered running infrared," Price said. "But since 'goyles are coldblooded…"

"Good thinking," John said, and slung the Daniel Defense DDM4 PDW, thanks to a pre-attached sling that he had to adjust.

"And on that note," Price said, reaching behind the chest. Almost simultaneously, the approaching thump of rotors in the night sky drew their attention.

Less than a quarter mile out, the white spotlight on

the Black Hawk's nose, and the strobe from its tail, became visible. A few seconds later, the red anti-collision light on its hull gained clarity, paired with the green navigation lights on its wingtips. And that staccato beat of its rotors evolved into a steady hum.

"As I was saying," Price lassoed their attention again. He had retrieved two fistfuls of scabbards. Inside each were different blades. A falcata, xiphos, two kodachis, and a kukri. The curved, pear-shaped blade of the carbon steel kukri quickly found a home beside Price's thigh, as he secured the black handle to his belt.

The others didn't need labels.

Reva accepted her twin kodachis, each with a 16-inch Damascus steel blade. John took his xiphos, a bronze-handled sword with a 20-inch leaf-shaped iron blade. And Nil his falcata, its curved brass handle feeling at home in his grip. He briefly removed the scabbard to observe the 5160 spring steel blade, its subtle curvature always reminding him of a woman.

The approaching Black Hawk's spotlight caught the blade and briefly blinded him.

"As a woman might," he would joke.

Except now that their ride was here, everything felt suddenly grim and heavy. They reminded themselves of what awaited them in Southampton, and that their own brothers of Boa Five were in danger. There was no active squad or fire-team in Forked Tongue's roster that didn't have Viper Three's respect and confidence, however, this op seemed fucked from the start. With what they experienced in Romania, and everything else that Calder had reported, things didn't really have that polished feel of good faith to them.

A lot to go wrong, and Murphy's Law was lingering above them like a bad omen.

As Lima-266 descended to the helipad, John equipped his own collar mic and inserted Peltor earplugs. As he paired his device with the others' comlink, the helo's skids touched down and the bay door slid open with a *clang*. Audible even over the roar of rotors. A crewman inside the helo beckoned them, shouting "let's go, let's go!"

Viper Four didn't hesitate.

They hustled across the helipad, and boarded the aircraft individually. Nil first, then Reva, followed by John. Price hoisted himself inside, and the crewman slid the door shut, locked it, and informed the pilot they were a go. He sat in his seat, beside Price, opposite the other three. They held their weapons barrel-down, safeties on. John was grateful for a cloth snugly wrapped around his rifle's $1800 suppressor, keeping it clean and unscathed.

The Black Hawk began its ascent.

During the flight, the scabbards for the operators' blades would occasionally clank against the pole frame of their seats. A muffled sound at best, once everybody had secured their headsets.

The cabin interior was lit, but dimly. Had the operators been running NODs, it would be a blue hue that wouldn't interfere with night-vision.

"Rudy Taggart," the copilot said. He had a young face but a no-bullshit determination to his eyes. He shared the same similarities in uniform as the main pilot, who remained quiet and fixated on his job. Taggart's insignia was not Navy, but Forked Tongue. This was comforting for Viper Four; not that they had any qualms with Navy personnel, of course. But this way, and given the gravity of the op, they assumed he and the pilot were in-the-know.

Which would help them.

"We'll reach Southampton in a hundred mikes, give or take," Taggart said. "Your pilot for the evening is a quiet kid, but is pure commitment. Ain't that right, Dickey?"

No response.

Taggart shook his head. "Dickey Worton. What a hoot. Anyway. Let's get down to brass tacks."

He brandished a ruggedly-cased thirteen-inch tablet, whose tempered glass screen protector had a myriad of shallow scratches on it, but with the brightness cranked they could still discern what they were looking at.

"This is your AO. Skyline Villa," Taggart said. Any iota of humor that had previously inhabited his tone had since deserted. "I understand you know *of* it, but not like this. We have a complete layout of the property, not just aerial but on-site, thanks to undercover familiars. Not the easiest job, mind you, and fortunately they were not present today. But thanks to them, we have a comprehensive rendition of the villa's interior, including a rough blueprint room-to-room."

The operators leaned forward to scrutinize the map. Their photographic memories studied it, appreciated its simplicity, and stored it for later use.

"Price?" Taggart said.

"Right. So, as you can see, a lot of high ceilings and open spaces. A few big staircases, too, but no stair-wells. We'll need to be extra cautious of our corners and balconies. The villa is only two stories, three if you count the roofs, which we should, because most of these double as terraces with furniture and low parapets. Since our primary hostiles are reavers and 'goyles, these don't pose the threat they normally would, *but*, if we get hit with a vamp cleanup crew, those spots become immediate concerns of enemy gunfire.

"Note the courtyard-like pool area, with the Jacuzzi overlooking the east hillside. And the floor-to-ceiling glass walls, neighboring hallways, including the sky-bridge connecting the two main structures. Upon arrival, I seriously doubt all that glass will still be intact, so that's even more open space. With reavers, this may be to our advantage, as they have a tendency to go nuts and charge, devoid of strategy."

"Unlike us," John said.

"Precisely. And Taggart? Our approach."

"We will reach the villa from the south." He extended a hand and John returned the tablet, so that Taggart could swipe to display the front of the estate. He flipped the device around to show the team. "The villa's anterior features a golf pad that protrudes from the structure. Not sufficient enough to be a helipad, so you'll fast-rope down."

"What about the posterior?" Reva asked, brow furrowed. She wasn't displeased with this approach, but her expression relayed immediate regret in even asking.

"Considered, but too many obstacles," Taggart said, understandingly. He swiped to display the rear of the estate. "Although the back deck is a broad terrace, and the second highest level to the villa, the area around the fire pit is adorned with high topiaries and a pergola to the east."

"Copy," Reva nodded.

"Boa has reported this area to be rife with 'goyles," Price said, indicating the greenery. Dense hedges surrounding tall conifer topiaries. "They seem to be periodically retreating and regrouping here."

"They may not be as methodical as vampyr," Nil said, "but it's arguable that they possess a thinking mind."

Everyone nodded.

"Speaking of which," Taggart said. "Since you'll be fast-roping in, the helo hovering, it needs to be brisk. We can't afford any contact with flying targets."

"Absolutely," Reva said.

"Any questions, concerns?" Taggart asked.

"No, sir. We appreciate it." This, from John, meant volumes to Taggart. He tried to handle it professionally, and nodded firmly.

"Can we hold onto this for the ride?" Reva asked, motioning for the tablet.

"Certainly," Taggart said. He began to get up. "If Boa, or Moyock, makes contact before we arrive, I'll relay immediately."

"Thank you, Taggart," Price said.

The copilot reentered the cockpit and sat adjacent Worton.

"Two hours is a long time in an active, hostile environment," Nil said, leaning forward. "I dread one of two things."

"And what's that, Nilsson?"

"By the time we arrive, Boa won't be intact," he said, his tone unenthusiastic. There was a pause as John and Reva shot him demeaning looks. And then Nil's voice lifted a little. "Or they'll have eliminated every target."

"Right. Then you won't be able to use your big-boy gun," John said.

Nil smirked dryly and rolled his eyes.

"I'd rather pray for the latter," Price said. "Regardless, the chances of a vamp crew reaching the villa within half an hour of our arrival is high. Don't worry, Nilsson—you'll get a chance."

Nil nodded confidently.

"How are we on vulnerability?" Reva asked. She was intermittently swiping through the images of the villa. "Skyline seems aptly named; it's on an incline, looks to be secluded. Can't tell, or remember, just how well."

"Very," Price reassured. "We're better off than the Atlanta situation, that's for sure. Everyone down there, from HQ's people to Cobra Five, is doing their best to contain the incident. Skyline should be safe from the public eye, though. Filthy-rich people like their privacy; filthy-rich vamps *need* it."

The operators nodded.

John hunched forward. "I was asking, back on the tarmac. What're you running tonight?"

"Oh, hell." Price sat back and pivoted the assault rifle on its three-prong flash-hider. "A favorite from SIG. The Spear, in six-point-eight SPC. Sixteen-inch barrel, hybrid EOTech, a thing of beauty. Should work great against 'goyles."

"Very nice. If I didn't have my Marlin as back-up, I'd be jealous."

"Speaking of thou-shalt-not-covet," Price said, and leaned to the side, then groped his hip-holster. "I said *fuck that, give me what Aguirre's got*."

"No shit? The TAC Ultra?"

"Gotta love a 1911. Can't shake it. I don't care what the nine-mil and Glock boys say."

John grinned.

"Forty-five gang," Nil said, clicking his tongue and patting his own holster. It wasn't a 1911, but the FN pistol was considered a top-of-the-line .45 model.

"Yada, yada," Reva said.

Price smirked. It was almost invisible, in the dark cabin, and amongst a shrubbery of graying beard.

As the Black Hawk tore through the night sky, maintaining an altitude of three-hundred feet, any semblance of humor amid its inhabitants began to dissolve. The severity of their op, and the fact they were coming to a larger team's aid, settled into their blood. It was usually the other way around; fire-teams occasionally required backup from a full squad.

At least they had been blessed with Seamus Price's company. Four to help five. They just prayed all five of Boa's members were still alive when they arrived.

7

Southampton, New York
August 10, 2024
10:08 PM

Muzzle flashes painted the scene on their approach. The Black Hawk had crossed the expanse of Atlantic Ocean facing the beachfront that the villa's anterior overlooked. Both side doors were already unlocked and slung open, providing Viper ample view, especially starboard. The property was inadequately illuminated, many of the exterior lights either off or broken, and although nearly forty-percent of the structure itself was glass, most of the indoor lighting appeared off as well.

Standing for a better view, the operators had removed their headsets and ensured their ear-plugs were on, synced with their collar mics. Even so, without headsets, the roar of rotors and twin turboshaft engines was almost deafening.

Perhaps the foreign dissonance of the approaching Black Hawk alarmed the creatures inside, because suddenly the muzzle flashes stopped.

Viper prayed this was the reason, and not because

they had been overwhelmed.

Then the comlink that Viper Four shared, inherently the same frequency that any Forked Tongue team used, burst with life.

"Boa Five, this is Boa Five. Any friendlies read?"

John and Price exchanged relieved looks, and then confident nods. Taggart exited the cockpit to reenter the cabin, and with Price's help they prepared the ceiling-mounted fast-rope equipment.

"Loud and clear, this is Viper *Four*, we read you, Boa," John said. "Approaching the south face. What's your status?"

He released his collar mic button and the team waited. They would be over the golf pad in ten seconds.

"Glad to hear it, Viper. AO is a shit-show. We are down two, *I repeat, we have one wounded and one KIA. My casualty is on the northwest rooftop, above a master bedroom. My other two men branched off to retrieve his body but I haven't made contact in five minutes. Me and my wounded are held-up in a fucking open-floor bathroom on the southeast corner. Got a skylight above us, but—"*

A crackle of gunfire carried over their comms, making Viper Four flinch.

Just then Worton directed the helo's nose-mounted spotlight at the golf pad. A cluster of dark figures scattered like humanoid cockroaches, springing acrobatically.

Taggart and Price had just about protracted the overhead fast-rope extensions when the rest of the team witnessed this.

131

"Looks like the cleanup crew got here just before us," John said. "Must've driven here, and crawled up the south face like spider-monkeys."

"God, I hate vamps," Nil sighed, and his right thumb kneaded the brass hilt to his blade.

Although vampyr were generally less a nuisance than the other Dreaded Five, cleanup crews were their elite.

The gunfire had ceased.

"Confirm, Boa. Are you still there?" John asked.

"Sure am, but Stav is bleeding real bad. Can you medivac?"

"Fuck," John mouthed, his finger off the collar mic button.

There weren't many Forked Tongue operators who didn't know the name, or the man, Stavros Bakirtzis. He usually went by Stav, and was a beast of a man that usually operated a shotgun or an LMG. On a couple of telltale occasions, both. But when he wasn't in the field, he was that gentle-giant archetype that nobody hated.

To hear that he was severely wounded hurt everyone aboard the helo. Possibly even the crew, too.

John looked to Taggart, who began to shake his head solemnly. Then he straightened up, touched his headset ear-cup, and glanced back toward the cockpit.

The Black Hawk's wing-like fast-rope devices had fully extended, and now dangled thirty feet of 40mm eight-ply nylon. Worton flew over the golf pad, and the helo gained elevation. The team held onto their seats and overhead bars, as they remained standing.

"So much for that LZ," Taggart shouted.

Even though the vampyr had scattered below, they were still teeming around the front of the villa.

"As long as we're boots-down within the next twenty seconds, I can't complain," John replied.

"We're gonna put you down on a terrace directly above the grand bathroom," Taggart shouted. "Shatter the skylight, and get Stav on that rope. I'll reel him in."

"Are you fucking sure?" John demanded, speaking slowly, but loudly. He knew how high-risk this last-resort maneuver was, especially with potential gargoyles in the vicinity. The only benefit being that the fast-rope devices, these anyway, offered a pneumatic pulley system for raising or lowering equipment. Or, in this case, someone that was wounded—as long as they had the strength to hold on.

"Just *do it*!" Taggart snapped.

John nodded, and exchanged grim looks with Price. Who then grabbed Reva's kit shoulder strap, pulling her toward the open side of the helo where he stood. She nodded at him.

John activated his collar mic.

"We're right above you, Boa. Sit tight. Vamp cleanup is on-site, we don't have much time."

"Copy. Watch out for 'goyles. Haven't seen 'em for a bit. They might be regrouping behind the pergola, northwest corner."

"Got it. You have any carabiners?"

A pause.

Some gunfire erupted toward the northwest corner of the villa. Not as far as the pergola, but just before it. Possibly the rest of Boa Five.

"Copy. A few on me. Sending us a rope?"

"Read my fucking mind. Frank, right?"

"John, that you? Fuck's sake, give us that rope, yeah?"

John smirked fleetingly, shaking his head.

Frank Santino was usually Boa Five's implicit SIC. Which begged to question where their assumed team captain was, Zac Gunnar.

Taggart touched his ear-cup again, indicating to the others that Worton was telling him something. From the aggressive look on his face, they assumed it wasn't splendid news. Hopefully just a statement for urgency.

"Incoming," John said, mic button pressed. He released it.

"Breaking skylight now. See you soon."

The second Frank's voice cut out, a muzzle flash lit up below the corner of the skylight. Thirty-five feet above, the Black Hawk hovered. The glass splintered, and another double-tap from Frank's rifle shattered it. The bathroom wasn't fully lit, but it wasn't pitch black, either.

"Us first, Viper," Price said. "Now move, move, *move!*"

The tips of Nil's boots were already gripping the metallic ledge of the helo's cabin floor. Both weapons slung, reinforced nylon gloves pulled on, he was ready to fast-rope down.

"Right behind you!" John shouted, and squeezed Nil's left shoulder. He leapt out, gripping the dangling rope with both hands and crossed arches of his boots. As he descended, Reva stepped off the opposite side of the helo, gripping the rope and descending briskly.

"Looking forward to your exfil," Taggart shouted at John and Price. "We'll be twenty-four klicks northeast, at the Klenawicus Airfield. Make the call with your sat-phone, Price has the number."

Taggart exchanged a forearm-shake with Price, and then stood by, ready to operate the starboard pulley.

John followed Nil as he said he would, while Price descended above and behind Reva, who was already boots-down and stepping aside. They were on the concrete terrace, lined with hedges and occasional topiaries, accessed via a stone staircase facing the anterior patio. Reva's attention fixated on this area, particularly the seating arrangements between their terrace and the golf pad, about eighty feet away. Anticipative of vampyr.

Like Nil, who covered open metallic double-doors left of where they landed, she kept her flashlight off and her laser on. The Black Hawk's spotlight occasionally fluttered over where they stood, while also scanning the area. The multitasking aptitudes of Worton at the helm of the helo did not go underappreciated.

"I'll drop down, help cover Santino," Price said, still gripping the fast-rope.

John nodded.

Price dangled the rope through the open skylight, and descended. Below, his boots crunched glass, and he stepped aside.

"All set, coming up!" Price shouted.

John looked skyward, where the Black Hawk hovered thirty feet up. Taggart loomed out of the cabin, illuminated by a red anti-collision light. John waved a forefinger in the air, and then gave a thumbs-up. Taggart reciprocated the last gesture and then withdrew. The rope went taut from Stav's weight, and milliseconds later the mechanical pulley did its job.

As the rope slowly lifted the 6'6" 270lb operator, often called the Gentle Greek Giant, or G3, what sounded like loud plinking caught Viper's ears. They looked up, momentarily bewildered. This didn't last long, as it occurred to them that the helo was being shot at.

Taggart shouted below, but his voice didn't register over the roar of rotors and engines. So he gestured with his hands.

"Reva! Golf pad."

She shot a glance over her shoulder, locking eyes with John, acknowledging that that was all he needed to say. And then she advanced down the steps, her Noveske N4 locked into her shoulder, one hand extended to clutch the vertical foregrip.

John followed five paces behind her, his DDM4 poised as well.

The gunshots coming from the front of the villa were not loud, but the second Reva peered around the corner, she spotted a cluster of muzzle flashes. Even the best suppressors reduced flash, but didn't eliminate it.

"Bang hammers, love," John said behind her.

Reva's green laser-sight beaded her first target, a dark silhouette in all black standing on the golf pad. She put two quick rounds into the upper chest, and the shooter staggered. Then she tracked her second target, who immediately noticed the unsuppressed gunfire from her N4, though equipped with an effective three-prong flash hider.

John stepped away from the building, left of Reva, and his compact rifle nailed a third shooter just as they began to target her.

The three vampyr went down with six to eight shots each, but would be back on their feet seconds later. It was quite possible they wore Level III ceramic body armor as well, still keeping them lightweight and nimble; bullets couldn't kill a vamp, but they still hurt.

Enemy fire had relinquished the Black Hawk, which had come dangerously close to its tail rotor.

John and Reva advanced into the darkness where they had originally planned to fast-rope down. A trio of armed vampyr clad in all black, balaclavas leaving only their pale upper faces and shiny gray eyes exposed, engaged the operators. The latter were superior gunfighters, and put rounds in them before they could squeeze the triggers on their suppressed weapons. This time, John and Reva aimed higher. Headshots could, in theory, kill a vamp, if enough were able to obliterate the skull or sever the spine; but their bones were notoriously resilient.

If center mass hits could stagger them, or even put them on their ass, sufficient headshots were like a disorienting migraine.

Meanwhile, at the top of the steps and behind a block of the villa's upper level, Nil watched Stav ascend. He had patted the man's back when he cleared the skylight, attached to the knotted rope via a carabiner on his belt. As far as Nil could tell, Stav had endured a nasty bite on his shoulder, near the neck, blood seeping through gauze, and been shot twice in the abdomen.

Fortunately they didn't have to worry about vampyr turning people with bites. In order to spread their disease, a vamp had to bite their victim on the neck or wrist, and then be fed on themselves. It was also a 24-hour process that felt like utter hell.

If nothing else, this assuaged Forked Tongue from dealing with zombie-like outbreaks. All the more fortunately, zombies were a thing of pure fiction. As if there weren't worse enemies out there that did exist.

A blur of motion in the dark sky above the villa caught Nil's eye. He jerked his submachine-gun up, and armed his flashlight. The narrow beam scanned the night, which was already being cut through every so often by the shaft of the helo's spotlight.

The shape lured his attention again, darting across his unsure beam. A vaguely humanoid mass with an immense wingspan arced toward the helo. Stav was maybe fifteen feet above the skylight, and an equal distance to Taggart, when Worton banked the Black Hawk left. Stav swung on the rope, almost colliding with a topiary. The helo banked right, then, as what Nil witnessed was a swooping gargoyle. Its bat-like wings flapped with a bellowing sound of wind, and it glided around the helo like a vulture.

Nil's flashlight tracked it, and he let out only his most confident shots from the suppressed SMG, careful not to shoot the Black Hawk. He also knew the rounds wouldn't do a damn thing against the 'goyle, except annoy it. This, he could accept, given the circumstances.

Anything to distract it from the helo.

Which Worton had stopped canting for the sake of Stav and Taggart. The pulley kept reeling the rope in, and the second Stav had reached the skids, the Black Hawk yawed away from the villa. The gargoyle snarled in the air, a sound that even over the thump of rotors, Nil could hear.

It was difficult to tell in the night, aided only by the illumination of anti-collision and navigation lights on the helo, but Nil believed he saw Stav be pulled inside by Taggart. And then the Black Hawk cleared the airspace above Skyline Villa.

A heavy sigh of relief exited Nil's lungs, but just as it passed his teeth, he remembered they were far from the frying pan.

The gargoyle tucked its wings in and swung through the air like a missile, redirecting to the villa. It could not leave the property, even if everything was safe.

Loyal to no fault.

"How we doing, Nilsson?" Price called out from below. Nil's heels were three or four feet from the raised lip of the skylight.

"Got a 'goyle in the air," Nil replied, keeping his eyes on the sky. "Helo's clear, though. I believe Stav made it up."

"Copy. Eyes on it?"

"Yes and no. Real dodgy."

"Coming to you. Santino's gonna lead the way."

"ETA two minutes," Frank said. "Best-case, thirty seconds."

They had to take into account possible run-ins with

the enemy. According to earlier reports from Calder, relayed by Boa, all the familiars working daytime security at the villa were dead. Including resident vampyr in the subbasements.

Now, it was just reavers and gargoyles.

At the front of the property, John and Reva had slung their weapons. The distinct sound of polished, sharpened steel drawing from airtight scabbards alerted the vampyr that these were not ordinary military.

This was Forked fucking Tongue.

John's xiphos had no light to reflect, but knew it would be more intimidating if it did. No such thought ever crossed Reva's mind; her dual kodachis occupied both hands like extensions of her arms. Her eyes had locked onto her target, one vamp slowly getting to his feet after taking so many rounds to the dome. Their blood was red like a human's, but thinner and less of it.

Reva made a barking sound as she charged her enemy. She swung the two kodachis in tandem, but each with a separate arc. Sixteen inches of Damascus steel cut through still night air with a voice of its own. Reva was agiler than even Nil in close-quarters, with her blades. The way her long, braided, dark ponytail danced in the night around her black-clad shoulders was something of an art form, if it could be seen.

The third swipe connected before the vamp could fully stand. He hissed like a reptile, his left hand rolling across the stone floor. Blood spurted from the severed wrist. The vamp glanced at it and then felt a second blade catch his right shoulder. The steel dug a trench in, locking into bone. Instead of letting this stall her, Reva used it as leverage and swung her body around the kneeling vamp, as if grappling in the Octagon.

She wielded her other kodachi like a handheld guillotine.

Muscles flexing, Reva managed to connect the blade with enough force to cut through half of the vamp's neck. A carotid artery burst and jetted blood across the stone.

Ten feet away, John had severed his enemy's arm at the elbow, making the vamp drop a rifle. He then kicked backwards, knocking a second one away. It was female, based on its frame and slightly higher inflection of hissing and grunting. Ignoring her holstered pistol, she instead leapt onto his back in hopes of sinking her fangs and delivering a more satisfying kill. Despite being half his size, her immortal strength counted for a lot.

In a rigorous sawing motion, Reva wrenched the kodachi through the vamp's spinal cord, and his head lopped off. The rest of the body went limp, but not as meat and bones. Along with the head, the body disintegrated into a slop of blood and mush. If Forked Tongue didn't get a mop-up crew here before local authorities arrived, there would be a lot of scratching heads. Not the first time, but at least vampyr didn't leave telltale signs of their existence. Just an absolute mess.

John grunted, wriggling his stout neck to avoid being bitten. His right hand swung the xiphos at the wounded vamp before him, while his left elbow repeatedly jabbed the one on his back in the ribs. The xiphos cut fabric and skin, but not deep enough to matter.

Then the vamp, despite his missing arm, managed

to grab John's kodachi and pull it out of his hand. By the blade. It cut the vamp's hands in the process, but the damn creature didn't seem to mind.

Hearing the xiphos clatter on the stone not far from her, Reva was alerted to John's dilemma.

She *threw* one of her kodachis at the vamp that had just disarmed John. The blade stuck in the creature's waist, entrenching between ribs. A shriek sprayed from his mouth, and he ripped his balaclava off, exposing his head. A mess of black hair above a ghostly pale face and gaping, fanged jaws shot toward Reva.

John drew his revolver at retention, firing into the distracted vamp with his elbow against his body. The close-range shot tore into the vamp's stomach, a grooved-copper .454 Casull devastating flesh. Even though a vamp healed fast, these would hinder that ability just enough to buy the shooter some time. In John's case, it was all that was needed, especially with a kodachi lodged between the ribs.

"Need some help here," a familiar voice in their ears. It was Nil. The occasional spurt of gunfire from his Scorpion could be heard within a hundred feet of where they were.

John resisted the urge to reverse-headbutt the vamp on his back, as he didn't want to crack his own skull. Instead he bent his knees and jerked forward, as if he was going to do a front-flip. Instead the momentum and his brute human strength managed to fling the vamp off his upper shoulders. She landed on her back, and didn't have a chance to pop up.

John drove the heel of his boot down, hard.

The top half of her skull caved a few millimeters, and she uttered a garbled, shrill sound of pain, her body writhing on the ground. He fired twice into her chest, .45 copper rounds surely penetrating her heart. Weakening that immortal clutch on life. And then he stomped again, while Reva reached the other vamp to drive her second kodachi into his throat.

John's third stomp crushed the female vamp's cranium, turning brain pulp into mortal mush.

When he dragged his foot away, he did so coarsely, as if trying to grind gum off the bottom of one's shoe. Crumbs of cervical vertebrate stuck into the soles of his boot, or otherwise rolled across the stone.

The female vamp's body disintegrated, almost in tandem with her comrade, thanks to Reva's decapitating maneuver.

"Appreciate it," John said, holstering his revolver. Reva nodded, the tiniest of smiles on her face.

"Nil," she then said, solemnity returning full-force. She gestured back toward the villa with her head, and John followed. As they moved, they wiped their blades on their pants and then sheathed them. Rifles slung forward, buttstocks planting against shoulders.

Reva bounded up the stone steps to the right of the villa's main anterior, which included a staircase leading up to a pair of metallic double-doors. Not the most inviting entrance, but there was another doorway that led into the foyer, at ground-level, left of this.

Regrouping with Nil on the walkway that overlooked a seating area to their right, John and Reva half-expected him to be waist-deep in shit. Instead, he was fickly pivoting on his feet, weapon scanning the night sky above them.

"You good, boss?" John asked.

"Gargoyle, goddammit," Nil snapped, under his breath. "It keeps evading me, but it's a big fucker."

John and Reva snapped to attention, their flashlights flicking on, beams searching overhead.

Though rigid in his posture, and keeping his attention high, John carefully moved toward the shattered skylight. When his boot reached the raised lip, he swung his aim down, flashlight scanning the bathroom below.

Empty, apart from large shards of glass and small smears of blood. Like a boot dragging below a wounded leg leaking through gauze.

John's brow furrowed.

"Stav got in, helo's clear," Nil said, as if reading John's mind. When in reality, just noticing that he was staring down into the bathroom. "Price and Frank are en route to us."

"Copy." John lifted his attention again. He moved toward the metallic double-doors left of the walkway. When he cautiously peered in, the first thing he noticed were the bodies. Familiars and reavers alike, although the former outnumbered the latter. The room stunk of bloodshed, and dead reavers were indubitably fouler than live ones.

Secondly, it occurred to him why that staircase out front led to such a banal entrance. Same as this one.

"We got a security room here. Some surveillance, a small armory. Metal roll-up doors on the far side, likely a balcony overlooking the foyer. And a lot of dead."

144

"Moving?" Nil asked.

John deliberated for two whole seconds.

"Copy. Better to engage a 'goyle on the ground than in the air."

It was a good call, however a close one.

Although gargoyle 'designs' varied, they were always winged and quadrupedal. This configuration and the ability to tuck their wings allowed them to navigate close-quarters effectively. The wings were densely membranous and while not invulnerable to gunfire, highly resilient to most calibers. When tucked, they acted as body armor. Additional, seeing as how their flesh was already melded with the stone husks from which they had changed.

Whether their heads were more like wolves, bears, or even Komodo dragons, depended.

All made terrible enemies indoors, but far worse when they owned the air.

"I have the rear," Reva said, and Nil didn't argue. He brought his aim down from the sky, following John into the security room. Reva closed the metallic double-doors behind her.

Indoor lighting was scant, but not nonexistent. Shell-like sconces arrayed the beige walls every eight feet. Some had been destroyed, by gunfire or physical contact, but those that were intact remained lit.

Most ceiling fixtures, where they existed, were still functioning as well.

The team deactivated their flashlights. Green beads from their laser-sights still danced around whatever surface they touched.

Back to Viper *Three* with Price detached, they moved with their weapons at low-ready. They needed to maintain caution of crossing paths with any friendlies. From the other two Boa operators to Frank and Price. What route they were taking up here, Viper had no idea.

Subconsciously recalling the interior map of the villa, John reckoned they would take a staircase that wound up a rectangular pillar between the security room and the skybridge.

Momentarily, they examined the area.

About the size of a conference room, if not a little bigger, the villa's security hub had a long table with chairs around it, half a wall of camera monitors, a small kitchen-like area in the corner, and a weapons locker near the hallway exit.

The latter was mostly gutted.

Familiars had put to use their arsenal, for better or worse. Boa seemed to have made an example of them, but the six bodies of familiars inside the room were clearly the work of reavers. They had been mutilated, and only partially eaten. That reavers were killing just to kill, and not feed, went against their very nature. They were usually starved and kept as rabid-like pets by vampyr. Mortally maiming their enemies was rare, without feeding; but doing so to the very familiars and vampyr that kept them was unheard of.

Fortunately—in a way—they had not yet had reports of gargoyles doing the same. Reavers could, by a stretch of the imagination, be accepted as mutinous. They were mindless, frenzied creatures deliberately starved and isolated until needed. 'Goyles on the other hand, were immensely loyal guard dogs raised from pups.

"John," Nil said, and Reva quickly joined him, too. He was observing the array of security monitors. Video feeds scattered throughout the villa. Half of them were washed away with static, suggesting the cameras were destroyed. The others still functioned, and the quality was above-board.

When John arrived at his side, he squinted.

A meaty forefinger pointed at one screen. Then that same finger withdrew and pressed his collar mic button.

"Price, Frank," John said. "We've got you on a security cam. Corner says *game room*. My memory of that map is fuzzy. Where are you in correlation to the security room?"

"Not far, as the crow flies, or in this case, walks," Price said over their comms. "But a lot of walls. If it wasn't for the stairwell, we'd be there by now."

"What's up with the stairwell?"

"Just outside the security room, if you hang a right and head to that corner, there are steps leading down. Right into a hallway outside the grand bathroom."

"Ceiling's collapsed," Frank's gruff voice came on. "Damn 'goyle tried to follow us, got hung up on a couple o' reavers attacking some familiars. Stav, in all his wisdom, shot his forty-mil. Blast annihilated that whole goddamn thing."

John nodded. "Sounds like Stav to me. Took out all those threats, though?"

"Not the 'goyle. Fucker crawled through, 'n we finished it off point-blank."

"Saw the remains myself," Price contributed.

Which would just be a pile of rubble, its original form gone. Not even the blood or flesh of a slain 'goyle survived its death.

"That must've been pleasant," Nil said, without activating his mic.

"Say," John mumbled, leaning forward to examine another security camera. "Who are your other two, Frank? Memory serves, it's either Zac, Ricky, or...?"

John's finger released the button for a split-second's worth of thought. And then Frank's sullen voice came on.

"Zac's no longer with us, John."

"Sorry, brother."

Frank cleared his throat over the comlink.

"I've got Ricky Bush and Jam. Joey Meyer."

John nodded. "That's right, hard to miss 'em. I'm looking right at 'em."

Ricky had dreadlocks gathered behind his head, and had a distinctly dark complexion. Jam—Joey Allen Meyer's preferred moniker—was a relatively short man with a solid build and long dark hair kept earlobe-length. He usually wore a headband to keep it back, when on ops, and was often the butt of "tiny Rambo" jokes.

"They made it to that rooftop above the bedroom, but they're still there," John explained. "Taking cover behind an AC unit. I see Zac not far from them, they've already covered him up. Got some 'goyles, reavers, and familiars still hashing it out opposite where they are. They haven't been noticed yet; exterior lights are out up there, camera feed's got infrared lighting. Looks like they're playing it safe, letting the bad guys finish each other off."

"Copy, this is…good news, I guess. Could be worse." Frank sighed. "What's the play, Price?"

Price's voice came on. "Stop playing voyeur, John. Cross the skybridge and make contact with them. Can't reach on comms, their mics must be trashed."

"Wilco, on our way."

"We'll head for the foyer, exit the villa, come up the front stairs, and meet y'all from behind."

"Kinky," Nil muttered.

Reva elbowed him.

"Copy. See you soon." John tore away from the camera feeds, and advanced to the hallway exit. It was a single metallic door, which opened with a creak. Nil followed suit, Reva maintaining the rear.

After clearing the immediate hallway, John headed toward the T-intersection ahead. The large open space to up on their right, about twice the width of the hallway, should be the skybridge.

Behind Nil, Reva lagged a few paces. She glanced back, noticing from where she stood that the dead-end corner of the hall, had they hung a right from the door, was a mound of gray and beige rubble. As Frank had said, the ceiling was collapsed and those stairs blocked off. She shook her head in disappointment, but was simultaneously glad the reavers and familiars had met such an unpleasant demise.

"Reva, cross and cover me," John said.

She came forward, crossing the gap of space created by the skybridge, putting her left shoulder to the corner of the wall. She knelt for better stability and extended her rifle's aim downrange. She kept her eye on the reflex optic, targeting the far end of the skybridge, which opened up to the outside, large glass double-doors now in pieces on the floor. Unlike the surprisingly intact floor-to-ceiling panes along the left side of the skybridge, overlooking the pool area. The right wall was solid, arrayed with intermittent sconces, all but two still illuminated.

The structure had a twelve-foot ceiling and stretched sixty feet across. Three adult men could stand elbow-to-elbow in the skybridge with still some space from either wall, glass or otherwise.

It was a spacious link between the two main wings of the villa.

Viper didn't look forward to crossing it, given the lack of cover on their left. Even if the windows were intact. And along the floor were littered bodies, albeit far less than they expected. Mostly familiars, and the occasional reaver, amid some bullet casings.

While Reva focused on the far end, she noticed an occasional shadow flash across the outside floor, twenty feet to the right of where Ricky and Jam hid. These must have been the "bad guys" as John put it, fighting. On a spacious landing at the top of a staircase leading to the back terrace.

John used his laser to get the attention of Ricky and Jam, through the glass panes along the skybridge. The refracted green light formed a rough beam that reached them on the rooftop, John just had to toy with it until they noticed from where they took cover.

About five seconds later, a small white light manifested from around the far end of the bulky AC unit. And
then it cut off.

John nodded to himself more than anyone else, although he knew he was more visible to them than they
were to him. Then he killed his laser-sight and waited.
Two seconds later, the white light on the rooftop appeared again, this time rhythmically flashing.

"Nil, you getting this?" John asked.

"Sure am. Your Morse still rusty?"

"Don't tell Price. It's embarrassing."

Nil smirked, as he shadowed John's left shoulder
and deciphered the considerably short message. It was
clear to Nil, and even John, that Ricky and Jam were being as succinct as possible for sake of efficiency.

The flashlight stopped flickering, and John looked
at Nil, whose eyes darted briefly as he deliberated. Then
nodded. When he spoke, it was just within Reva's earshot, too.

"One G, three R's, may be more on-site, two to
three, low ammo, no comms, one wounded."

"One 'goyle taking on three reavers," John said,
shaking his head. "Bold of them. Won't be long 'til it's
not distracted anymore. And can't fuck with a 'goyle on
low ammo, much less at their capacity. They didn't say
which of them is wounded?"

Nil shook his head.

"Alright. Send this: *Copy. Meet on bridge. Coming
to you.*"

Nil nodded and knelt by John's left ankle, flickering his flashlight mount in Morse code. Dots and dashes;

quick flashes, and longer ones. He remained low, as had Boa, since they didn't want to broadcast their position. Mindless as reavers were, they still had the basest instincts of most predators.

And were skittish as hell.

The second that Nil confirmed his message was sent, John gestured at Reva and then advanced onto the skybridge. He moved briskly down the center, keeping his DDM4 trained on the far opening they approached, while Reva gave the glass along their left more attention.

A quarter the way down and they began to hear the animalistic sounds of the gargoyle battling three reavers. Possibly less by this point. And another ten paces, John glimpsed movement, adjusting his eye, simultaneous to glass crunching beneath boots.

He looked completely clear of his optic.

Ricky was being helped along by Jam. A dense bandage wrap coiled Ricky's left leg, and half of the white was stained red. Now against the light of sconces along the skybridge, which reflected off the glass to provide even more illumination, the condition of Boa's missing operators became clearer. They were both drenched in sweat, and Ricky's wound appeared worse than a first glance would suggest. It was possible he had been stabbed or shot in the thigh. That he was up and walking at all, despite a limp and the support from Jam—who was a few inches shorter and at least fifty pounds of muscle less than Ricky—hinted that his femoral artery was fine.

Still, the injury was debilitating.

They didn't just need another medivac. They

needed to bail altogether.

As long as the reavers were killed, they could. Gargoyles posed no threat of leaving the property, although if local police arrived on-site, they would face that threat with all the confusion and fear in the world.

A look of relief came over Ricky's face, Jam's face, and John's—

"Get down!" Reva shouted.

Chills surged down John's spine and he threw a hand out, palm facing Ricky and Jam who were about twenty feet away when Reva exclaimed.

Reva threw her back to the wall, a sconce bathing her in a yellow glow, as her rifle pointed at the nearest glass pane. She had not even had a chance to squeeze the trigger when what she had seen collided with another window fifteen feet away. It buckled and shattered in the same motion, a gargoyle the size of a pickup truck crashing through it.

Had she not said anything, John would have been history. Unfortunately, when its wings swung out after it had breached the glass—shattering three panes in its wake—a talon at the tip of its left one speared Ricky in the sternum. Jam hollered in anger and frustration, holding onto his friend. The gargoyle turned toward them, snarling, its head reminiscent of a hyena, only four times as big. When it turned, its wings did, too, tucking inward slightly. This tug didn't cleanly remove the talon from Ricky's chest, but took a bulk of his sternum and broken ribs with it. Gore gushed from the poor man's mouth in an airborne arch of red and yellow.

He hit the floor a few feet from the edge of the sky-bridge, sliding through a carpet of broken glass.

Jam staggered back, fumbling to bring his weapon to aim. The KRISS Vector SDP rattled in his hands as he hosed the gargoyle with 10mm rounds. Less effective than rifle ammo against the gargoyle's hide, the fast rate of fire and meaty cartridges from the Vector SMG still proved a point from a mere ten feet away.

Although the massive gargoyle's amalgamated stone and flesh composition only twitched against the impacts, it was better than nothing, or just a pistol.

John slung his DDM4 and put the Marlin in his hands. He fired a round into the gargoyle's hindquarters, and it flinched, but kept its attention on Jam. Meanwhile, Reva joined Nil and together concentrated their fire on the gargoyle's tucked wings. These were pure membrane, and the most susceptible of its anatomy.

If nothing else, their work was annoying and thus distracting the 'goyle from Jam. This, paired with Jam's own bursts from his Vector, kept the creature from outright charging him. Then his boots crunched glass again, which meant the beast was forcing him back into the open, knowing full well another 'goyle was nearby.

John tucked the Marlin and rushed to Ricky's body, ducking as he neared it—

The gargoyle's serpentine tail swung toward him, cutting through the air where he had previously stood, only to lash back, lacerating the wall and destroying a sconce.

"Fuck's sake," John groaned, freeing his hands in an impulsive attempt to help him. His eyes searched

154

Ricky's brutalized body for where to begin.

The man was dead.

His expression was frozen in a moment of unprecedented pain and dread. It was the worst way to see someone, especially a man so beloved and respected by his peers, friends, and *family*.

John repeatedly shook his head, and eventually returned his hands to the Marlin.

"Fuck!" The word cut through his teeth like a Doberman's bark. It seemed to echo in the skybridge, despite the gaping space to the outdoors to his left.

When he stood up, John bolted the Marlin's buttstock to his shoulder, cocked the lever, and fired. This time a 45-70 round caught the 'goyle in what would be the 'armpit' of its left wing. The bullet snuck into a crevice of where flesh and stone melded.

The beast made a grunting sound and faltered.

Then it swung its hyena-shaped head around, tail burrowing a trough in the dense wall along the skybridge. Two more sconces shattered. Any amount of darkness cloaking the gargoyle made it even more intimidating.

Consistent, albeit staccato, shots from Reva's N4 and Nil's Derya provided additional light thanks to muzzle flashes. Nil's semi-automatic shotgun and the slugs it packed were especially helpful in pestering the gargoyle, but not so much wounding it. The segmenting slugs were ideal for actual flesh, not the resilient chimera that was a gargoyle's anatomy.

The thing growled at John and stopped advancing. It sunk back on its haunches, preparing to pounce.

In a moment of poor timing, Reva had to reload. Nil's shotgun expunged the last of its magazine, the slug ripping a bloody hole through a membrane on its left wing, which helped distract it. John fired his Marlin, and from ten feet away the 300-grain 45-70 took off the gargoyle's right ear.

The sound it made was a high-pitched snarl, reminiscent of an aggravated tiger.

"Get fucked," Jam all but shouted.

John looked his way, far left. The other 'goyle had rounded the corner outside the entrance to the skybridge, and was almost within a wing's reach of Jam. This one was a little smaller but bulkier around, about the size of a polar bear, and seemingly composed of *brick* and flesh, rather than stone.

Suddenly Jam slung his weapon and *ran*. He sprinted back to the rectangular rooftop where he and Ricky had been taking cover. The 'goyle became airborne in its pursuit of him. Jam had nowhere to go, but his impulsive evasion happened so fast.

John watched Jam reach the far left corner of the rooftop, and vault into the air. From the base of the structure encasing the bedroom to the nearest corner of the pool, was about eight feet. Jam made the leap when the beast's stout jaws snapped shut inches behind him. He landed in six feet of water with a splash, and the gargoyle flapped its burly wings ten feet in the air. The surface of the pool water rippled but Jam didn't come up yet.

The 'goyle directly in front of him regained John's attention. It had not yet bitten his head off thanks solely to Nil and Reva, who were back to firing at it. They focused on its wings, and the base of that limb, such as where John had previously wounded it.

When it charged them by the wall, Reva dove away, but Nil waited until the last nanosecond. As he did, the 'goyle inadvertently slammed its snout into the wall. Its entire skull sunk into a forced divot. As it used its heavy, clawed forelimbs to help push itself out, Reva emptied another magazine into the base of its right wing.

The moment she ejected the mag, John marched forward. He drew his xiphos with a distinct *shing* and then buried the first eight inches of its twenty-inch leaf-shaped blade into this armpit-like wound. Now a cavity of exposed flesh, it widened to accept the broadest width of the xiphos, and with both hands on the grip, John twisted it. Steel grated stone and chewed through meat.

The gargoyle howled in pain.

Outside the skybridge, the other 'goyle shifted its attention from the uneventful surface of the pool—despite Jam's faintly visible mass within the clear water—to John. He finished plunging the entircty of his sword into the wound, and the gargoyle's powerful stony limbs buckled.

Nil stepped forward, with a freshly loaded Deyra mag, and dumped two quick slugs into the beast's ear wound.

The head went slack on its neck and its entire mass slumped to the floor.

"Jesus," Nil griped.

"John!" Reva snapped.

In the blink of an eye, if that, John spun on his heel.

The hovering gargoyle above the pool had angled itself to come at him in the same fashion the other had burst onto the skybridge.

And then gunfire erupted *below* it, two assault rifles in full-auto. Bullets tore into its spread wings, and despite the collective mass of the creature, it didn't yield the same might as the one on the skybridge. It faltered midair, yelping like a hurt dog, and then plunged. It tumbled through a glass partition separating the pool area from an open-floor kitchen below the skybridge.

An unusual silence casted a pall over Skyline Villa.

No reavers hissed or garble-growled, no footfalls from familiars or vamps, and no bellowing flaps of gargoyle wings.

If Ricky and Jam had been correct in deducing there were as many as two to three more on the property, that meant those numbers were now down to one or two. Still unpleasant when it came to 'goyles, but something to work with.

At long last Jam came up for air, but not gasping theatrically. Although he had applied to the Navy SEAL program twice, he had never graduated from BUD/S but eventually found his calling as an unexpected Raider. His superiors at MARSOC underestimated him time and time again, but Jam enjoyed proving them wrong.

So he wasn't SEAL material, but he could compose himself in situations where most would otherwise crumble. Which wasn't to say that when Jam finally crawled out of the pool, he didn't have to battle the urge to shed tears for Ricky.

Or Zac.

At least now he had confirmation that Frank was alive and well. John was joined by Reva and Nil by the shattered edge of the skybridge to peer down at the court-yard-like pool area. Frank and Price had convened on the deck there, and were assisting Jam. About twelve feet off the ground, Viper Three was too high up to simply hop down and regroup with the others.

They *were* within earshot, though.

"Appreciate the assist," John said.

"Any injuries?" Price asked.

"Just my heart. Ricky didn't make it." John's voice was grim. Then he clenched his jaw and Reva could literally hear his teeth grind. "I *shouldn't* have told them to move."

"We would've anyway, boss," Jam said, soaking wet. This didn't diminish the solemnity in his disposition at all. And 'boss' was just what Jam called pretty much anyone he had any respect for.

"Don't put that shit on you," Frank said. "If anyone's gonna wear the brunt of Ricky and Zac's deaths, it'll be me."

"Not a day will go by that I won't carry Ricky's pain in me," Jam said, almost growling it. To nobody in particular.

Frank squeezed his shoulder, and then informed him that Stavros got clear and should be flying high on morphine somewhere right about now. This helped assuage Jam to some extent.

"Listen," Price raised his voice a bit more. Hoarse but commanding. "I hate the phrase, but what's done is done. Pack it up. *Use it*. Right now, we get to the highest point of this fucking place, and phone our bird."

John nodded. He sniffled and looked to his right. Past Ricky's corpse, past the gargoyle's rubble, and to the open night air outside the other end of the skybridge. Then he looked left, and his eyes darted down toward the foyer. The glass panes separating it from the pool deck had long since been shattered.

"Suggest you guys take the foyer," John said, pointing. "Cut outside, up the front steps, through the security room…"

Then he pointed at the floor by his feet.

"Bing-bada-boom," he finished.

"Read my mind," Price said. He secured the butt of his rifle into his shoulder. "See you in thirty seconds."

Price led Frank and Jam away from the pool deck. Jam's rifle was still functional, even waterlogged. Their boots crunched glass as they entered the spacious foyer, out of Viper's line-of-sight.

"How many 'goyles have you encountered in your day, John?" Nil asked. There was sarcasm hidden in there somewhere.

"Four ops, can't count individuals, though."

"And how many of those ops would you compare the 'goyle behavior to *that* fucking behemoth?" Nil pointed, while still staring up at John, at the rubble in the middle of the skybridge.

"Not one, Nil," John said, blandly.

Nil scoffed, poorly suppressed a cynical laugh, and then paced while he performed weapons maintenance.

"You good?" John asked Reva.

"He's got a point," she said bluntly. "Reavers attacking 'goyles and vice versa, on the same property? Much less vamps themselves. And 'goyles being *that* aggressive? *That* bold?" She shook her head. "Something is off, love. *Way* off."

"Preaching to the choir. Fortunately, it seems we're not alone in that assumption. Hopefully HQ is putting their big, fat, paper-pushing brains to the test and coming up with more than just theories."

"Hopefully," Nil muttered.

"Hopefully what?" Price's voice startled him.

Despite not hearing Price or Frank's approach, as soon as Jam caught up, his still-dripping body was impossible to silence. Time would have to do, as it slowly dried in the summer night.

"Nothing," Nil sighed.

"Hopefully HQ has some answers to this whole fiasco," John said anyway.

Price nodded, and looked at Frank.

"Hopefully indeed," Frank mumbled.

"Let's get topside," Price said. "According to Santino, Boa's transport flew *over* the villa before dropping in at the posterior. And there's a way to the highest terrace back there."

"Let's get it, then," John said.

Santino took the lead, and then Price patted his own head, a ubiquitous "on me" gesture. John followed, trailed by Reva. Nil greeted Jam more intimately, and then convinced him he would accept their six. Brandishing the semiautomatic shotgun helped convince Jam of this decision.

Reva wasn't necessarily thrilled to be followed by Jam. As great an operator as he was, as friendly a person, he was a notorious flirter. As long as he didn't overtly try to hook up with other operators or trainees, his behavior wasn't condemned, within a realm of reason. And he was never the kind that couldn't take a hint; he played rejection like a violinist. All that said, there were only a few specific circumstances that presently kept Jam's attention from slipping down to Reva's backside.

The death of his friends and teammates.

The unavoidably dire situation at hand.

And if absolutely nothing else, her all-black attire in the poorly lit environment.

The second they cleared the skybridge—passing over crunching glass with some caution but not a lot of deceleration—nightfall enveloped them. One by one, they activated their flashlight mounts but kept their weapons at low-ready so as to no telegraph their position or approach as they moved. This also helped them mind their footing—

Dead reavers and familiars scattered the stone walkways this side of the villa.

A slain gargoyle's pile of rubble at the base of an ivied terrace caught Price and John's attention after Frank passed it with no regard. Then he paused, glanced back at them, and shone his light at the remains.

"Zac and Stav put that one down before me and the others regrouped with them." Frank shook his head once. "I'm missing them already."

"I hear that," Jam murmured.

They proceeded, Frank leading them off the beaten

path and onto the ledge of a decorative terrace covered in foliage. Left of them was a seating area around a fire pit, and beyond that a pergola. An intact exterior light bathed this space in stark white, providing a glow that washed over the area where the operators were walking.

They deactivated their flashlight mounts and slung their weapons, after Frank did. Then he stepped off to the side and bent his knees, cupping both hands.

"This way?" John asked for confirmation, pointing to the upper ledge of a concrete terrace. Identical to the one they stood on now, almost like tall steps layered with creeping ivy.

Frank nodded.

John sighed, and accepted Frank's boost. John was easily the biggest guy present, and didn't need much assistance to reach that ledge. He extended his arms best he could so as to exert as little as possible on Frank. Once he had pulled himself up the smooth concrete surface, he impulsively reached for his revolver, ready to face a threat. Instead, the next terrace was clear of activity. A flat platform unadorned by foliage, there was the aftermath of a quarrel that briefly distracted him.

"What is it?" Price asked, noticing John was distracted.

"I'll show you. Who's next?" John looked down, knelt, and then extended a burly arm.

Price shrugged and followed, with Frank's help. After which Nil accepted this responsibility, moving toward the front of the pack. In his mind, he wasn't about to let Jam give Reva a boost. She was like a half-sister to him, and as much as he saw a lot of himself in Jam, as well as not expecting him to 'try anything,' he knew it would comfort Reva more.

Frank went next, who thanked Nil for replacing him. It was evident that Frank was easily the most fatigued of the group, having been on-site for nearly four hours and in that time suffered one casualty—their team leader, no less—had to medivac another, and then Ricky.

He wasn't having a swell night.

Nil was the last one up, having just boosted Jam. Who was, thankfully by then, much drier. John helped every one of them up, and once Nil was pulled to his feet, too, their weapons had all returned to their hands.

The topmost terrace was before them.

Price was already pacing along its longest edge, the platform about twelve by sixteen feet, with his sat-phone out. As he connected with Lima-266, likely Taggart, the others looked at what had distracted John earlier. The rubble of a lion-sized gargoyle, surrounded by two vamps clad in black, their suppressed weapons still in-hand. The gruesome wounds on the vampyr's necks suggested reaver.

Before anyone else could vocalize a conjecture, Reva spoke.

"Last of the cleanup crew," she said, her laser-sight pointing at the two vamps. "Ambushed by reavers after they took down the 'goyle."

"And the reavers?" Frank said. There was a dull hopelessness to his voice. Plighted by exhaustion. "You think they're all dead?"

"After something like this," John said, "they don't just go dormant like *that*."

He snapped his fingers.

Frank nodded. "So we'd have crossed paths by now."

"Presumably."

"We're good," Price said, convening and returning his sat-phone to a back pouch. "Bird's on the way. And Stavros is at a medical center called Atrium, off of Montauk Highway. Stable."

"Thank God," Frank sighed, his head bowing. Jam gave him a sort of side-hug, an arm thrown around his shoulders. Then they straightened for the other good news.

"Exfil should be twenty minutes, tops," Price said. "They just got done refueling. Then we'll RTB. Stavros will have to stay put, for now."

"Any updates from Calder?" Reva asked.

"Negative, not over the sat, anyway. Maybe once we're in the air."

Reva nodded.

"Right now, we just sit tight, stay alert, just in case, and wait 'til we hear that sweet symphony of Black Hawk rotors."

It was something they could cheer to, if they had beer or wine to make a toast. Anything would help momentarily take the sting out of losing two operators in the span of three hours.

All of Forked Tongue would mourn them.

And the night had only just begun.

8

Not ten minutes after they had boarded the Black Hawk, the same way Stav had, the six operators were being replenished. Water and protein bars, excavated from their own kits. Assisting with their headsets, which involved fetching extras stowed away, Taggart was silently relieved to see Viper Four again, intact. Although he compartmentalized well, it was still evident in his face that he empathized Boa's losses. And their inability to transport the two bodies was silently mourned. Something that softened his heart a little was when Frank spoke into his headset's attached mic.

"Taggart, right? What's your buddy's name?"

"Worton. Dickey Worton."

Frank nodded. "I know it often goes unsaid, but after the shit-show we faced down there, and the threat of 'goyles in the air, I really fucking appreciate what you did for my guy. I imagine Stav was vocal about it himself. Risked your bird, Worton, and you and Taggart's lives. Means a metric fucking ton. Won't forget it."

Taggart's head bowed with respect and speechless-ness. Then a surprise voice entered their ear-cups.

"He called me an angel," Worton said. "I told him, ain't nobody said that to me but my mama. He asked if there were any other resemblances. I just can't with y'all sometimes."

Everybody in the cabin smiled ear to ear.

Jam's eyes welled a little above his own grin. If he shed a single tear, at least he knew his grizzled stubble would absorb, and hide it.

"Fact is," Worton added, "we don't do what we do for each other. We do it for everyone else."

"And this," Taggart said after a few seconds of re-flection, "from a guy that, I swear to God, says *maybe* four words a flight."

A few of them smiled again.

Taggart took a deep breath and glanced out the window behind him. The midnight sky was glazed with light from a moon that would be wholly full in three days. Worton was keeping the Black Hawk at three-hun-dred feet, going a steady 165mph.

"I've got some good news and some bad," Taggart said, gathering everybody's attention as if fish to an an-gler's lure. "The esteemed Calder reached out while we were refueling. I shit you not, *minutes* before Price rang. I'll hit you with her update, but it's scant. All I know is all she told me. Worton contacted Moyock the second we had y'all in the air again, just to confirm. Calder should be calling again, in the next few minutes, with more info. Almost surprised she hasn't yet."

Taggart paused and glanced back at the cabin.

"You're not holding anything back from us, are you, Dickey?"

Morton simply shook his head once.

"Anyway, he'll patch her through once she does," Taggart said. "So, bad news is we won't be going to Fentress just yet. Y'all probably won't see home 'til daybreak."

Frank's head bowed and he let out a deep, haggard breath. His hands clutched his assault rifle tighter, as the muzzle device pressed into the textured metal floor.

"Good news is," Taggart continued, "we'll be stopping much sooner. You'll resupply at McGuire Air Base in Burlington County, Jersey."

"Almost there," Worton stepped in. "Five mikes."

Taggart nodded. "Making great time. From there, we'll fly you to Coyle Airfield, thirty-eight klicks southwest. Right at the heart of the New Jersey Pine Barrens."

John shook his head.

"Full-mooner territory," he said, his mumble barely picked up by his mic.

"That's our guess," Taggart said. "But the way things been going, past twenty hours, who the hell knows."

Reva nodded repeatedly. She bowed her head in a moment of concentration. Meditation, even.

"Where to from there?" Nil asked.

"A small unincorporated community called Woodmansie. Seven klicks northeast of Coyle. There's a sand and gravel quarry just west of the houses there, only five according to our scans. And a lake."

"We're to reach those houses, then, and ensure the residents are safe?" Jam asked.

Taggart shrugged.

"Guess is as good as mine. Calder should confirm."

"Seven klicks, huh?" John asked, but not Taggart. He was looking across at Price. "On foot. In the Barrens."

"I imagine we take the road. Should be a two-lane highway, cuts across Coyle. Been before."

"Same, last year," Frank said, dully. "Jersey Devil shit. Another false report."

"Overrated," Jam said, shaking his head. "Lycans have 'em beat."

"Far and wide," Nil muttered.

About three minutes of contemplative silence followed. Only the kind of quietude available aboard a Black Hawk at three-hundred feet.

When John noticed Taggart shift on his feet and turn to stare out the window, he got a tickle in his gut. Something was off. And then he noticed it, too. The helo had yawed, making a distinct redirection.

"Talk to me, Dickey," Taggart said, pulling the mic toward his mouth.

No immediate response.

"Dickey, goddammit," Taggart said, and moved toward the cockpit. Worton raised his right hand, and from where Reva sat she could see the pilot's head turn, his mouth moving.

He was talking on a separate line.

Taggart slipped back into his copilot seat, and flipped a toggle above his head. Then his left hand turned a knob by his knee, gingerly.

The operators sat, waiting in relative silence.

"Everyone read?" Taggart's voice came on. "Just got an urgent message from Moyock. We're to avoid McGuire altogether, and go straight to Coyle. No resupply—no time. Reports are spreading like wildfire. Worse, we're getting a lot of interference. Can't say why just yet."

Worton cursed under his breath, coming through his mic like a ruptured sneeze. He jabbed something on the instrument panel, but fortunately the Black Hawk continued its path steadfast.

"Patching Calder through now, just keep in mind, a lot of interference." Taggart sighed. "She knows, and has been advised to keep it concise."

There was a click in their headsets, and then a wash of white noise that quickly subsided. It rose in volume, slightly, every few words. Calder's voice was tinny but intelligible, when the static was at bay.

"Viper, Boa, you have my deepest sympathies for ...losses you've...terribly sorry for sounding so...and cold, I hope you understand my..."

"Let's hear it, ma'am," Frank said.

"Two hours ago...reports of full-mooners in...Barrens, along Savoy Boulevard, attacking passing cars, then dragging...woods."

Taggart shook his head.

"Taggart here, ma'am. It's getting worse. Advise you—"

"Serpent One," Calder said, her voice firmer and

louder than before. These two words moved the operators to their core. They didn't need to inquire to confirm their assumption. She had, likely with a SIC present for witness and documentation, assigned them an official call-sign. They were now one unit. Six operators under one name, a rare element of superior tactics and firepower authorized by Forked Tongue.

A force not to be fucked with.

"Serpent One," she repeated. *"You are...secure Woodmansie...escort...possible to...quarry, deploy flares and call...exfil, RTB...Carolina needs...help...can get."*

The call sputtered out.

"It's gone," Taggart said painfully. "Attempting to reconnect, but…"

Everyone aboard the helo, including its crew, felt a tension exacerbate in their stomachs. Jam leaned forward, kneading his temples.

Although the official assimilation of Viper and Boa had initially rejuvenated them, it was short-lived.

A long moment passed before anybody spoke.

"We're less than ten mikes from Coyle," Worton said. "Advise everyone prepare for landing."

The operators safely performed weapons maintenance and gear checks. At least, finally, their LZ would be a complete touch-down and not a drop-off or the like. The Black Hawk crew would even disembark, too.

"Any post there?" John asked.

"Small staff, single structure, low security," Taggart said. "They've been notified, military credentials and the whole nine yards."

"They turn their heads real nicely," Frank said, re-calling a memory that offered a crumb of comfort.

John half-smirked.

Good. As best they can, avoid exposure of Forked Tongue ops with those not in the know. Not just civil-ians, but other government fields.

"So," Reva said, "we've got full-mooners attacking *cars*, outright? Then dragging them back into the Bar-rens. The literal fuck?"

"That's my line, babe," Nil clicked his tongue.

It was a bit out of character for her to talk like that, especially in the presence of someone like Price, but no-body could blame her. She was as befuddled about it as everyone else.

"It doesn't track," Price said. The equilibrium to his voice was enviously flawless. "But right now, for us, it doesn't need to. We land, make haste, and prioritize the safety of the residents in Woodmansie. Escort them, if feasible, to the quarry. This time of night, shouldn't be any crew there, but possible. Phone our flyboys, pop flares, and wait for the bird. Try to keep the civvies as closed-minded as we can, and calm. We RTB, stack up, and figure out how best we can serve humanity next."

A key point was that Price said 'humanity,' not 'country.' Because their work, although Forked Tongue was an American program, opened an umbrella that cov-ered nations worldwide. Often without their knowledge.

It hearkened back to what Worton had said earlier. That their commitment to this job wasn't as black-and-white as "keeping each other safe," or even "protecting the homeland." It was to ensure a way of life, even bliss-ful ignorance, for humankind as a whole.

More than anything, on the surface, Price's suc-cinct speech worked like a drug that the operators desperately needed. Especially Frank and Jam. It set them straight, put their minds and hearts back on path. Fatigue was not a privilege they could afford at the mo-ment.

Serpent One was above that.

Two minutes later, and maybe about five from reaching Coyle, the Black Hawk juddered. Worton cursed, but his and Taggart's mics were no longer linked to the others' headsets. They proceeded to bark back and forth at each other with a crescendo of vigor that worries the operators behind them.

John began to stand, but Price extended his hand, stood instead, and walked to the end of his seating row. He peered into the cockpit, noticing an array of small flashing lights, most notably what he recognized as an infrared sensor. It went off to indicate potential collision with another aircraft. The actual dissonance of so many alarms was exclusive to the pilots' headsets.

Price reached out, ready to grab a hold of Taggart's shoulder, or at least his uniform, and demand some open communication.

Then Worton cursed louder, and pushed the stick. The Black Hawk pitched forward, Price colliding with the back of Taggart's seat. Cumulus clouds fluttered around the canopy, and by this time John was standing, too. He saw, through the mesh backing of Price's seat, the helo's spotlight illuminate the night sky.

A violent *whoosh* caused the helo to shudder, as air pressure warped in the thin atmosphere. And then the spotlight didn't need to exist. A yellow-orange pulse preceded the descent of a commercial airliner. It plunged nose-first, but in a tumultuous spiral. Its starboard wing was missing, from the engine to the tip. Fire and smoke roared from the massive wound, illuminating the 'Delta' painted along the hull. This jarring, tragic light trailed the 767's cyclical descent. John's initial reaction was profanity, but he wasn't the only one to notice.

In milliseconds, everyone aboard the Black Hawk was aware of the travesty, or assumptive of it.

Worton leveled the helo at two-hundred feet, and significantly reduced speed. They flew over the Pine Barrens, but canopy coverage was scarce in this region.

"Whitesbog just west of us," Worton said, his voice tremulous. "Wheatland ahead, and then, uh, then Woodmansie. Might have to land in the quarry, I don't know what—"

Taggart's mic was on when he shouted "Jesus Christ" and his eyes opened wide enough to hurt. Worton cycled the pedals, banking the helo. An immense, almost serpentine shape cut through the night sky in front of the Black Hawk. The roar of wind alone was deafening, and distorted the air pressure around them. The helo wobbled in its flight path, Worton struggling to maintain control.

"Wyvern, wyvern, wyvern!" Taggart hollered, grabbing his mic and practically biting it. Then both of his hands shot forward, and up, and down. The myriad of controls in his purview called for attention.

Worton yawed east, and Price staggered back. John

clutched Reva before catching Price, and joining Nil behind their seats. Nil was already rummaging through the Black Hawk's aft storage, passing parachute packs down to the others.

Taggart's unnerving exclamation would forever live in Reva's skull, enrobed in terror, just thirteen days after telling a trainee about wyverns. How beautiful they can be, and how reclusive. How they *don't* casually fly around, and how averted they are to human contact.

"Mayday, mayday, mayday," Worton rattled off. "This is Lima Two-Two-Six, declaring emergency just south of Wheatland, New Jersey. Coyle, McGuire, anyone read? Mayday, this is—"

"Sucker's big, he's coming back around!" Taggart shouted, trying to track the creature's movements, visually. Wyverns were coldblooded. They could not be detected via aircraft's infrared sensors. Worton was literally flying blind, so far as the threat went.

Even when a jarring explosion rocked the woods below them, from the airliner.

Worton banked again, preemptively.

It was bad enough that this wyvern was a dark burgundy, almost a burnt brown color. An earthy blemish in the night.

And then Jam saw through the portside window a sight he knew would stay with him—supposing he survived this.

The dragon subspecies had an arrow-shaped head with wavy horns cresting from its brows. A long neck connected to a slender yet muscular body, powerful hindquarters tucked along the base of its tail in flight. No traditional forelimbs, only the webbed 'arms' branching from its shoulders, operating the vast membranous wings. These limbs converged to a scaly knob of three talons, technically its hands.

Its latter traits were invisible in the night sky, even when dully illuminated by surrounding moon-glazed clouds. The wings were utterly horizontal, periodically flapping. Otherwise it glided—

Directly toward the helo's left side.

"Port, port!" Jam shouted into his mic.

Worton dipped and yawed simultaneously. The helo was less than two-hundred feet above scattered canopies. A dense, dark green blanket of New Jersey wilderness beneath them. With the Whitesbog Preservation just west of them, the immediate region was rife with scattered marshes.

Serpent One suddenly felt inaptly named given the wyvern's superior threat.

And then a long, spindly tail ending in a spiked club like a mace clipped the Black Hawk's tail rotor. A spark of flame burped from the mechanism, then a gush of black smoke tarnishing stratus clouds they dipped through. Worton struggled to balance his aircraft as they cleared the lowest level of cloud cover.

Moonlight dappled the terrain below them.

"Eyes on, anyone have eyes on?" Taggart asked, almost choking on his tongue in the panic.

A few "negatives" scattered through the cabin, while half the operators secured parachute packs.

"Aft, Dickey, af—" Taggart shouted, but it was too late. The wyvern, despite yielding the length of a 747 and the wingspan of a C-130, had not even been glimpsed until it was within a hundred feet of the helo. At the speed it moved, far too close to evade.

Its narrow jaws clamped on the tail, for a brief moment. Immediately the wyvern realized this thing wasn't viable prey, nor an edible threat, and flapped its wings with such strength that it worsened the helo's path. With a mangled tail, the rotor free-falling a hundred feet, the Black Hawk's descent was a violent spiral.

"Attempting to arrest speed," Worton declared, through grinding teeth. The controls at his feet, and the stick in his left hand, juddered audibly, even with everything else going on.

"Bail, bail, bail!" Taggart shouted behind him.

John, Price, and Frank were still without parachutes, but nobody had forgotten their weapons. Nil had a pack half-on, after trying to push it into John's hands. Fact was, they didn't have enough parachutes for everyone on board. But that wasn't all. Now, time was a fatal factor.

Price yanked the starboard door open, elbowed John out of the way, grabbed Jam's shoulder, and jostled him out of the helo. Then he reached for Reva, but John impeded him, while Frank pushed Nil in the back, trying to herd him toward the open door, wind violently gushing in. It was utter chaos.

"Fuck the packs, bail!" Taggart shouted. "We're over water, *we'll* ditch, but—"

"Too hot, too hot, can't…" Worton exclaimed, once more through a clenched jaw. His bottom lip bled from an accidental bite.

177

Fumes and smoke began to seep into the cabin from the destroyed tail rotor.

"Sixty feet!" Worton practically screamed.

The starboard door rattled against the hull, and then the portside one jolted open during the spiraling descent. Worton had miraculously managed to reduce their speed, as they plunged at an obtuse angle—but only a fraction that wouldn't matter in the next four seconds.

Survival instincts and tactics regained control of John's brain. His lips brushed Reva's right ear without a sound before he shoved her out of the helicopter. Frank bailed next, so closely followed by Nil that Price almost tripped on them both. The three men plunged forty feet, landing separately in the grassy bog below. John was attempting to pull Taggart out of his seat when he noticed the copilot had engaged his three-point harness.

Taggart's left hand was clutching the sleeve of Worton's right arm.

John staggered away from the cockpit and rebounded off the nearest seat. He exited the helo backwards, about a single 'Mississippi' before it collided with the shallow water thirty-five feet away. Reeds and cordgrass crumpled around him, his right elbow dragging through the soft waterbed about nine feet below the surface.

They could count their scarce lucky stars later, for having landed in a particularly deep stretch of wetland. Most marshes had an average depth of three to four feet, depending on the season and recent precipitation.

Lima-266 was another story.

John had not cleared the surface in time, as Jam and

Reva had, to witness the wreckage of their helo. The Black Hawk tumbled through shallower waters, and moments after it rolled to a stop two-hundred feet away, a turboshaft engine caught fire.

The tapering tongue of flame licked at the night sky quilting the marsh.

Frank helped John out of the brackish water, which they had to tread with full gear on. Together they looked around, grateful for the moonlight, but not so much the ample red-orange glow from the helo's fire. Jam had turned away from the direction of the aircraft to help Nil clear his head from a clump of cordgrass. He must have landed head-first, as soaked peat soil from the marsh's bed clung to his blonde braids and scalp.

Reva was still transfixed by the helo, but finally cleared her mouth of water and peat to call out. Despite the direction of her gaze, she hollered for John.

"Here, I'm here, on your six," he responded, treading until he could walk. The waterbed was soft but dense enough for his boots to find purchase. He waded for a few seconds, then the water levels eddied only around his waist. They were level with Reva's hips, and finally she turned away from the glow of fire two-hundred feet away to embrace John.

"Thought I'd lost you," she murmured.

"I said I'd find you, regardless."

"When was that?" Her brow furrowed as she gazed up at him. The flames from the helo casted a subtle amber hue to her dark eyes, and a stronger glow on her wet face.

"Before we bailed," he said.

179

"You mean…before you pushed me," she said, almost smiling. There was a sadness there. Not from his actions, of course, but the whole debacle; from the loss of life in Southampton to the 747 and now their own helicopter. But a faint glimmer of personality seemed to have survived. "I couldn't hear a fucking thing, anyway."

John kissed her, holding her head.

"Price!" Someone shouted.

"Price!" Another.

John and Reva disconnected. They turned and realized everybody was accounted for except Price. Four long seconds later, Frank hushed them and shouldered his rifle. The attached laser-sight emitted a red light. The beam itself was scantily visible given the smoke sullying the air. Everyone followed the path of the laser, and then noticed what Frank had.

Price was fine.

He was on the move, though.

His weapon slung, he marched through the shallow march toward the helo. Price was maybe sixty feet from it when a bellowing sound caught their attention. Price immediately knelt, reducing his profile by more than half. The water went from being level with his knees to rippling around his ribs.

"Everybody, *low!*" John snapped, under his breath.

In the next split-second, the terrifyingly vast wingspan of the wyvern cut through the clouds eighty feet above the marsh. Its dark bronzite body had a burgundy undertone that was almost lost in the darkness, and would have been superior camouflage if it weren't for the moonlight and helo fire.

The burly haunches extended to cushion its landing, then the serpentine dragon perched its clawed, knobby 'hands' in the marsh—about as quadrupedal as it would ever look. The immense wings were only slightly folded; the membrane could be compared to a dense leather, incapable of being snugly condensed. Instead they jutted up like webbed triangles of reptilian flesh, a hue or two lighter than the rest of its body.

Somehow appearing so much larger now, than in the air, the wyvern barely moved. Its head yawed, forked tongue flickering through a narrow gap between its scaly lips, the jaws almost perfectly shut.

Even a hundred and twenty feet from where most of the operators stood—sixty from Price—its piercing yellow eyes were starkly visible. And haunting; this was horror, not beauty.

Should Reva live to tell this tale, she would enthusiastically amend her wyvern narrative to Mitchell.

The massive creature's slender neck diverted its head toward the Pine Barrens, the nearest treeline two-hundred yards to its left. About twice that distance glowed an amber light from what the operators assumed was the wreckage of the airliner.

It appeared to pulse intermittently, possibly setting trees ablaze, although this area was too wet for a wildfire to spread. Thankfully.

The tongue of flames sputtering from the helo suddenly flickered, and there was a sound of metallic crunching. A bulk of the aircraft folded in on itself, splashing water and singing reeds surrounding it.

The wyvern flinched, jerking its head toward the wreckage and snarling. Price felt so close he could reach out and touch the astoundingly big, sharp, carnivorous teeth lining the wyvern's jaws. He couldn't, of course, and he wouldn't dare try, much less move.

He remained undetected by the beast.

It had been theorized that wyverns perceived the world in infrared, but it was pure conjecture. This marked the most evidence in recent history.

Suddenly the wyvern's wings extended, nearly giving Price a heart attack. He stayed still as a statue. The surface of brackish water around him, appearing as if oil in the flame-kissed night, eddied away from him. With powerful bucks of its winged arms, the wyvern lifted itself into the air. A few flaps later and its curled toe-claws with eighty feet above the marsh. The long tail curled behind it, like a whip at the ready.

What occurred next made John wish he had a camera present. However, it simultaneously made his heart break for Worton and Taggart.

From two gum-housed apparatuses in its palate, the wyvern spewed a flammable toxin in hosing fashion. A literal belch followed suit, so quick that it was virtually impossible to distinguish one from the other. The liquid ignited ten feet from its snout, and a churning fireball engulfed the wreckage of Lima-266.

The marsh, however shallow, managed to keep collateral damage at bay. Were they on dry land, Price feared he would've been swallowed by the conflagration.

With each vicious flap of its giant wings to keep it

airborne, the flames leapt back. Moments later the wy-vern's head had vanished into cloud cover, and a second more its entire body was reclaimed by the heavens.

Haste spurring them through the shallow waters, the operators went from wading to running until they caught up to Price. He had since moved closer to the wreckage, but only as far as the beating heat would al-low. And then he staggered back some, and sunk once more to his knee. Holding onto his weapon, the butt of it pressed firmly into the waterbed, he bowed his head in silence.

Dickey Worton.

Rudy Taggart.

Their pyre burnt on, scarring an otherwise still night in the Jersey wilderness.

Breathing heavily, the rest of Serpent One looked at each other before individually kneeling, too. Reva was the first to go down, and then John. Frank, Jam, and Nil bowed their heads once on their knees as well.

Residual ripples in the water came back to them minutes after the wyvern had departed.

Somewhere in the distance, at a range far too close for them to ignore, a wavering howl split the night sky.

9

Having recalled Worton's distress call when he was upright in the helo, Price informed the others of where they were. Just south of Wheatland, a small community north of Woodmansie. According to the compass in his wristwatch, they were headed in the right direction. Woodmansie was four to six miles from where they were, Price's conjecture. With no indication of roads, or civilization for that matter, the operators just had walk, albeit through the woods. Price and John took point. The rest of them followed in a rough echelon formation, maintaining good barrel discipline while keeping their heads on a swivel.

Flashlight mounts were armed, beams cutting through the midnight woods. Each one gave their position away, but without NODs or thermals, it was their only option. Moonlight stippled the pitch pines, but it was dense out here.

That silvery luster only penetrated so far.

A mere two minutes into their walk and Nil spotted Jam go down. It was like he was being swallowed by the ground. Jam even called out, though reservedly. Nil cut a quiet whistle through his teeth, alerting John up ahead, and the others rushed to Jam's aid.

Mortification flooded his face pink when they realized what had happened. After tripping over a log, Jam's other foot caught a soft spot in the earth, like a muddy sinkhole. It devoured his leg, all the way up to the knee, and surely he thought the ground had come alive to eat him whole.

Then reality came to.

Nil and Frank helped him back to his feet. Jam hunkered over briefly, caught his breath, shook his head, and stood up straight. He pushed his long hair back away from his face, still damp from the marsh.

"Fuck me, sorry fellas, ma'am," Jam panted.

Frank sighed and squeezed his shoulder.

John looked around, and then nudged Price with his elbow. Price followed John's gaze, then the green bead of his laser-sight. John was pointing at a tree ten feet away. There seemed to be an opening in the canopy overhead, providing a nimbus of moonlight.

"Follow," Price said, and led the team to this spot. They gathered around, close but not assholes-and-elbows close. Then Price unslung his SIG and looked at the others. "Gear check, tip-to-butt, mags, everything. Comms, too."

Nods preceded compliance.

Previously they had only performed the bare minimum. First ensuring their ear-pro was dry and relatively clean, then reinserting them. Next they ensured their magazines were secure and racked firing levers. Now that they were drier, albeit still damp, the operators could better assess their gear. The concentrated shaft of moonlight helped, too. They deactivated their Modlite mounts so as to not blind each other.

Price finished first, briskly, and quietly stepped away to provide lookout. He kept his flashlight off, but traced the surrounding pitch pines with his green laser.

"What is that, Frank?" John asked, nodding at the assault rifle in Frank's hands. "Don't recognize it."

"Model 1, from Radian Weapons. New manufacturer out of Oregon. Sexy, ain't she?"

"Looks aren't everything," John said, sternly at first. Then he found himself appreciating the arctic gray lower receiver and the urban camo upper. The canted foregrip, EOTech holo, magazine window, and rubberized K2 grip. John clicked his tongue and added: "But she sure is."

"Shoots sexy, too," Frank assured him. "Seventy-seven grains, TMK."

"Can't beat five-five-six," Reva smirked.

"Debatable," John shrugged.

"Y'all ain't runnin' silver, are you?" Jam asked. He had finished confirming the operability of his Vector, and was now onto his pistol. "Because I'm not, and if we've got full-mooners out here, can't say I'm thrilled."

Their ear-plugs twitched with activity.

Price's tinny voice came through. There was mild

distortion from possible water damage, but the communications equipment itself remained functional.

"Coyle was supposed to provide some," he said. "Given the area, and past ops involving full-mooners, Coyle's always maintained a steady supply of Forked Tongue gear. The guys at the airfield know nothing about it, ain't like the crates are marked *werewolf-killers*, but that was the deal. Now Coyle is twice the distance from where we are, at least. Best case, we reach Woodmansie without any run-ins. Worst-case, we resort to our blades. And John's Marlin."

Price made great points, even if most were not comforting.

If all else failed, John's 45-70 could theoretically annihilate a lycanthrope skull—even if it took a couple of rounds. And their bladed weapons, while not silver, could decapitate a lycan if enough damage was dealt to the surrounding meat first.

"Well," Nil sighed, trying not to let himself sink into the soothing clutches of pessimism. "At least our comms still work."

"Gear, too," Frank said, racking the slide on his pistol. A 9mm round popped out, but he caught it. Then he ejected the mag, reinserted the cartridge, and secured it into the grip again.

"Nine-mil?" Reva asked, nodding at the pistol.

"Y'all running the same model?" Nil's brow furrowed, once he realized the identical similarities between Frank and Jam's pistols.

They both nodded.

"Boa is, was, partial to Springfield Armory," Frank

said, shrugging. He brandished the black semiautomatic handgun. It was a sleek full-size 9mm platform, bearing a faint resemblance to Reva's Ruger-57. "The Echelon, probably the best nine I've ever fired. Yes, better than a Glock. Don't get me started."

John smirked, shook his head, and raised a palm. "Wasn't gonna."

"All set?" Price asked, sounding impatient.

"Let's move," John said, tacitly pulling his proverbial game-face back on. He led the others into the clutch of trees again, navigating around trunks and occasionally ducking from a low branch, or striding right through underbrush.

Although they gradually returned to formation, now that their comms were working again, they could speak freely, and reach everyone, no matter their distance. John and Price led, thus about thirty feet ahead of Jam and Nil, who kept their rear.

"So, uh," Jam said, holding his mic button. "Nobody's gonna address that, huh? A *wyvern*, out in the open?"

A few seconds of quiet, apart from their wary steps, followed.

"Let alone *targeting* an airliner, and then us?" Jam added, scoffing before releasing the button.

Reva tentatively pressed hers to respond.

"Actually, that part tracks. I can't say how or why one's roaming about, now, but...supposedly they see infrared, so...that plane, our helo—big heat sources at an altitude like that. Not shocking it attacked us. It was more curiosity, if anything, I think. If it really thought we were a threat, it would've lit us up in the sky."

Reva released the button and returned both hands to her N4. She swallowed and her eyes darted back and forth through the dark forest, their flashlight mounts providing only a hint of awareness and security.

"Well said," Price acknowledged. "But I'd rather we not discuss *possibilities* in the field. Only focus on certainties."

John nodded.

Everybody collectively, implicitly, agreed.

And then Price sighed, without opening the com-link. John heard him, though, as Price walked parallel to his own path, about eight feet to his left. When Price did speak, it was on comms. There was a slight relaxation to his gruff voice.

"John, Reva, I know your story. Montana, two years ago. Flyover, didn't actually engage. Anyone else see a wyvern before?"

A pause.

"Once," Frank said. "Been three years, feels like yesterday, though. Running reconnaissance for a skin-walker op in the Appalachians, Maryland side. Flyby in a Little Bird. Was, uh…me and Zac, actually. That boy hated flying, but…"

Frank smirked, shook his head.

He looked up briefly, and then continued.

"Green. It was a dark, almost olive green shade. That wyvern down there, just…perfect camo. Was eating a deer when we passed over. Looked up, tilted its head, then dragged the carcass into its den. Vanished. Didn't give two shits about us, huh? No big deal."

They reflected on this story, and certainly envied that sort of experience with a wyvern. Far less traumatizing than what they had gone through. Jam and Nil certainly wished they had seen a wyvern before tonight; now they hoped they would never again.

"What about you, Price?" John said, once more just barely catching himself from saying 'sir.'

Price sighed before caving and contributing.

"Five years. My third active-duty op. It was like…a dream come true, until it wasn't. A juvenile had gone rogue up in Nepal, outside of Manang. Thing was the size of a tractor trailer, but underdeveloped wings. Couldn't fly. Thank God for that. Still, something was wrong with it. A brain sickness, I don't know. We'd eventually find the mother, throat torn out. But we tracked the juvie to a small village twenty klicks from Manang. This place was detached from the rest of the world, nameless. Talk about an ideal place for an unideal situation. I know that sounds rough, but…"

Price shook his head.

"The juvie tore it up. By the time we arrived, we just…I mean, I was new to being in the field. Seeing shit like that, ya know, different than SF. We were two squads, eight units. Three had tranqs, tried to use 'em. Juvie fluttered, dizzy-like. Then shook 'em off, and wouldn't go down. Had to kill it. A goddamn shame."

Price clicked his tongue and spit off to the side.

"If nothing else, we were grateful for its age. Which sounds cruel, but…it couldn't fly, that was a plus. And couldn't breathe fire, either. Glands come in at a certain age, much later than the maturity of teeth. Those things were *big*."

Price's fingertip had started to dull. He released the mic button and shrugged his shoulder into the buttstock of the SIG Spear. He let a relative silence take over, not caring or minding if anyone said anything afterward.

To nobody's surprise, it was Jam that eventually spoke. John and Reva suspected it might be Nil, but with Jam in the mix he was the one to bet on.

"I didn't even realize they bred," Jam said. He chuckled awkwardly.

John shook his head, noticing a wry smirk on Price's disheveled, damp-bearded face. Then both of their gazes locked forward, relieved to see a clearing ahead. About thirty yards. It seemed big enough to park two pickups in. John recalled Viper's op in Siberia, and wished they had quads to hop on and take them to their objective.

He felt as though Reva might be fantasizing the same.

"Like, how the hell does that even work?" Jam scoffed, reminding John and Price he had even brought it up in the first place. "I mean, I don't even know how bats—"

A decaying log crushed under the weight of something. A nanosecond later, underbrush shuttered and leaves sprayed in the wake of a big object.

Price averted his gaze far right. He swung his weapon—

The snarl was what interrupted Jam. That wet, salivating, guttural sound mid-pant. Then the lunging lycanthrope collided with a tree, just as Price side-stepped. Had he not, the momentum would've likely broken Price's shoulder. Instead the beast clipped him, and he tumbled back. The pitch pine trunk juddered, leaves and green needles sprinkling through the moonlit night.

John crossed over to reach him, but kept his flashlight trained on the wilderness.

"Contact!" John shouted, disregarding his comms.

A big hand and burly arm helped Price back to his feet. Price's flashlight washed over a brown-furred shape, an anthropomorphic wolf. It rose to its feet, immensely bipedal, like a Kodiak bear in the intimidation phase. A lupine snout widened, roaring and flinging saliva.

Price's rifle opened up. Muzzle flashes joined the beam from his flashlight mount. Single-shots banged from his SIG Spear with power and accuracy. The lycan recoiled, fleeing as 6.8mm rounds pursued it.

A spine-tingling howl spun the attention of the other operators.

And then a second.

Two more lupine shapes cut through the woods, occasional splashes of moonlight illuminating their routes. Modlite beams enhanced their vision, sporadically, catching the wolves' eyeshine and making them seem more like monsters than beasts.

Nightmares incarnate.

Quadrupedally, they charged Serpent One.

Two converging from opposite sides.

Gunfire ripped into trees, and around them. The beasts were agiler than they ought to be at that size. Darting around trunks, rebounding from them, launching faster. Stronger. Closer—

Crossing rounds intersected on one lycan, forcing it into a wounded tumble just short of Reva. Price had detached slightly from the head of their formation for a better angle. She nodded at him with gratitude. Then Price noticed John's back was to a tree, and he was jerking his rifle to and fro, tracking a *third* lycanthrope. It slalomed around tree trunks, bursting through underbrush.

Reva convened on his position.

The operators remained in a column-like cluster.

Price's attention shifted from Jam, Nil, and Frank—their backs to the same fat tree, shooting methodically in every direction—to the clearing ahead.

"Stagger, on me," he said into his mic.

The sound in their ears triumphed over the muffled gunfire, thanks to their Peltors.

Jam and Frank left the tree. The latter snapped at Nil, who finally followed, his shotgun roaring as a nimble lycan approached. It just about reached him when his heel caught a stump and he fell back. The beast lunged, Nil's eyes in terrible awe of how light reflected off its dense, curved talons.

A five-petal slug opened up as it bore through the lycan's chest, decimating a lung in the process. The creature fell close to Nil, and then tumbled past him. Almost tripping Frank as he went back to help Nil to his feet. The lycan whimpered in pain as it struggled to collect its bearings, blood slopping from its jaws and the slowly healing cavity in its chest.

"Hell of a shot," Frank said.

Jam's Vector hosed out rounds in full-auto, albeit in bursts. He had backtracked to provide cover fire for Frank and Nil when another lycan rushed toward them.

Price, John, and Reva were, respectively, approaching the clearing in a staggered column. Likewise, they fired shot-by-shot, in alternating directions. The number of their enemy seemed overwhelming, but also unsure. Whenever one was terribly wounded, however not mortally, it would retreat and another took its place. Which begged to question if they were receiving true reinforcements, or just recycling their charges.

Presently, a confirmed three, not including the one that Nil had severely wounded, were in their line-of-sight.

Price backpedaled into the clearing, and stark moonlight bathed him as if kissed by Luna's gaze. He didn't let this distract him too much, keeping his flashlight just left of John's shoulder.

A fourth lycan howled somewhere unnervingly close, and then the splitting sound of a branch gave way. Chunks of wood and periderm bark showered Jam as Frank and Nil neared him.

The beast descended, but Frank released himself from Nil, throwing his right shoulder into Jam's chest. Jam tumbled back and the lycan landed on Frank. Amid a flurry of flashlight beams from both Jam and Nil, who were in the midst of catching their balance, the burly beast tore into Frank Santino. Its jaws snapped in a frenzy, never fully clamping on anything, tearing away layers of Frank's screaming face. Part of his scalp flew off his head, landing on Jam's thigh, blood and pus forming a layer of makeshift glue.

Jam yelped in terror, the voice catching in his throat. Two rounds jerked out of his Vector, one punching into the lycan's right shoulder. Nil stumbled to the left for a clearer shot, and unleashed two rounds at almost point-blank into the lycan's upper back. Slugs flowered through fur, skin, and muscle, but not bone. The lycan flinched and seemed to have whimpered but kept bearing down on Frank, its toe-claws sinking into his thighs, the talons on its hands ripping through body armor and gouging troughs into his chest.

John's Marlin thundered twenty feet behind Jam, a startlingly well-placed shot catching the lycan below the left ear, above the eye. Although it glanced off the skull, denting it over ocular nerves, it tore off the pointed ear, taking a chunk of scalp with it. The lycan yipped in pain and tumbled back, fleeing.

Two others were pushed back by John's Marlin, and merely cocking the lever intimidated a third enough to make it flee.

He convinced Reva to join Price in the clearing, while he assembled to help Jam and Nil address Frank's condition.

Except there was no condition.

Whether he had died just then, or moments ago during the attack, couldn't be determined. For his sake, they hoped much earlier. Although, the sputtering, jarring screams under the weight and flurrying claws of the lycan would eternally haunt Jam nonetheless.

Despite his short stature and size, he required both

John and Nil to haul him away from Frank's brutalized corpse.

Jam didn't give in until he had dug a family photo out of Frank's vest pouch, and torn the Radian Model 1 from his hands. The sling was ripped, but the weapon intact. Jam's teary eyes were joined by John's when they hovered over what remained of Frank's photo.

His wife of eleven years and 9-year-old son gathered in his arms. It was hard to tell, though. The photo had been torn, each rip flayed at the edges, exacerbating the distortion of the image. And it was caked with fresh blood, even the pulp of flesh. An attempt to wipe it clean only muddied it more.

Tears not fully absorbed by Jam's stubble dappled the photo.

John embraced him with one arm, briefly.

Then he gave him a firm shake, once, and pulled away. A two-second, hoarse "fuck" broke from his mouth. Had he not been wearing long sleeves, one would see the veins embossed along his thick arms. They momentarily peered out along his neck, above the collar of his shirt.

John paced near the center of the clearing, which was about thirty feet across, a rough circle.

The grass here was coarse and dry, clumps of peat visible through the loam. It wasn't called the Barrens for no reason.

"Jam!" Reva suddenly snapped, in his ear. He flinched, but looked at her steadily.

While Reva convinced him to "nut up," Nil standing by and keeping an eye on the nearest treeline, Price tended to John.

"You good?" Was all he said at first.

John nodded until he couldn't anymore. His neck muscles slackened and he stopped tensing. Then he stopped pacing altogether.

"Full-mooners attacking people in their territory is one thing," John practically growled. "But dragging them from their *cars*? Nevermind the wyvern. If it wasn't for that thing, we'd have landed in Coyle fine, resupplied with silver, and no lycan, let alone a *pack* of full-mooners, would've stood a chance against the *six* of us!"

Price took a deep breath and nodded once.

"Be that as it may, we are where we are, regardless. Answers will come, but right now, we need to advance. There literally is no…other…option. Understand?"

Now John imitated Price's composure with his own slow, deep, reorienting breath.

Somewhere a twig broke, and a bush shuddered.

John snapped his Marlin up, and swept the flashlight beam across the curving treeline surrounding them.

"Then we have to move faster," he said quietly, his cheek not leaving the rifle.

"And we will." Price whistled, then beckoned the others. They assembled. Price sized up Jam, but not for the reason others might have guessed. Jam *appeared* to be in the throes of getting himself together. He could mourn later. But then Price asked: "How are you on ammo, Jam? Pouches look empty."

Jam shamefully brandished his Vector. The protruding stick-mag held forty rounds of 10mm, but everyone could guess it wasn't full.

"Last mag," he said, his voice phlegmy. And then he thumbed over his shoulder. "Must've dropped the rest when we bailed from the helo. Not that I had much after Skyline."

"Splendid," Nil sighed.

"Who's faster on their feet?" Price asked, his eyes darting between Reva and Nil.

They both furrowed their brows and struggled to answer. Neither wanted to, suddenly.

"Third-party perspective?" John said. "Depends. What's the task?"

Price painted the tree trunks between which they had emerged minutes ago, with his laser-sight.

"Jam needs ammo for his Radian," Price said, and then dropped the green bead of his laser-sight down to the Model 1 assault rifle that Jam had taken, only to drop on the ground. Price's eyes shifted between the members of former Viper. "And Frank should have some in his kit. Even if it's just a couple o' mags."

Jam's head bowed and he kneaded his brow. When he lifted it again, he began to say "I'm small, I'm fast" but Price and John shook their heads.

"Fat chance," John said bluntly. Then he looked at Reva, and shrugged. "Strip the kit so you don't get caught on anything. N4, too. Just the Ruger, and the kodachis."

Reva mouthed 'fuck' and began to disrobe her gear. Subconsciously, she relished the challenge. But she was also in her own way mourning Frank's terrible death. Losing the helo crew was bad enough; the unexpectedness of it made the casualties worse. As many of them as there were, they shouldn't have been overrun by lycans, even full-mooners. *Especially* full-mooners. After all, they rarely ran in packs; they preferred the rogue life out here.

One thing after another went against everything they had learned and been taught at Forked Tongue.

"Naked enough for ya?" Reva asked John, having shed her entire kit, from vest to pouches, and rifle. Only her Adra knife, kodachi blades, and pistol remained. Her long-sleeved all-black attire made her look sleeker in the night, her frame lithe but not without its curves and muscle. She even tucked her braided ponytail into the back of her snug shirt, without anchoring her head.

"For now," John replied.

Reva tried not to smirk. She turned around, but paused a few strides from the treeline. Behind her, flanking both sides, were John and Nil. John raised his Marlin, and Nil racked the firing lever on his shotgun. Between John's 45-70 and Nil's 12-gauge slugs, they had the most powerful ammo in the squad, both with great range.

"On your light," Reva said, knees bent and torso hunched forward.

John and Nil exchanged nods. Behind them, Price and Jam kept their eyes on the surrounding treeline. If they were ambushed here, it wouldn't be pretty—especially with Reva in the woods, and the other two covering *her*.

The second that John and Nil's flashlights shone forward, Reva darted into the forest. She navigated tree trunks and vaulted logs with impressive footwork. When she reached Frank's mutilated corpse, about forty feet from the clearing—which felt like sixty, given the wooded density—she immediately hunkered down and began rummaging his kit. There was an inherent, unavoidable shame to her actions, like stealing from the dead. Even though she knew he would do the same; any operator would, even soldiers.

Consider it a parting gift.

Reva was expecting, or at least hoping, for three to four mags. Instead she gathered a mere two; there was a third, but it had been brutalized by the lycan's claws, the sturdy plastic ripped open and cartridges spilled onto the bloody forest floor. She had no apt pockets for the mags, so she stuffed them into the snug waistband of her pants, which couldn't have been more uncomfortable.

When she stood, her teammates' flashlight beams cutting through the forest on either side of her, Reva's breath shuddered.

Movement in her left peripheral.

She jerked her head, noticed a shape darting from tree to tree, past a flashlight beam that tapered wide.

Hands free, she raised one to her collar mic.

"Got one, at my nine," she said. As if on cue, another sign of motion, and then a third glimpse. Her pulse quickened. "Another, eleven o'clock. Third, two."

She lowered her hand to the Ruger, and slowly unholstered it.

The two flashlight beams rerouted.

"Got 'em," Nil said. "Move your ass, Rev."

She didn't hesitate. Reva spun and mad-dashed back toward the clearing. A howl ruptured the still night somewhere to her far left, and then an audible snarl approached her right. Heavy, clawed footfalls tore up forest floor, even scored tree bark, and crushed logs in their wake. Panting, rugged breaths from massive lungs through toothed jaws.

Gunfire, ahead.

Muzzle flashes.

Heavy bullets and slugs ripped through the woods to her left and right. She prayed most of them avoided trunks, and had all her faith in the men firing, but there was reason to doubt. Full-mooners were far nimbler and more resilient than lycanthropes that still lived in their human form. These had not known any semblance of human life, let alone shape and function, for years. Decades, some.

Reva was within twenty feet of the clearing when a bullet whizzed through the night past her right ear. It caught the edge of a tree trunk and made a distinct sound, especially when it sprayed fragments and bark into the face of a lycan. It yelped and bounced off another trunk, raining pines and twigs.

Then Reva's right ankle caught a log and she staggered forward.

Her hands had to literally push herself off a tree to keep from slamming into it, only she found herself tripping through a dense bush. When she landed, she sprang up, arms extended and both hands on her Ruger. Its own flashlight mount scanned the dark forest with a sweeping beam.

The gunfire behind her had ceased. Their own beams were shakier, suggesting they were reloading.

Just before they straightened out again, a guttural snarl jerked Reva's attention to the left. A lycan sprang at her, and her pistol swung toward it. The beam of light illuminated its long snout and the saliva trailing from exposed fangs. She squeezed the trigger with no intent other than to kill. A brisk volley of 5.7mm rounds struck the lycan at 1,700 feet-per-second, from a mere ten-foot range. The creature's imposing snarl was reduced to a whimper as it faltered, and Reva avoided its momentum after dumping four rounds from her gun.

When it struck the tree that had been behind her, it bounced off and messily regained its footing. Blood poured from wounds, including a decimated eyeball. It shook its furred head as if merely wet, and then growled at her again.

Gunfire returned to mar the silence of nightfall, this time far more reservedly than before. John and Nil were picking their shots with greater faith in their own marksmanship, and that Reva was engaging one of three known targets.

"Fuck this," she growled under her breath, holstering the Ruger. Both of her hands then hovered over the grooved handles of her kodachis. She thumbed the brass guards clear of their scabbards, but didn't draw them.

The full-mooner's throat uttered a croak of a snarl before launching itself at her. She drew the short swords and sprung from where she had hunkered. The right kodachi swung at the lycan's head, the left jabbing upward. Reva ducked and slid forward, her left knee gliding through dry soil.

When she came to a stop a mere eight feet away,

the lycan had landed awkwardly where she had been. She turned, and in the scattered moonlight could vaguely see its mass shift. Blood glistened around its thick neck, dripping through dense fur. More of it dripped from under its right arm.

Her kodachis were wet, too.

But the lycan was a seven-footer, and must have been at least four-hundred pounds of meat, muscle, and bone. It didn't fall, not yet. Another growl, and then it pounced.

Reva screamed as she held her ground, until the last damn second. Her heel planted against a root, knee bent, she launched herself airborne when time mattered most. Reva could've never anticipated *riding* a lycan like a bull, but she did for a fleeting two seconds as she drove one 16-inch blade to the hilt between its ribs, and the other across its throat once more. The bucking lycan rid her of one kodachi, and flung her from its back.

She landed with a painful tumble, bouncing over a stout stump rather than into it.

As she struggled to her feet, Reva noticed that one of the two mags previously stuffed into her waistband had fallen out. And her other kodachi was still lodged into the lycan's ribcage.

It turned to face her, and a flashlight beam not hers lit it up. A gunshot rang out, muffled by her ear-pro, catching the lycan in the hindquarters. It whimpered and faltered. When it turned to flee, Reva shook her head.

"Oh, no you don't," she said, and ran after it.

She slowed down as she neared it, and the lycan detected her approach. It spun around to face her, but when it did, Reva thrusted her kodachi forward, in a perfect fencer's lunge. The canted tip punched into the lycan's empty eye socket, penetrating its brain cavity. The full-mooner's body went limp like a heavy sack, and slid off her blade.

"Bad dog," she said, bending over and twisting the other sword out from its ribs. She wiped both of them on its fur, wherever blood didn't sully it, and sheathed them.

The gunfire from her comrades had ceased.

She hunted down the other Radian mag and returned to the clearing with haste. Once she emerged from the treeline, to John's far right, she stood akimbo and caught her breath.

"You good?" John asked, jogging over to her. He held the Marlin high, its hefty buttstock resting on his hip.

Nil backpedaled toward them, flashlight scanning the curved treeline. Still wary.

"Better than them," she said.

"You kill one?" Nil asked.

She nodded, and then pulled one of her kodachis from the scabbard, about halfway. Some residual blood tarnished the otherwise gleaming Damascus blade.

"How?" John asked.

"Let's just say…it couldn't *see* too well."

John relaxed, and smirked. "Lovely."

Price and Jam arrived behind them.

"I don't know what to say," Jam said, making tentative, avoidant eye contact with Reva.

She brandished the two AR-15 magazines, which Jam accepted. He had detached the sling from his Vector and adjusted it to fit the Radian. With the rifle slung, he secured the two mags into pouches on his kit, adjusting them, too, to fit the bulkier shapes compared to the sticks for his Vector.

"That'll do," Reva said, slapping his shoulder.

John handed her the gear she had disrobed, and she felt eager to don it again. Her remark earlier about being 'naked' was only half a joke. In the field, on an op, being without her gear truly felt like going nude. Had she been forced to shed her Ruger and kodachis, too, for whatever reason, she might have mutinied.

"Everyone set?" Price asked. He consulted the compass in his watch, and indicated with his flashlight beam the direction they were to head. About halfway across the clearing, the motion of a sluggish object caught his gaze, hard right. Then another, and a third, lured the others' attention.

Before they knew it, Serpent One was being surrounded on all flanks by lycans. Full-mooners were emerging from the circular treeline, squeezing between pitch pines, some reared up on their hind legs, but most on all fours.

Drool dribbled from their jaws.

"Fuck me," Nil mumbled, just within earshot of Reva and Nil.

John had already advanced closer to Price, ready to ask him something about their progression. Maybe regarding his guess on how far they were from Woodmansie. God could only say, now; John had lost all train of thought.

"Cluster," Price said, in his mic. His hand had

moved up to press the button about as slowly as he could.

No fast movements, the others assembled on him. They were, more or less, in the center of the clearing. At thirty feet across, they didn't exactly have a lot of room to move. And with each pivot of their heads, it appeared that lycans had emerged all around them, no more than six feet apart from each other.

Ever patiently, they raised their weapons.

Somewhere, in neither a direction nor range they could quite place, a sound interrupted the lycans' growling. It was a cacophony, really. Not just one noise, but a crescendo of them. Ripping. The tearing of something great and coarse. Too loud and tumultuous to be fabric. But it wasn't metallic, either, ruling out a collision or crash. The ground didn't shake, so it wasn't a quake. It had the faint semblance of lightning cracking the sky, but a glance above them revealed no indication of a storm.

Chills ran down their backs as a new form of confusion struck them.

Moreover—

The lycans showed mixed reactions. Some yipped and even barked, some snapping their jaws at each other. One or two retreated into the woods without hesitation. Previously on its hind legs, another lowered to all fours and lurched toward the humans, almost drawing a shot from Jam, but instead it bounced back and fled into the Barrens.

"What the hell is going on?" Nil asked, without activating his mic.

"Just…hold," Price said.

Then one of the full-mooners abruptly howled before tearing off into the woods. On that note, all but one of the lycans scattered into the embrace of the Barrens. Vanishing, with no indication of a return. A lone beast remained, appearing puzzled. But it went beyond that; the creature seemed rattled, as a rabid dog might behave.

Suddenly it charged the group, loping at a startling speed.

Nil knelt and blasted it with two quick shots from his Derya. The shotgun slugs slammed into its limbs, as John's Marlin blew a round that caught it high in the skull. The beast reached the group in a tumble, and the operators fanned out. All but John. He stepped forward instead of back, placing the muzzle of the Marlin against the beast's right temple, below its pointed ear. He cocked the lever and squeezed the trigger before the lycan could even flinch. The blast shattered its skull and painted the dry grass with brain pulp. From his shins down, John's pants were now a ruddy pink color.

He used a boot to push the lobotomized lycan onto its back.

"On that note," Price said, nodding toward the treeline behind him. "Let's fucking move, yeah?"

He was within arm's reach of a tree when his sat-phone chimed. It wasn't a full-fledged ringtone, but a two-tone sound that nonetheless caught his attention. Those strange ripping sounds had ceased six seconds after they began, leaving utter silence in their wake. Making the sat-phone even more noticeable.

Price displayed a befuddled expression as he dug it out of his pouch, cradling the SIG rifle with one hand.

John hovered over the phone, Price tapping buttons. The display illuminated.

"Calder," he said, looking up at Price, brow furrowed. "She sent you an encrypted text."

The others were keen to know more, but kept their eyes and weapons on the surrounding treeline, not trusting the complete desertion of the lycans.

"Why not call?" Price asked.

John pointed at the display, and then the digital clock in the top right corner.

"First message was delivered twelve minutes ago. Must not have heard it during the gunfire. Before that, I bet she tried to call, but couldn't connect. The fucking Barrens."

Price nodded.

"Fuck's it say?" Jam asked.

Price would excuse that, given the rattled nerves, jarring curiosity, and due impatience.

"First message says…*Caution. Cambion activity suspected behind everything. Comms interference to worsen over next hour.*"

Price shook his head.

"Second message, received now. Reads: *Cambion coup confirmed. Not just I, but B and C, too. They're on the news. Get airborne.*"

Price took a massive breath, extended the antennae from the phone, and proceeded to text a response. John watched the letters accrue on the screen.

Lima is down. Wyvern in the air. Need a bird for exfil. Low ammo. Woodmansie.

He sent it, retracted the antenna, and then looked

up at the others.

"I, B, C," Jam said, perplexed. "What the hell is—"

"Not just *imps*," Reva said. "But *Barons* and *Centurions*, too."

"Ah…"

"Good catch," Price said. "Was my best guess, too."

"I…don't understand, though," Reva said. "A *coup*? Imps don't have the authority to…"

Her heart sank. The realization hit her moments after it appeared to have manifested in John and Price's minds. Nil seemed unsurprised, like he suspected all along. Knowing how cynical Nil was, still, at heart, this wouldn't shock anyone.

"What? What is it?" Jam asked, a bit slow.

"The imps didn't call this play," John said. "They've been *used* by their higher-ups, like sentries. Probably, what, a dozen Barons could pull a move like this?"

"A single Baron's charge is a Legion. Which is…anyone?" Price said.

While John and Reva did the mental math, Nil stepped forward. When he spoke, it was with a disturbing nonchalance. Like he went to bed every night with this information teeming beneath the surface.

"Six Centurions," he said. "Sixteen imps each. Which makes ninety-six imps total, per Baron."

"And…in what number do Barons move as a unit?" Price asked, at this point deathly curious himself.

"That's pure theory," Nil said. "We only know the

arrangement of imps, Centurions, and Barons based on knowledge from the Jordanian Assault of 1897. There hasn't been a cambion incursion since."

"What about Dukes?" Reva asked.

Nil shrugged. "Supposedly, they reign over Barons. Anywhere from six to thirteen per Duke. Accompanied by rachnids."

Jam batted his eyes. "Come again?"

"What, you never ran through cambion history in your spare time at the facility?" Nil said.

Jam scoffed. "No. Why would I? Imps are basic training. Like you said, a Centurion hasn't been sighted since the late 1800s. Why waste—"

"Enough," Price said. "Speaking of wasting time, we're doing that now. Best not dwell on the doom and gloom. We need to *move*. We're in no condition to be engaging Centurions, let alone Barons. A few imps, sure. A *platoon* of them? Hardly."

Nobody could argue.

The unmatched ability of imps of influence the weak-minded was one thing, but having this sort of effect on cryptids across the globe was another. That kavū had been driven out of their habitats from the organization of a mass coup by cambions almost made sense. That wyverns and full-mooners were acting uncharacteristically was another. It suggested what none of them wanted to admit—

That this was much bigger than a few Barons marching infantry onto their plane. Cambions didn't have projectile weapons. They were no match for modern militaries, unless they moved in forces of *hundreds* of Barons, and dozens of Dukes. The latter were twenty-foot-tall beasts that could likely withstand tank rounds, and perform untold feats of interdimensional power.

"They're on the *news*, for fuck's sake," Price pressed. "We're no longer dealing with something that can be swept under the rug. The rug is *gone*."

A brutal reality they couldn't have fathomed in their lifetime was suddenly upon them. Nobody knew how to handle it, especially given their current circumstances.

They moved as one, back into the woods.

Weapons ready. Hearts playing catch-up.

10

Not even a crumb of lycanthrope presence since they scattered from the clearing. If nothing else, this assisted Serpent One's urgency. Some ten minutes after returning to the woods, they heard more ripping and tearing sounds. Louder this time, more discordant, and closer. Maybe a hundred, two-hundred yards out. Disconcertingly, the dissonance was not alone. In its wake, the faintest hint of screams among screeching tires and blaring horns. A certified panic of the human kind. Although indicative they were headed in the right direction, and not terribly far, it was inarguably *not* good news.

Within sightline of artificial light seeping through the trees as they became scarcer around them, Serpent One paused midstride.

Price's sat-phone chimed again.

The two-tone notification sound was one they had been eager to hear again.

"Grab it, read it," Price said, implicitly to Reva,

212

who trailed him. Price was intent on keeping both hands on his weapon, the SIG's barrel and optic trained on the fence line of trees sixty feet ahead of them.

Reva did, without ado.

"Calder again." She cleared her throat. "*Copy. Dispatched an armed BH to the Woodmansie quarry. ETA 4-0, barring fuck-ups. Godspeed.*"

Reva paused.

"Should I reply?"

"Negative. Put it back, and let's push. Hopefully we're not too far from the quarry."

Reva returned the phone. She patted his shoulder, indicating he was good to go. As Price and John advanced, their vanguard, the other three followed in arrow formation.

The artificial light flowing through the trees ahead turned out to be from a convenience store across the street. It was a narrow two-lane backroad that a nearby sign showed was *Mt Misery Rd.*

"Pleasant," Nil mumbled.

Poorly-lit letters fixed to the front of the store read *Woodmansie Supplies*. The property occupied maybe half an acre. There were two gas pumps out front, with no awning. Not even a prices sign, only the Citgo emblem on a post. It was no Wawa, but likely a resourceful hub for the rural homes scattered out this way.

The operators were in awe of what they were seeing. A scene of disarray.

Most disconcerting were the rifts.

Fire-orange ovals searing through the cambion dimension to reach Earth's plane. They were usually a few feet off the ground and anywhere between three to seven feet tall, permitting the passage of an imp. They sealed, vanishing completely, once passage had been fulfilled. If a rift remained open, it meant more were waiting to cross through from the other side. But in all the years these operators had been with Forked Tongue, and of all the stories they had heard, rifts never remained open for more than ten seconds.

Imps were about five to six feet tall, but more often than not crawled on all fours, with the mobility of a spider despite their gaunt human frames, and half-skull heads. So their passage through a rift was usually very quick; they were also a creature typically devoid of strategy, notorious for acting on whims.

Although a rift here and there was common wherever imp activity had been reported, *seven* of them in a half-acre space was an unnerving sight. Neither Price nor John could recall a time they had seen more than two rifts open at once.

From these leapt or crawled imps, one after the other. The area wasn't congested with people, but enough to make the scene an absolute nightmare.

"We've gotta be close, rural homes down the way, both directions, probably," Price said, pointing left and right down Mt Misery.

"We need a map," John said, his body language indicating a strong urge to advance.

Price nodded. He looked at the others.

"Conserve your ammo—but don't hesitate to save a life."

Everybody nodded.

"Now *move!*" He snapped, and they surged forward. A sedan tore out of the store's small parking lot, tires screeching and a smokescreen pouring out the back. An imp was crawling on the roof, hissing and drooling. Bony talons scored the windshield as it crept toward the hood, despite the car's building speed. Screams spewed from inside the car.

John's posture straightened like a statue.

Marlin shouldered, he fired. The 45-70 struck the imp in its rump, splitting it nearly in half. The creature made a foul screech and tumbled off the car, black blood not unlike tar leaving a mark on the car. It fishtailed before the driver regained control and sped off, down Mount Misery Road.

"Nice," Jam said, in passing. He and Nil moved together, darting across the road.

Only two more vehicles in the lot.

One hopped the curb and reached the road while two imps pursued it. The pickup truck skidded across pavement, almost spinning. As the driver got control and straightened out, westbound, Price nailed one of the imps leaping through the air after the truck. His SIG Spear put two rounds in its chest and it dropped like a ragdoll. The other imp ignored the truck and crawled toward him with disturbing speed.

It evaded his next shot, and then Reva punched a few rounds into its left shoulder with her N4. It stopped, screeched at her, haphazard fangs in its half-skull slick with saliva. That it was capable of producing any was disturbing in its own right. Imps always appeared on the verge of fatal starvation, everything about them dry and coarse. Even their exposed brains were a desiccated labyrinth of rot.

Price fired his SIG, a single 6.8mm catching it in the right temple as it was distracted by Reva. The rest of its head tumbled across the pavement in a mess of black and gray goop.

"Thanks," Price said.

Reva nodded and they, John to her right, finished crossing the street.

There were imps on the roof of the convenience store, a couple by the pumps, and two crawling over a van attempting to leave the lot. Far right, presently being handled by Nil and Jam. Nil swapped his Derya for the SMG. The slugs were overkill for imps, and not the most accurate with civvies in the line-of-fire. As their select-fire bullets tore the imps off the van, flustered civilians thanked them under haggard breaths, and then sped off.

"Forked Tongue is either gonna get raped by the media for this shit-storm," Nil said, into his mic. "Or thanked, after we mop up the mess."

"Is that optimism I hear, Nil?" John said.

"Half-and-half, man."

"We'll take it. If anything—"

"Up top!" Reva snapped. She backed up, dropped to one knee, and raised her shouldered N4. An imp on the roof of the convenience store was maybe a nanosecond from pouncing on Price or John. She put a tight cluster into its upper chest and the creature fell to the pavement in front of them.

"Good looks," John nodded at her.

She returned the gesture and stood.

Inside the store, glass shattered and a man screamed. Price rushed in, John fast on his heels.

A man's body was slumped over the front counter, his spine ripped clear from his flesh. He was also missing his right arm.

By the refrigeration section, an employee or customer, difficult to tell, was being ravaged by an imp. Its feet were *inside* his hips, clawed toes latched onto the exposed bone of his pelvis. The imp's humanoid jaws were taking cookie-cutter bites from his neck. Arterial blood showered the contents of the creature's exposed skull.

Price and John's faces contorted.

John unholstered his revolver, and Price stood down. The hammer cocked audibly, and the imp looked away from its victim to sneer at John. He squeezed the trigger and the .454 Casull obliterated it from the neck-up. Both the imp and the poor man's body slumped to the floor in a pool of gore.

John holstered the revolver, and turned around. Price had plucked a local NJ map from the front counter. Then they exited the store. In time to see Jam executing a wounded imp with his newly acquired Radian Model 1. Behind Jam, Nil was nudging a recently slain imp with his boot.

Apart from the two casualties inside the store, there was a sedan by the pumps with a pair of bodies in the front seat. They were disturbingly mauled, partially feasted on. Blood painted the inside of the splintered windshield.

Likely the imps responsible littered the pavement

217

around the car, slain by Reva. She had not followed Price and John into the store, but instead turned at the sound of…

Flesh tearing.

The civilians inside had been killed well before Serpent One's arrival.

"Where are we?" John asked, his nose wrinkled with anger. And the unavoidable fetor of bloodshed. Dead imps reeked awfully, too. Until their bodies were reclaimed by their dimension, via a sizzling evaporation, leaving nothing but embers in their wake.

Many traits made it difficult to not call cambions *demons*. However, to Forked Tongue's limited knowledge, their realm was far viler than the pits and flames of the biblical hell.

"A klick from the quarry. If that, hard to tell with that lake. See?" John followed Price's finger. "Cut through the woods, save a few minutes by avoiding the road. Have a feeling lycans won't be active around here. They're scared of cambions, much as humans are."

John nodded.

"Down this road, Savoy Boulevard, our main highway out here." Price used his pinky to indicate smaller routes in the local map. "See that line, there? Just before Egg Harbor Road. Dirt path, probably. For tractors and shit. Take that left of Savoy, down into the quarry. Maybe a fifteen-minute hike."

"We better get going, then, yeah?" Nil said.

Price stuffed the map into a pouch and led the way. John followed suit, trailed by Reva. Nil and Jam kept their rear. Once they were back in the embrace of the

Pine Barrens, their pace dampened some, but not significantly. Warier under the canopies than they were in the open, this caution diminished with each passing minute. It became crystal clear that Price's deduction earlier was on the nose. That no creature, no matter how fierce on their lonesome, wanted to risk a run-in with cambions. So they steered clear, madly so.

About ten minutes later, Price and John emerged from the woods and began to trek down the side of Savoy Blvd. Behind them followed the others. Under the luster of moonlight, they deactivated their Modlites and focused on their path.

Spotting the narrow dirt road snaking off from Savor and toward the quarry was their first sign of good news. While John led the others across the two lanes, Price held back to examine the map some.

Once he regrouped with John, he explained himself.

"The residences we were originally tasked with securing, and evacuating," Price said, tapping the paper map. "Maybe three-hundred yards down that way. Just past the quarry, this side of the road. "

John shook his head.

"We just can't. Like you said. We're not fit to, not like this."

"You reckon we'd do more harm than good?"

John sighed. "Harm to us, yeah. Say we evacuate two people from those houses. Maybe even more. *Kids*, I'll say. But we lose half of us. What good's that do for everyone else? Price, you know as well as I do…we have to resupply. Or we'll be dust in the wind, all the same."

Price sighed hoarsely.

It was strange, for him, being on this side of reason. Strange for John, too. He abhorred admitting those things out loud. Just glad he didn't have to do it in front of the others, or worse yet, trainees. Forked Tongue hopefuls.

"Then we go," Price said, gesturing across the street. "And make ourselves rocks again."

"Tou-fucking-ché," John said.

They hustled across the road, until their boots scuffed dirt and pebbles. Then they rushed to catch up with the others, relieved nobody had waited for them. There was no crossing canopy-cover down the dirt path, but not for lack of trying by the trees. The Barrens weren't thinner this way, because of the quarry. If anything they were denser and greener, likely because of the lake and an accumulation of moisture.

John wouldn't be shocked if the government pressured the Jersey Wildlife Preservation to surrender the lake, too. Drain it and extend the quarry.

"No bird, not yet anyway," Reva said, into their ears. "Popping flares regardless."

"Good call," Price said.

"Let's hope they didn't encounter any interference along the way," John said.

"Or, as Calder herself put it," Nil said, borderline satirical, "*fuck-ups*."

It was undeniably uncharacteristic of Calder to use that sort of language, let alone in a professional manner over a secure line, but the circumstances were sound.

Reaching the quarry about twenty seconds behind Reva, Nil, and Jam, John and Price found them standing around sizzling flares fifty feet from a mobile trailer. Like an office for whoever managed the site, the squat structure sat opposite a bulldozer and crane, both unoccupied. A pickup truck stamped *Chatsworth Construction* on the door was parked between the trailer and bulldozer, but nobody was inside.

Avoiding eye contact with the searing flares in the moonlit night, John instead navigated toward the crane. He figured he could get a nicer viewpoint on top of the cab, should any enemy find their way down here.

He was maybe twenty feet from it when a familiar ripping sound rattled his eardrums. The Peltors served no purpose with that kind of noise. Then a rift opened right where the trailer was, halving the structure with a flash of flame.

Serpent One backpedaled.

All but John, who faced them on the opposite side of the trailer. He backed up, too, and quickly wished he had not walked away from the others.

This rift was much bigger than the ones around the convenience store. That it was only one should have been good news, but wasn't.

The oval portal was at least fifteen feet tall and eight wide. Its fiery border continued to burn, and a few of the operators achieved a glimpse into the other side from where they stood. What they saw was equally bewildering and terrifying. Structures composed of vermilion flesh and mauve organs dripped with slime, over which teemed hissing imps.

Then two larger shadows manifested, and a pair of Barons individually stepped through. They were nine-foot creatures with bodybuilder frames, massive shoulders and big, round, hairless heads that closely resembled human skulls. Only eyeless; not even sporting the cavities where eyes ought to be. Just small holes across the forehead, possibly sensory organs, like a pit viper's. The mouths seemed humanoid until they stretched wide in a snarling roar; pronounced canines bracketed by sharp incisors.

If the Barons had skin it was difficult to discern; their bodies appeared to be connected chunks of pale bone, bound by the occasional revelation of taut muscle.

Hands ended in giant fingers, four each, tipped with claws fit to rip a bear in half. The feet were hooved, and from the knee-down were identical to the third abomination that followed them.

"Duke, we, we have a Duke," Nil mumbled.

The sandstone floor of the quarry reflected moonlight with no reservation. This made the area much brighter than anyplace else way out here.

Setting their human eyes on a Duke, however, almost begged there to be more darkness. It was grotesque, and with each cloven step the earth vibrated. Shaking loose their last grips of hope.

The sixteen-foot-tall beast had to duck through the rift, its giant yellowish horns clearing the sides by turning its head. Once fully upright, the two-legged two-armed Duke revealed what occupied one of its massive, clawed hands. A massive flanged mace, black with terrifying barbs down the shaft. With a single low swing, the Duke not only demolished both halves of the trailer, but shoved their debris aside as if Styrofoam.

Despite its evident functionality, the Duke's stomach area was composed of a gaping, spiked rib cage, and no visible internal organs. This pained the operators' strategic minds, as they didn't know where to aim, supposing their weapons stood any chance.

Its skull was vaguely anthropomorphic, but its jaws were mostly fangs, and the goatish horns protruding from where its ears ought to be were curved like tusks. They swooped low, parallel with its chin, and then rose high, past eye-level.

Scattering past its hooved feet were two six-legged beasts. They were a dull, rugged pink in composition, their skin stretched over a spiked, bony spine that arched high above the shoulders and tapered toward the rump. Past this was a swinging tail, each ending in a spiked club of bone.

That of an Ankylosaurus crossed the back of Jam's mind.

"Rachnids," Nil said, pressing his mic button. "I swear, I always thought they were more myth than anything."

"Not as spidery as I feared," Jam said, noting the ram-like horns that jutted forward, as if deliberately sculpted for impaling enemies. Let alone the under-bite jaws, inarguably carnivorous. He gulped. "Still bat-shit terrifying, though."

The skulking beasts were each about the size of a small car, reminding John of kavū in that manner. Nothing else about them were alike, though—except for the row of gray fur sprouting along its spine. And these abominations had no redeeming qualities...

The *only* positive outlook Price could find was that there were 'only' two rachnids, two Barons, and one Duke.

"Feasible numbers," Price said, his voice sounding hollower than usual. "But not with this gear. Calder said she sent an *armed* helo. Any chance it's—"

With a screaming twist of flame, the rift behind the Duke sealed. And the massive beast roared, a sound that put raging thunder to shame.

One of the rachnids tore away from the others, setting its orange orbs of eyes on John. The two Barons targeted the rest of Serpent One, while the Duke hung back. Possibly to bear witness the satisfying view of its subordinates killing these humans.

Even John's big-bore Marlin was struggling with the rachnid. Each shot that landed only seemed to annoy the creature. It was *bleeding*, this much felt comforting, but its bones were as if impervious.

Meanwhile, if anyone was surprised about anything, it would be Jam miraculously killing the other rachnid by his lonesome. It took some impressive footwork to begin with, but for anybody to outmaneuver a cambion it would be Jam, or Reva. He had to evade a few chomps of its jaws, the swinging of its tail, and those damned horns, but eventually the Radian delivered enough hits to make it falter. When it did, Jam chanced a closer encounter, slung the Radian, drew his single kodachi, and wrenched the blade into an amber eyeball; once he sensed some give, Jam *jammed it* the rest of the way. The beast made a croaking sound, and then went limp on the sandstone ground.

About the same time, the two Barons were engaging Price, Reva, and Nil. Price seemed dead-set on a particular Baron, and his 6.8mm rounds were performing beautifully against the exposed musculature of the beast. Periodically Reva would tear away from the other to assist Price, her steel-core 5.56mm rounds eventually achieving penetration against the Baron's breastplate.

Angrily, the Duke witnessed the death of its two rachnids and one Baron. The other was being irritably wounded by Nil's 12-gauge slugs, and then John's Marlin into its back. The Duke moved out of recession to swing its mace at John. Incapable of not noticing such an immense motion, John acted swiftly; he ran, first, and then dove once he realized even he wasn't fast enough.

The gigantic flanged mace annihilated the crane, decapitating its arm with a shrill, loud, distressing metallic sound.

It almost overwhelmed the thump of approaching rotors. But when Jam noticed it first, he put two fingers in his mouth and ripped a strident whistle.

Heads turned.

"Helo, inbound!" Reva screamed.

Damn their mics, she needed to let that out.

The Duke didn't notice, as the helo approached well behind it. The cambion's attention was fixated on John. It swung the mace again, this time overhead. The sharp, terrifying tip of it crushed the sandstone ground a mere six feet from where he had been. Sweating, panting, and more fearful for his life than he ever had been, John scampered to his feet and fled in the direction of the others.

Nil spent his last slug killing the second Baron, the slug petals chewing into its abdomen. With the help of Reva's kodachis to the backs of its knees, and Price's 6.8s to its skull, the Baron finally went down.

This, the Duke noticed.

When it turned, so did the approaching Black Hawk. Portside. The gunner's door was open, and on a platform that the GAU-19/A was mounted, he stood. The three linked 36-inch-long barrels, electrically driven, spun and sprayed muzzle flashes through the moonlit sky. At two-thousand rounds-per-minute, armor-piercing .50 BMG rounds hosed the sixteen-foot Duke below. The pilot had the mindfulness to keep the helo out of the Duke's reach, analyzing its extended capabilities with the mace.

The sound of the rotary gun was comparable to a chainsaw, only tenfold the volume.

Massive brass casings littered the quarry below.

Serpent One scattered, ensuring the hot metal didn't burn them. Price had experienced that once before, prior to his SAS days, and never wanted to relive it. He didn't have the option of forgetting it, either; the scar on his neck remained.

The Duke roared at the helo, swinging its mace but missing the aircraft. The pilot deftly swung the helo around it like a condor, and the gunner intelligently held his fire during the mace swing so as to not waste rounds. The BMG bullets were devastating, chewing through the Duke's flesh as if it were no more than the dense meat it was. If a brickhouse was composed of flesh and muscle, the Duke was its equivalent. Eventually the spewing .50-

caliber rounds shattered its bones, too, and the Duke collapsed in a quaking heap.

Price gestured at Reva. She collected one of the flares and threw it at the seemingly dead Duke, by its massive, horned head. One of the horns had been shattered by bullets, exposing the marrow within. Then she handed the other flare to John; both fuses were moments from going out. John hurled the flare in the opposite direction of the Duke, but still in the confines of the broad quarry.

A new LZ for the helo.

But before the Black Hawk landed, its gunner lit up the fuse with a burst from the GAU-19/A. A tracer caught the flare and a flash of flame engulfed the Duke's head. It writhed in pain, more evidence that these creatures weren't demons of the Good Book, and were mortal, not to mention vulnerable to fire.

Another burst from the rotary gun split the Duke's skull open and it stopped moving entirely.

By the time the helo's skids touched down in the quarry, the Duke's corpse was joining its brethren in a vanishing act of embers.

"A shame I didn't bring my camera," Nil shouted, over the roar of the helo's rotors. "I'd have liked proof a Duke had walked this earth."

As a crewman rushed the operators aboard the helo, the gunner, still on his platform, rose Nil's attention.

"Don't have to worry about that," he said, loudly. The others heard, too. "For every major city, six Dukes are marching."

227

Nil's face was suddenly devoid of color, and all humor had been sapped from his arteries. John had to pull him aboard the helo. With everybody but the crewman and gunner seated, the bird lifted into the night sky.

"Then why the hell did a Duke show up way out here?" Jam asked, now with a headset on.

"Got me," the gunner said. "My guess? 'Cause y'all were out here. They got eyes on us, remember? From their side."

Jam shook his head, bowed it, and kneaded his temples. John and Reva exchanged grim looks. Then Price got the crewman's attention, noticing the Forked Tongue patch.

"What's your name?" Price asked.

"Richie Fields."

"Fields of Dick," the gunner laughed.

Fields rolled his eyes. "You're Seamus Price, aren't you? Have only seen you in passing at Moyock. It's an honor to fly with you, sir."

Price looked at the others, who, even in this grave situation, struggled to hide smirks.

"The world's gone to shit, kid, you can cut the 'sir' crap."

"Then you can cut the 'kid' shit, if you don't mind."

Price's head recoiled.

Reva laughed. John nodded, smiling.

"Well, fuck me runnin'," Price said.

"I'd rather not," Fields said. He then gestured at the gunner. "But Homo-way over here might."

"It's *Holloway*, smartass," the gunner said. "Lance

Holloway. At your service, ma'am."

"Normally I'd put you in an arm-bar for a remark like that," she said. "But considering the shooting you just did, and that phenomenal flying, whoever your pilot is, I'll concede and express my gratitude."

"I'll take the W."

Fields shook his head. "Our pilot's Billy Easton. He's probably busy right now, hailing Calder about your pick-up."

"We *are* going back to Moyock, correct?" Reva asked.

"If it isn't compromised," Fields said.

The look on everyone's faces sunk.

"Moyock's a small town, no major city—but it *is* the home of Forked Tongue. And the cambions know this. Raleigh's getting hit hard, though. Just like the other capitals. Inland, too. Rachnids come by the dozens. Hundred imps, at least. And Barons have axes."

Price buried his head in his hands.

The others had never seen him like this.

Once more, all signs of humor had been stripped away. Jam felt his throat close up, but Nil was driven to a point of manic vexation.

"They're not supposed to do that," he blurted, almost laughing his way through the statement. "It's not like they're in endless supply, either. There's a chain of command on the other side, and here, on fucking *Earth*, it's CAB...*all*...*day*. Checks and *balances*, not *free reign*."

Nil scoffed in disbelief.

John squeezed his shoulder, but eventually tightened his hand to the point that it hurt Nil, and shook him from his episode. He ran a hand through his braided hair, fingers coursing along the grooves.

Moments later, John mustered the voice to speak. His tone was parched and shaky.

"Any reports of wyverns flying about?"

"A few, here and there. They're not deliberately attacking anyone, mostly just startled. The Dreaded Five, apart from the cambions of course, are being erratic more than anything. Spooked, maybe."

"Or frantic," Reva said. "Like the end of the world, even theirs, is upon them."

Price lifted his head and shook it.

"Our military is too mighty. Not even a thousand Dukes could crush us."

"Unless," came a new voice. The pilot's, likely. John, Price, and Reva had glimpsed the cabin earlier. They were flying without a copilot, unless that position belonged to Fields. "They march on our depots. Get us before we can assemble and deploy. Holloway was right; they have had eyes on us for some time."

"Even if they caught us with our pants down, which seems like they have," Price admitted. He looked at nobody in particular, since the pilot was not within sight. "Our tech is still superior. This *will* be a short coup."

"Possibly. But word is they have more than 'just' Dukes to offer. Bigger things. Gargantuan things. And firepower, even. We know less about them than we've liked to believe, all these years."

"If that's the case…then surely there's a plan. If

Raleigh's being razed, how's HQ holding up?"

"I don't know, but there *is* a plan…in the works."

Price sighed and looked at the others. Their eyes shone only a faint light, and that light was not of hope.

"Easton, right?" John spoke up.

"You got it."

"Any idea what this so-called plan might entail?"

"What they're doing to us…we do to them."

A few very long seconds of relative silence in the cabin. And then, just as Price was about to speak, Jam blurted a word.

"Invasion?"

"More or less. Think a strategic infil. Not just Forked Tongue, either. We gotta figure out their weak point, assuming there is one. Maybe a stronghold, a heart we can rip out. So to speak."

"And…that's the word on the street, per se?" John asked.

"Far as I've heard. Been utter chaos back home, last two hours. It's all unfolding real quick, real bad."

"I understand. And how long before we reach Carolina airspace?"

"Little over an hour. Best I can offer, sorry."

"We get it," Price said. "Just get us there in one piece, matters most."

"Wilco," Easton said, and then took a breath. "I'm going to see if I can get a hold of Calder; comms have been shit since we left. Radio towers are being attacked, too, demolished by Dukes. Even the sat-phones are having trouble, suggesting something far worse."

None of them could fathom cambions in space.

Unless Easton was implying that rifts were opening in government facilities where these satellites were being monitored. Somehow this was equally unnerving.

"Fields, tell 'em about Mamba Three," Easton said, and then there was a click in their headsets, insinuating he had switched his mic.

"What about…Mamba Three?" Price asked, leaning forward.

John and Reva, too, dreaded hearing bad news about another beloved fire-team from Moyock. Mike Laszlo, Trevor Brayton, and Bailey Evans. If anyone was better with a rifle than John, it was Laszlo. There was a reason he managed the gun range back at the facility.

"Just before Raleigh was hit, Moyock getting it 'round the same time, Mamba Three was deployed on a last-minute op to relieve a reaver problem in southern Virginia. We passed over their AO on our way up here, it's like a ten-minute flight from the facility."

Fields paused, the expression on his face grim.

"It was bad. Vamps are staying underground, or flocking elsewhere, but the reavers are going nuts, and the cambion problem is off-the-wall down there. Fallout from Norfolk, I assume."

"Mamba was deployed to Norfolk?" Reva asked.

Fields shook his head. "Rural community of Carrsville. Fifty klicks west of Norfolk."

Reva nodded. She looked at John. There was a dire, yet reluctant, tacit response in his eyes. Price seemed to be noticing this silent exchange, and read right through it. He returned his attention to Fields.

"Is it likely we'll pass over that area again, on our

way back?"

"Very. Normally we'd cut over Norfolk, since Moyock's a forty-klick straight-shot south of it, but given the activity they're experiencing…" Fields shook his head. "We've adjusted our route for a more diagonal approach. Why?"

"If the air space is clear, we want to check up on them," Price said. He nodded toward Holloway. "Maybe even give 'em some support, if needed."

"I think I can convince Easton to do that," Fields said, showing the smallest sign of a smile.

"We appreciate it," Price said. When he looked at the others, there was an implicit gratitude and under-standing in their faces. And then Price put his hands on his headset. "I know this is gonna sound absolutely fuck-ing bonkers to you all, but I have to catch some shut-eye, and I'm going to, no bullshit. Barring a call from Calder, or a goddamn wyvern, don't wake me up."

Nobody protested.

Price removed his headset and slumped in his seat some. Seconds after he closed his eyes, he seemed to be lights-out.

"Wish I could fucking do that," Nil muttered.

"We all could," Reva said. "Only problem is, at this rate, I fear that shutting my eyes will invite those damn things into my dreams."

"Or that I'll never stop seeing their faces, hearing their screams," Jam said, reflecting on Frank's death, and the rest of his team.

Nobody said anything for a while.

"No," Price mumbled. "That never stops."

11

Alarms wailed, but that wasn't what stirred Price. He might have managed to sleep all the way to Moyock had the rifts not started manifesting in the sky. From them, imps fell, along the route of their helo. One sprayed into blood and limbs when it passed through the main rotors. Curtains of black liquid painted the cabin windows. The bisected torso of an imp tumbled down the front of the canopy, smearing half the glass with its tar-like blood. Price was woken by shouting, as panic gripped the operators inside the helo.

It shook, as more imps landed. Some clinging to the tail, others on the skids. Easton's attempt to keep the helo level wasn't a major struggle until their tail rotor screamed and a bursting sound went off behind the cabin.

John could picture one of the imps suicidally shoving its upper half into the tail rotor.

"We lost it!" Fields shouted, from the copilot's seat. He was frenziedly hitting switches and buttons.

The helo's tail wobbled severely, but they didn't go into a spin, suggesting it wasn't completely fucked. And that Easton was a talented pilot.

Seconds after Price became fully conscious, a rift opened *inside* the helicopter. It remained, instead of passing with the helo's route, or cutting through the hull; possibly because something was constantly occupying the portal. First an imp emerged, immediately latching onto John, who was the only one standing. Meanwhile, a large clawed hand gripped the side of the rift, unbothered by the fiery brim.

John parried the imp's snapping jaws with his Adra knife, and then wrenched the blade inside a cheek, ripping its face nearly in half. It would be appropriate, given the 'natural' state of its semi-skull.

The imp reeled back, slamming into the copilot's seat. Fields cursed, and then Nil charged the creature, somehow putting it in a headlock before stabbing its gaunt armpit with his own knife at the speed of a psycho.

With the rift still open, the other operators could see into the cambion world, as if a glimpse of a future they loathed.

It was a putrid dimension of flesh citadels and necropolises teeming with grotesque organisms.

Suddenly a Baron's huge head emerged from the portal, and Price lifted his leg to slam the sole of his boot onto its dome. He tried to push it back in, terrible and futile an idea as it was. Reva took the opportunity to draw one of her kodachis and drive it into the Baron's snarling, salivating mouth. The blade excavated its brain through the back of its skull, and the Baron returned to its world.

235

The rift closed quickly, likely sensing a threat.

Nobody could fathom how those things worked.

Reva was without one of her kodachis now, but at least had kept her hand, and Price his foot.

"Everybody good?" Nil shouted, without his headset. He returned to the main area of the cabin. And then glanced back toward the cockpit. The dead imp on the steel floor vanished into harmless embers.

John slapped Nil's back, nodding.

"Mayday, mayday, mayday," Easton announced. "This is Echo One-Four-Two, we've lost our tail rotor and are flying half-blind, over Windsor, V-A. Requesting LZ—Garner, Franklin, Suffolk—do you read?"

"Déjà-fucking-vu," Nil grumbled, returning to his seat. He looked over at the others. "Those evil ass-hats really have it out for us, don't they?"

"I'd say," Reva shook her head.

"I'm not getting *shit*!" Easton shouted. He reached over and grabbed Fields' uniform, giving him a shake. "We're gonna try to ditch in Drummond! But not before giving Mamba some reinforcements!"

Fields nodded fervently, and detached his harness. He got up, his legs shaky with the destabilization of the helo, grabbing overhead rails for balance. He reached the seating and shouted at the operators, none of them wearing headsets anymore. They wanted to be mobile, ready to bail if needed.

"We're just ten klicks north of Carrsville! Gonna drop y'all off as close as we can to Mamba, supposing they're still there!"

"What about you guys?" Reva asked.

"Gonna maintain low altitude, slow and steady as possible, then ditch in Lake Drummond, thirty klicks west. Get your asses ready! Price, fast-ropes out!"

Price didn't hesitate.

Easton had already reduced altitude dramatically.

They were now flying over the highway leading into Carrsville, about eighty feet up.

When Price banged the starboard cargo door open, a gust of wind hit him in the face, drying his eyes. Air rushed into the helo fleetingly faltered the others. The consistent imbalance of the Black Hawk didn't help, although Easton was doing a hell of a job.

Occasionally Holloway's thumbs went to work.

The rotary gun zipped out six to twelve rounds each burst, muzzle flashes scarring the night. He was concentrating fire on the unfurling chaos below, likely saving civvies in immediate need. When John opened the portside door to his left, to extend the fast-rope device, he could see it more clearly. Headlights and taillights alike illuminated the road that cut through Carrsville. It was congested with vehicles both ways—civilians trying to get out, but also coming in. Probably after fleeing Norfolk.

John appreciated that Holloway's focus was on everything but imps. They were too skinny a target, and too nimble. The occasional Baron took the brunt of his shots, most of their heads or torsos erupting in a spray of blood from each burst. Centurions were more frequent, but less targeted.

It was devilishly difficult as it was, hitting his mark with such a big gun at this range, civvies in the vicinity, and at night. Car lights only helped some; at times it was disorienting, especially as the helo flew overhead.

John only had about eight seconds to take all of this in, while simultaneously securing the fast-rope wing. And then the helo bucked and he damn near fell out. In addition to catching himself, Nil was right behind him to grab the back of his vest.

"Pedals are wonky as fuck, y'all better hurry!" Easton shouted from the cockpit.

"No luck reaching anybody?" Reva asked.

"Negative," Fields said. "Comms are FUBAR! You'll have to find Mamba another way."

John and Nil looked at each other disappointedly.

"Luck of the draw!" Reva shouted, looking at John and Nil.

"Let me come with!" A new voice called out.

It was Holloway. He was already unharnessing himself from the gunner's platform.

"Negative!" Price shouted.

Holloway's expression sank.

"Nothing personal," John said. "But if you're as good with a rifle as you are with the GAU, Easton and Fields deserve your company!"

Holloway nodded firmly. "You got it!"

"Good hunting, fellas!" Fields shouted from his seat. "Now yeet!"

Reva couldn't help but smirk and shake her head. Jam was in the same boat. Price was puzzled, but distracted by the enveloping bedlam.

The Black Hawk neared a large building near the outskirts of Carrsville, but away from the road. And then

238

Easton fought to keep it stable enough to hover. He did and he didn't. The attempt, given the condition of their tail rotor, put the Black Hawk in a slow spin.

"Fuck's sake," Nil griped.

There was no order to them fast-roping out of the helo, onto the vast, flat roof fifty feet below. Price had all but shoved Jam out the door, and then followed suit. They had no time to don their reinforced gloves for the maneuver, using their standard ones to descend. Starboard, Reva went first, when Nil hesitated. Then he followed, but as John reached out for the rope, a rift opened ten feet above the helo. Two imps poured out before it vanished, and the creatures landed on the helo's canopy.

Inside the cockpit, Easton and Fields exclaimed.

The cambions shrieked and clawed for purchase as they slid down. Bony claws grated the canopy, half of it still caked with black imp blood.

The Black Hawk wobbled worse then, and John exited messily. He managed to clutch the rope, but it swung like crazy. The imps finally fell, one leaping for John but not making it; its inability to fly left it to fall to its death, when its back broke over the parapet lining the edge of the roof.

Before the helo fully departed the area, John let go. He didn't set down like the others—he *let go*.

Fortunately, the rope was only about ten feet from the nearest surface. To his surprise it was a parked eighteen-wheeler, the rear of the twenty-foot trailer backed into a docking bay on this side of the building. When his boots collided with the roof of the trailer, there was a hint of give as metal dented with a distinct sound; then his legs bucked and he rolled. The presence of his xiphos scabbard and revolver holster didn't do his body any favors, pain-wise. But they might have slowed his momentum. John nearly tumbled off the curved lip of the trailer, but caught himself at the last moment.

Grimacing as he slowly rose into a three-point stance, using the Marlin as a crutch, John counted his scarce blessings. He then looked around, noticing a 7-Eleven across the street from where the semi was parked. It seemed to be experiencing its own level of mayhem, sadly. On the plus side, he appreciated the amount of illumination on the property where his team had landed. It was not a warehouse as he suspected, but a store. One open 24-hours, clearly. An unavoidable blue and yellow sign that was still lit up caught his eye at his ten-o'clock, visible well above the roof of the building.

"God bless Walmart," he mumbled, and then hoisted himself to his feet.

He heard a burst of gunfire in his left ear, very nearby. Not from the rooftop, either. It sounded like a handgun, followed by the distinct blast from a shotgun. The range of both, he supposed were from the parking lot on the other side of the Walmart. Probably customers, or just civilians in the area. It was suburban Virginia, after all, John wouldn't be shocked if a third of the population carried.

It did dawn on him that he heard the gunfire with lopsided suppression because his left Peltor had popped out when he fell. There would be no finding it on the asphalt now, even with the lights.

A sudden throaty hiss interrupted his perception of Reva calling his name. When John lifted his attention from the ground beside the trailer's wheel chocks, he noticed a quadrupedal shape loping up the truck's cab. It passed over a row of orange light stubs, not currently illuminated. The property lights surrounding Walmart left no need to activate his Modlite. He stared at the reaver ten feet away, bloody saliva dripping from its segmented mandibles. The toothed drinking apparatus squirmed in the open, eager to dig into a wound and imbibe its victim's blood.

"Not mine, buddy," John huffed, turning on his knee to fully face the reaver.

Its body was pale, a color between taupe and gray. Completely naked, but sexless. This changed when they were forced to breed; it was a filthy thing to witness, and John wished he could strike the memory from his brain. As if the rest of reaver anatomy wasn't repulsive enough.

He had not had to engage one in nearly a full year of ops. But he would never forget what he lectured trainees about in Moyock. The impenetrability of a reaver's sternum, and the need to destroy that vital hub of organs beneath it, from an angle.

John's right hand slowly relocated to his revolver. His left navigated to the handle of his xiphos.

Behind him, the sound of scratching.

He impulsively glanced over a shoulder. A second reaver had scaled the trailer to flank him. This one showed less patience than the other, snarling and hissing as it charged him.

Nearby, he heard Reva's voice and some of the others that had landed on the roof.

"Here!" John roared, and rose into a squat.

The reaver behind him reached first, and it would've leapt onto his back had he not side-stepped last second. There wasn't a ton of room to move on the roof of the trailer, but he made do. The two creatures collided. One almost slid off the trailer, but pulled itself up in a feat of dexterity. John's revolver was drawn, and thundered, triggering tinnitus in his left ear. Worth it—

The .454 Casull caught the reaver in the shoulder, almost sundering its entire arm at the intersection. The other reaver charged him, swiping claws and splaying its mandibles inches from his face. John rose higher on his feet, kicked it in the chest, and unsheathed his xiphos. The revolver boomed again, a round blowing off the reaver's right mandible in a spray of gleaming red blood. During its disorientation, he angled the xiphos, and jammed the first eight inches of its twenty-inch leaf-shaped blade into the reaver's left ribcage. He twisted the handle, and the breadth of the steel parted its ribs, letting it sink deeper.

The tip penetrated the reaver's hub of protected organs.

"Sweet spot," John growled under his breath, and shoved the blade so far that a few inches of the tip exited beneath the reaver's right armpit. It shrieked a painful sound, wretched life abandoning its bleak eyes.

A single gunshot erupted behind him, startling John. He looked, not back, but forward. The other reaver took a rifle round to the dome, and its head whipped back. The spine didn't break, but was awfully malleable. It returned its head to place, bleeding from the cranial wound. Then it hissed and leapt at John; he dislodged his sword, and slid left. Two more shots from Reva's rifle punched into its upper chest.

John lunged, revolver holstered, and squeezed the reaver's neck before digging the sword into its right rib-cage as he had the other. Despite its wounds, and being dwarfed by John, the creature still fought. Its slick, flex-ible neck somehow slipped free of John's grip, and its grotesque tongue-like apparatus shot toward his throat. John replaced the emptiness in his hand with one of the reaver's mandibles, not just breaking it, but ripping it off the thing's face.

It made an awful squealing sound of confusion and pain.

Then he wrenched the blade the right way, and it slid under the dense sternum, impaling that union of or-gans. The reaver convulsed a few times, and John hated how close he was. Then it went limp, and he gladly shoved it away. While the body rag-dolled down the cab of the semi, John got up and met the others at the edge of the roof. The trailer's rear wasn't flush with the para-pet, but down a few feet from it.

Reva and Price loomed above him, ready to give him a hand. Nil and Jam were covering their six.

A hissing, soft churning sound briefly distracted John. As his extended hands grasped theirs, he noticed a waft of ash in the illuminated night air; even reavers dis-integrated like their vampyr brethren.

Once hauled back onto the roof, John thanked them

and gave Reva a kiss.

"Where's mine?" Jam asked, his naturally gravelly voice and nonchalance making the joke somehow funnier. If even so briefly.

"Find us Mamba, then get us home all together, and we'll talk," John said.

"Oh, it's a deal."

"Alright, lovebirds," Nil said, dropping the aim of his SMG to low-ready. "So how do we do that?"

"Do what?" Jam asked.

Reva sighed. "Find Mamba."

"Proximity, hopefully," Price said, and made his way across the rooftop, toward the front. That long side of the Walmart overlooked the vast parking lot. They didn't get too close, in case a startled civilian with a gun acted on a whim.

Then Price pressed his collar mic button and raised his voice some.

"Calling Mamba Three, Mamba Three, do you read?" He held a long pause. Erratic gunfire popped off through the area, only distinctly loud for John. While Price continued to try hailing Mamba, he informed Reva and Nil of his missing Peltor.

Finally Price made it back to them, shaking his head.

"So much for that. I say we dismount, and—"

"Wander aimlessly?" Jam said, scoffing. "Sorry, I just don't understand how we're supposed to find them. It ain't a big town, but they could be *anywhere*. And let's say they're *not* running cans; we won't be able to distinguish their shots from the civvies'."

"I could," John said.

"Likewise," Price added. "But I get your lapse in hope. Just don't let it show again. We have to make ends meet, somehow."

Jam took a couple of deep breaths.

"What about the safe house?"

Price's brow furrowed. "What safe house?"

"Oh, yeah," Reva said. She slapped Jam's shoulder. "I forgot about it."

"Suffolk, right," John nodded. He looked at Price. "It's no vault, but has some resources, an ammo cache, and a few—"

"I know what a safe house is, Aguirre," Price said, almost condescendingly. He was just frustrated, and for once in his life *not* in-the-know about something job-related. "But where exactly?"

"Suffolk," John said. "I…don't know *exactly* where, but—"

"I do," Jam and Nil said, simultaneously.

"When in doubt, the brain in this guy *sometimes* serves a purpose," John said, nodding at Nil.

He shrugged. "Ten months ago, right? That Windsor op we had. Rowdy skinwalkers. Two went from pumas to deer, can you believe that shit? Evaded us at sundown, tore ass southeast. Toward Suffolk. We were scant on ammo, misjudged the op. A rare moment."

"I don't need the whole tale," Price said, once more snappy. "Just so long as you know where it is, exactly."

"We do," Jam said. Nil nodded.

"Good. We need a map so all of us can be in on and this knowledge."

"Walmart's definitely—"

"No chance in hell," Price cut off Jam. He strode back toward the spot on the roof that overlooked the docked truck. Two of them, actually, about sixteen feet apart. Price pointed, indicating a 7-Eleven across the street. It was maybe thirty yards from where they stood, far as the crow flew. "Our best bet. Sorry, just won't be risking our asses in the confines of a Walmart that's probably teeming with as many civvies and imps."

John nodded.

"I know it's grim," Price said, as if reading the others' minds, "but we can't help everyone here. Our best bet is to convene with Mamba, reach that safe house, stock up, and be at better odds. Either we'll hoof it to Moyock from there, or, best case, be retrieved. Raleigh getting plundered by cambions doesn't mean HQ hasn't already hatched something. Or is in the process of."

Nobody protested.

"Good. Let's kick it. Nil?"

Nil nodded and took point. He dismounted the roof and strode across the trailer, to the cab, sliding down the windshield to stand on the hood. While his SMG swept the area ahead, his keen eyes spotting no threats, only scurrying humans across the street, lit by the lights on 7-Eleven's property, the others followed suit.

Next Reva, and then John.

Jam after, followed by Price.

One by one they dismounted from the cab's hood, using the robust front bumper as a step, and the Kenworth swan hood ornament as a brief handle if needed.

"Contact!" John shouted.

Before everyone was boots-on-pavement, Price and Jam still descending the cab, a throb of imps swarmed the team. Two came from across the street, and three arrived from both sides of the loading area behind the Walmart.

Price hesitated on the hood to engage with a better vantage point than his teammates. Jam adapted swiftly, following suit.

None of the creepy-crawly imps ever got within arm's reach of the operators, they were so on-point. They really had the surrounding lights to thank for visibility; their flashlights would only provide so much.

With the creatures slowly disintegrating into embers, Price and Jam successfully dismounted.

"Great work," Price said. "But how's everyone on ammo?"

"Low as hell," Reva said.

Nil nodded. "Shotgun's almost dry. Two more full mags for the EVO."

"Marlin's about capped," John said, shaking his head. Then he patted the AR mags in the pouches along the front of his kit. "Have barely touched the DDM4, though. Set on that."

"Same for Frank's Radian," Jam said. He shrugged. "More or less; got a mag and a half, but better than nothing, thanks to Reva."

"And you?" John asked Price.

"Not looking great. Seems we need to hit that safe house sooner than expected."

"Maybe Mamba felt the same," Nil suggested.

"Possible," Price said. "Let's go get that map, see

from there."

Everyone tacitly agreed.

Nil accepted point, his shotgun now in-hand. He was on his last ten-round mag of slugs. Behind him, the others followed in a broad arrow formation. They crossed the street, periodically checking abandoned vehicles for survivors or lingering enemies. The occasional sight of bloodshed tightened their stomachs and honed their senses with ire, with resolve.

The 7-Eleven was far less rife with activity when they reached it, than it was earlier.

A couple of civvies looting the store scrambled to their vehicles, or off on foot, when they saw Serpent One. Their military garb, postures, and weapons could be terrifying to some, or comforting to others. That none of them spoke to any of the passing civilians added an air of sternness and resolve.

The stark white fluorescent lights within the 7-Eleven were momentarily blinding. The operators' eyes adjusted and they quickly began hunting down a road map. Along the aisle of magazines and newspapers, as well as behind the counter.

No avail.

"It's 2024, no shit we can't find a map," Jam said, defeatedly.

"We did up in Jersey," Nil said.

"Yeah, shocking," Jam joked wryly.

Nil shrugged in acceptance. And then Reva whistled, and they assembled toward the back of the store. She crouched by a slain man, next to a few dollops of black blood. Unlike the imp's bodies, their blood did not dissipate. In one hand, the man held a Glock. In the other, his phone.

Reva took the phone, swiped the screen, and looked up. She handed it to John and Price loomed beside him. John navigated to Google Maps and then turned.

Although neither Nil nor Jam were offering their hands, John held the phone out to them. Not that Jam had anything to redeem, Nil let him take it and accept the responsibility. Jam entered the address for the safe house in Suffolk, then rotated the phone for everyone else to see.

He zoomed in and rotated the map in almost a flaunting way. As if he was a cartographer.

"Right, I remember the area now," John said.

"Same," Reva said. She shrugged. "Barring a Duke encounter, we could get there in twenty minutes, if we had wheels."

"We will," Price said resolutely. He had seen enough of the map to stow the information in his head. Although not discussed, John set the phone down with respectful care, as if it was an heirloom of the diseased. And then they flocked out of the 7-Eleven.

Much to their initial surprise, the night was still and quiet when they emerged. No distant gunfire, screams, or cacophonies associated with panic, car collisions, the like.

Reva momentarily removed her Peltors to confirm this, and in a way, appreciate it. Nil did the same, if nothing else than to give his eardrums some relief.

"I can't be sure if this is good or bad," Nil said.

"Dead or fled," Jam said.

"What's that?"

"Either everyone's dead," Jam said, lackadaisically, "or everyone's fled."

"Probably a bit of both," Price said. "We can hope for the latter."

John nodded firmly to that. Reva reinserted her earplugs, Nil following suit.

With Price on point, they crossed the street, but not toward the Walmart. A squat Dunkin' Donuts building drew their attention. The property was sparsely illuminated by security lights, but the business was closed. Reasonable for this time.

Unlike the surrounding businesses, the Dunkin' was untarnished by death. John had replaced his Marlin with the DDM4, figuring that the suppressed .300 Blackout option would be more befitting of the quietude. He surveyed the area, laser-sight skimming wherever the security lights didn't reach. His Modlite off—there was enough collateral light that it was unneeded.

And then Reva was on the move.

The rest of the team followed her without protest. She had noticed a glimpse of light creeping around the edge of a drive-thru to a Citibank on a neighboring property. It was across a backroad, and everyone looked both ways as they moved.

"Talk to us," John said into his mic.

"Lights, one one-o'clock, see 'em?" She danced the bead of her green laser-sight on the bank. Far enough from the corner where the lights shone for her laser to be seen in the dark.

"Copy. Stay frosty."

They did. Not a single one of them had a lapse in vigilance as they moved through the night, following Reva's lead. They slowed dramatically upon reaching the bank, and hearing a low rumble sound. Closer they got to the drive-thru, louder another sound became. Slurping. Ripping.

Reva turned the corner, suddenly awash in the LED headlights of a parked Kia. She squinted, and spotted a low silhouette off to the left. When John turned the corner, he hugged it, navigating out of the headlights' beams. The second he cleared them, his view of the silhouette clarified. In this same moment, Price shadowed him, and the lone reaver lifted its mandibles from the body of a woman on the asphalt. Blood dripped in excess from its mutant mouth.

"Wanna keep that kukri clean, or…?" John said under his breath, the DDM4 still firmly pressed to his shoulder. His laser-sight fixated on the reaver's pale forehead.

Price slung his weapon and suddenly lunged forward, drawing his TAC 45 at retention, and firing into the reaver's chest. The pistol bucked in his firm grip and flashed beneath his face. The reaver screeched and faltered briefly before charging. Price met it first, his kukri machete drawn with a concurrent swipe. The curved blade tore an open gash across the reaver's bullet-riddled chest, exposing bone through a glistening sea of blood.

Then he stuffed the robust steel barrel into a wound, and fired two more times. The reaver gargled its own blood and shook fiercely, clawed hands incapable of getting a grip on him. Before the creature could register what was happening, Price had holstered the pistol, swapped hands on the kukri, and driven the tip of the blade into the wound. He used it like a crowbar, the blade catching the base of the reaver's sternum, and then twisted it. The reaver screamed, before he plunged the curved machete four inches deeper. It didn't impale the reaver's vital hub, but cleaved it.

A gush of blood and even pulp from the organ itself spilled out of the wound channels, sliding down the black blade.

Price shoulder-checked the reaver off the kukri and it fell with a wet thump.

"Beautiful," John said, walking past him as he sheathed the kukri. Then he looked toward the Kia, and Reva stood on the driver's side, opposite him. "What've you got?"

"Driver's dead. Male, twenties. Over there?"

"Female, same."

Reva shook her head irately, and seemed to mumble something but he didn't catch it.

"Is the car operational?" John asked.

Reva ducked inside, through the window. The driver's door was shut, unlike the passenger's. The woman must have been hauled out, and then killed. The man was decapitated, and not cleanly. The head rested awkwardly on the center console cup-holders.

"It is," she said. The engine was idling in park. "Who knows how long it's been neutral. Gas is at twenty, thirty percent. Should be good without filling."

John backed up to look over the sedan. A recent

model, probably '22 or '23. Price stood beside him and shook his head.

"Better than a two-door, but," he said, and didn't follow up.

John looked around, wanting to provide a sound rebuttal. He struggled, though. With all their gear, Nil and Jam could squeeze into the back; Reva could fit, but it wouldn't be pleasant. John and Price up front.

When he posed this to Price, Reva overheard it.

"That's not gonna happen," she said. "I'd sooner sit in Price's lap while you drive, John."

A couple of seconds passed. Somewhere, maybe about a quarter mile away, a sputter of gunshots echoed.

"Nothing, really?" Price asked, looking at Nil.

"I think I might be broken," he said.

Price smirked dryly and shook his head. He moved to the back of the car, and pressed the keyless trunk entry. The lid lifted. He shrugged and gestured at Reva, who met him behind the car.

"Now hear me out," he said.

12

Reva had tried to contain her awkward excitement to try Price's idea. Once they hit the road, she knew her faith in John as a driver—especially with her in this current position—was solid. The Kia K5 wasn't anything like the Revology Mustang he owned, except somewhat comparable in size. Still, he drove it with equal care and assertion. Their urgency was unbridled, but they also had to be diligent about their surroundings. Whatever hell Carrsville had been going through seemed to be on its last legs.

Dead or fled.

For the next twelve minutes, driving through the community brought them only four kills. All imps. They were scattered, too. Two pursued fleeing pedestrians, one was attacking an inhabited car, and the other seemed to be lingering, sniffing the air even.

That one was eliminated by Reva.

She sat in the trunk, the backs of her knees hooking

the edge, heels of her boots against the rear bumper. John and Price had brought the spare tire up out of its compartment, so she could use it as a booster seat. This gave her a better vantage point and made her aim almost perfectly eye-level should an imp rise on its hind legs.

As the one sniffing the air had been.

Nil and Jam in the backseat, their windows rolled down, weapons protruding. The same for Price, in the passenger seat. John was the only one not utilizing his weapons, as he drove. The DDM4 stood barrel-down beside Price's left leg, and the Marlin rested on the dash, snugly below the windshield.

Circumventing abandoned cars, or vehicles with casualties in them, was all John had to do. But this was scarce; there weren't loads of people out at one to two in the morning, when Carrsville was initially hit.

Passing an elementary school down the street from a fire station made all of the operators subconsciously glad this incident had not happened during the weekday.

After winding down roads in the Kia for what felt like an inordinate amount of time, to no avail locating Mamba, they deduced it was in their best interest to reach the safe house.

Their drive out of Carrsville occupied Holland Road, or Route 58. It was a two-lane passage that cut through farmlands between Carrsville and Suffolk. Every twenty to thirty feet, a couple of cars had to be driven around. A truck stop near the outskirts of Suffolk slowed their approach, as muzzle flashes lit up the interior of the small structure.

John brought the Kia to a lurching stop twenty feet

255

from the front entrance. Reva hoisted herself out of the trunk, and Price exited only to stand behind the open passenger door.

"Nil, join Reva," John demanded. "Jam, get out, but stay put. Watch our ass."

Nobody objected.

Nil followed Reva, cautiously, into the truck stop. Just as she reached for the glass door, a gunshot boomed inside and the pane shattered. She exclaimed, retreating. Shards had sprayed her, but only little stings on her right cheek, a few tiny cuts. Nil pulled at her rig, and they hunkered behind a brick façade under more windows.

"Fuck's sake," John said through his teeth.

"Movement inside," Price said, peering through his SIG's optic. "Not all human."

"Clear to proceed?" Reva asked, via her mic.

"Can't confirm."

Too many ad posters plastered the windows.

"Advancing, low," Reva said.

Nil followed close, their boots crunching glass. The second they passed over the threshold, another gunshot rang out, this time going nowhere important. The owner's voice vaulted in a painful scream that tapered into a messy gurgle.

Reva straightened her knees and rushed toward the sound. Nil took her right flank, and they converged near a narrow hallway leading to bathrooms.

A trucker had just been killed, after his revolver seemed to have took the life of an imp. But a second imp now crouched over him, a clawed hand gripping his esophagus through the jugular.

It looked up at the operators, its eyeless gaze searing. Reva and Nil didn't hesitate to pump it full of rounds, neither overkill nor conservative. Just the right amount to ensure its death.

Reva advanced to clear the bathrooms.

"Status?" John asked in his mic.

"All clear," Reva said, emerging. She and Nil passed through the truck stop, disappointment on their tired faces.

Seconds after exiting the small building, Price opened his mouth to speak. He was interrupted. A staccato, almost rhythmic judder of gunfire in the near distance.

The operators' brows furrowed and they exchanged inquisitive looks.

"That *had* to be military," Nil said, hope a rare ingredient in him.

"Or police," Jam said.

"This far from Norfolk, that well-armed?" Nil countered.

"Hey, I'd love to be wrong," Jam said. A pause. "For once."

Nil tried not to smirk. He hastily returned to the car, Jam and Price ducking back in. The second Reva was resituated in the trunk, she confirmed to John with her mic. His operation of the Kia was put to the test.

Everyone dug a Peltor out for better sound reception. The K5 had a stock turbocharger and a little bit of power to it, enough to make aggressive maneuvers growl from under the hood. This crippled John's full awareness, and Price's. Reva was too near the muffler to be of

257

much help; Jam and Nil were, once more, who they relied on the most.

Two blocks down the road, it became more apparent they were closer to Norfolk than ever before. The bleed-over from whatever cambion warpaths were being waged in the city was explicit here.

Gunfire popped off again, this time to the car's far left. Even John thought he heard it, but Jam confirmed in the seat behind him.

John uttered "hang on" and veered left. The Kia hopped the curb, and Reva bounced uncomfortably in the back. Although she didn't say anything into her mic, and he couldn't hear her vocalize a complaint, he suspected as much.

"Sorry, luv," he said into his collar mic.

Price looked over at him. John shrugged.

There was no point hiding their relationship now. And John was relieved when Price's reaction was nothing but a firm nod. There was respect in his eyes, and above all else, a sort of understanding. That some things were unavoidable, and ultimately came down to how it was handled.

Reva's perception of the car's progress was backwards, of course. She noticed they were passing under small trees, and over grass. Then, seconds later, the tires screeched against pavement again, and she spotted a basketball court. Past that, a soccer field and bleachers.

This time, when the gunfire sounded off, it was not only tremendously nearby, but clearly military. The methodical semi-auto bangs, the mix of rifle and pistol and even shotgun ammo, all on top of an absence of screams.

Comforting, at last.

"Pour out," John snapped, and everybody exited the Kia. He killed the engine to save gas, but all the doors were left open. And the key fob stayed in the cup-holder. Something John had already thanked the slain driver for, after subconsciously apologizing while removing his headless body from the car. Then his actual head.

A memory sure to stay with him forever.

They reached a backdoor entrance to Lakeland High School, noticing a lack of destruction to the property or brick structure itself. Also, virtually no signs of death around it, at least from the posterior. All great signs.

"On me, on me," John said, assembling everyone between two heavy steel doors. He looked at their faces, and nodded. He had but two words for them before they burst in through the doors. "Bang hammers."

Serpent One funneled in through these two push-doors. They entered a gymnasium, their boots echoing beneath the high ceiling. Some blood smears from dead cambions on the polished hardwood floor, and not a single dead human. More good signs.

They exited the gymnasium and proceeded down a hallway that eventually led them behind the cafeteria. More reports rang out, which inside the school were amplified with an intense echo. At times confusing on direction, especially now that everyone's ear-pro was firmly secured. All but John's left ear. This was one reason he took point.

They cut through the ground level, and in hindsight should have driven the Kia around to the front of the building. As they neared the lobby, Price tried his comms again. It sputtered briefly before sending into the ether.

Seconds later, their Peltors received a trickle of someone's voice. It was deep but smooth, and loud. So loud they thought they could hear it reverberate through the hallways themselves; lockers weren't very forgiving with the passage of sound.

"...Three, this is Mamba Three. Say again. Serpent One? Do not recognize."

Price sighed. "This is *Seamus Price*, goddammit. With Viper Three and company. Location. Over."

"Front office, lobby. Need assistance ASAP, Viper."

"Laszlo," John said, shooting his eyes at Price. "That's gotta be Laz."

Price nodded and they hurried. John could not remember the last time he heard Mike Laszlo sound so stressed. He was comparable to John's build, if not a little bigger. Mocha-skinned and bald, with a jet black goatee darker than the Pine Barrens at midnight with no moonlight. His rigor and austerity at the Moyock gun range often carried over to ops, but he rarely repressed his lighter side around tenured members.

Reva looked forward to seeing Bailey again, since they were last at the facility, being resupplied. She was only a Cage Troll when an op didn't call for Mamba Three.

Brayton was one of Moyock's more reserved operators, a bookworm that always wanted to know more about Forked Tongue's history. Much like Nil, but far less cynical or egotistical. Brayton was newer to the fire-team, and the program, having only been active in the field for eighteen months. Whereas Laszlo and Bailey each had over four years.

Bailey was, in fact, a transfer from the Salem facility. She became Moyock-official just last year.

The group's incentives to meet up with Mamba could be aligned to one final thought: self-preservation. The more the merrier sort of deal.

Except that under these circumstances, there was simply nothing merry about any of it.

Emerging into the front lobby was a nightmare. Two pairs of glass double-doors had been shattered, their aluminum frames warped. Part of the wall was even missing, in rubble. Recently slain imps littered the tile floor, and a wounded Centurion was struggling to its feet. Essentially a horned Baron but slightly smaller—standing maybe seven or eight feet—with armor and a bladed weapon of some kind, Centurions were no gentle foe.

Nil fired his shotgun at its head from ten feet away. The slug flowered, shattering its left horn and angering it to no end. But the slug didn't penetrate its helmet. The cambion beast snarled at them, rising to its feet and swinging a double-edge battle axe.

Reva darted left, dropping to her knees and sliding across the tile just as its axe came around again. She heard the air slice above her head, spun on her left knee, kodachi drawn. She plunged it into the creature's right hamstring, where there was a gap in its leg armor.

The Centurion wailed, limping.

Behind her, in the front office, more gunshots

barked.

With a cushion of time and space, the rest of Serpent One moved in that direction. Behind Reva, although Jam stayed behind to assist her. Having circled around behind the Centurion, he concentrated fire on its wounded leg, until the 77-grain TMK rounds from Frank's Radian blew out that knee. The Centurion toppled to the right. Its axe skidded across the tile, and Reva wrenched her kodachi free. One of its meaty, clawed hands reached for her leg; two-handing the kodachi, she buried the blade into the center of its wounded horn. The steel dug into the marrow, split the horn the rest of the way, and then punctured its underlying skull. There was a sickening *crunch* and the Centurion went limp.

Inside the office, close-quarters was given new meaning. Half the walls were inches thin at most, or glass. They shattered or broke whenever a Centurion got in the way, or an imp leapt.

There were three imps maneuvering the office, and one Centurion.

Upon entering, John and Price realized that Mamba Three was in increasingly worse shape. The Centurion wielded a sword-type of weapon with dual tips, except that the blade itself appeared to be sharpened bone, and barbs along the edges could be curved teeth. Possibly from dead Barons, or the like.

Nil immediately found Brayton in a corner, tending to a bad wound. Nil had to dig a sword-tooth from Brayton's neck, and then help pack it with gauze. Some of the operator's blood misted Nil's chin. He grew angrier with each millisecond that passed; angry that they had not arrived sooner, or that it had come to this in any way, to begin with.

Angry that he knew he could not save Trevor Brayton. A man eight years his junior, who he had seen many times at the Moyock library, but only struck up a conversation on two occasions. And they were all too brief.

"Stay, c'mon, stay with me, brother, it's not that bad, you've…" Nil continued to lie to the dampening color in Brayton's face.

Between the principal's main office and the little foyer in front of it, the Centurion had demolished most of the drywall. Laszlo was inside the office, behind the principal's desk, likely grateful it was empty, anyway. But he couldn't safely fire at the Centurion with Bailey on the opposite side, engaging an imp.

The other imp was being distracted by John and Price, who collectively used barrel discipline with their handguns, while intermittently deploying their knives. Not their bladed weapons, even those were too big for these confines. Their seven-inch Adra knives could do a number to imp flesh, but might not be fatal enough.

A considerably loud pistol went off inside the office. Bullets pounded into the Centurion's leg armor, until some got through and penetrated meat. The cambion roared, turning its back on Bailey to march toward the desk. Laszlo dove out of the way in time for the beast to lumber right through it. The sound of splitting, crunching wood was awfully loud.

Back in the office, Bailey finished killing the imp, the very last bullet in her Walther pistol seeming to do the trick.

At which point the other imp succumbed to its wounds from a myriad of .45-caliber bullets and .454 Casull rounds, exacerbated by any number of knife cuts and stabs.

Walking through its slowly disintegrating body, John reached Bailey and nodded firmly. In passing, though. He entered the principal's office and locked his elbows. The stainless steel revolver roared, and a round caught the Centurion as it towered over Laszlo on the floor, in a narrow space between helmet and epaulette. Black blood squirted from the wound and the Centurion twitched before facing John, taking its eyeless stare off Laszlo.

A mistake in itself.

Laszlo sprang to his feet, and used his own knife to lift the Centurion's breastplate. Before it could register his movement, he pressed the muzzle of his Glock 40 against the cambion's left peck, and squeezed the trigger in rapid succession, three times. The Centurion staggered back, and John's 460 XVR bucked again. This time a round met the creature in the face, where the helmet arched over its mouth. The mandible blew off in a spray of blood and saliva; preceding the collapse of its body after the bullet expanded at the base of its spine.

"Gotta love the mortality of these things," John said, digging a finger into his left ear and wiggling it.

"Ear-pro?" Laszlo asked, casually, as he walked toward John.

"Fell out, long story."

They met, and exchanged firm but fleeting hand-shakes.

"I bet," Laszlo said. Then he pressed his mic button. "Sound off, Mamba."

"Brayton's bad, real bad," Bailey's voice came through, both comms and in person. Her voice shook.

When Laszlo and John emerged from the principal's office, it was right behind Price. He seemed to half look over the decline of Brayton's health, those fruitlessly trying to save him, while also keeping an eye on their six. He faced the rest of the front office, outside of the principal's foyer. This area was essentially an antechamber within the lobby surrounded by glass panes and half-walls. A seating area arrayed with chairs, end tables, and photos of the student body during key events over the years.

Very vulnerable.

Price refused to take his eyes away, at the cost of appearing indifferent to Brayton's condition.

Meanwhile, Nil and Bailey actively tried to mend Brayton's wounds. It was more than just a Centurion's sword to his neck and shoulder, but an obscure gut wound, as well.

"How the hell did this happen?" John asked, almost angrily, squatting beside Brayton and indicating the abdominal injury. It looked like a deep cavity, not caused by any blade. Something…blunter.

"Damn imps…f-fucking imp p-punched me, boss," Brayton mustered, answering John directly. He then laughed painfully, blood framing his teeth. A hand gripped John's uniform, but John quickly transitioned the operator's fingers into his own. They locked and held the man's hand, knowing full well Brayton's last moments were upon him.

"You hit back, though, yeah?" John said, his teeth audibly grinding. Once more, Reva could heard it, after she had entered the office behind the others. Jam followed, slowly, but also kept pivoting to maintain vigilance about their exposed sides. Not unlike Price, who noticed this and took it to heart.

"H-Harder, you bet, b-brother," Brayton managed.

"Goddamn right you did. No shutting down you Mambas." John grinned crazily and looked up from this man he so barely knew. When his eyes connected with Laszlo, it was clear that the tenured operator was struggling to keep his face dry. His empty fist clenched so tightly John could hear the tension.

"Stopped, I, I think I stopped the bleeding up here," Bailey finally said. "Now let's look at—"

Her voice dried up.

Brayton's head had lolled forward, between his shoulders. Blood and saliva fell from his slack mouth.

A deep, rugged breath crawled out of John. He stood up. Wobbled briefly. Reva clutched his shoulder from behind. His eyes met with Laszlo, who then shook his forearm in a different kind of gesture.

"How…How did y'all end up in *here*?" John asked. He glanced over at Bailey.

"Let's, uh, get out of here before more come in and it all repeats," Laszlo suggested.

"Solid. We've got wheels."

"No shit?"

The group began to exit the all-but-demolished front office, although Bailey and Nil hung back. Bailey was trying to close Brayton's eyelids, but they were being stiffer than she expected. Her own hand shook a little, and it took her a moment longer to succeed.

Nil offered a hand to help her pop to her feet. Then she let herself be distracted by the coldness, the comforting simplicity, of armaments. She was, after all, a Cage Troll at heart.

"You're rocking the Nexus, too, I see," she said, nodding at Nil's EVO.

"Uh, yeah."

She showed him that so was Brayton. It rested on the hard carpet floor beside a secretarial desk, few feet from where he sat upright in death.

"Trust me," she said. "He'd want to be useful, even when he isn't here. I think that was Trevor, all the time, even in life."

She lifted the submachine-gun, and detached the drum magazine, setting the SMG on the desk. Then she handed the drum to Nil, who tentatively accepted it, and gently pulled another drum from Brayton's kit. She also ejected a mag from his Walther, the same model as hers, which Nil noticed.

"Group compatibility," he said. "Good touch. Boa Three had that, too."

"Just us," Bailey said, as she gathered more spare 9mm mags from Brayton. "In love with the PDP Match. Not Laz, though; he'd never go for a nine."

"Don't tell me the big man's got a Desert Eagle."

She smirked, shook her head.

267

"No, no. Glock 40, ten-mil."

"Still nice."

"On me," Price said, distinctly for Nil and Bailey, who had not realized they were the only stragglers.

"Appreciate it," Nil said, nodding. He looked over the second drum, which had to have a capacity of fifty, far better than his twenty-round stick-mags.

"Definitely," Bailey said, moving with him toward the others.

"I was talking to Bray," Nil said.

Bailey smirked and nodded.

As the group exited the lobby, Bailey found herself glancing at the others. She made eye contact with Jam, whose face she had never seen so downtrodden. And then her brow furrowed.

"Wait...Where's the rest of Boa?"

"Skyline," Reva said, her voice rough. "K-I-A."

Bailey's expression muddied. She gripped Jam's shoulder briefly in consolation.

On their way back through the high school, Laszlo explained Mamba's situation. It only took him a moment to get started; neither he nor Bailey could barely believe that they were just leaving Brayton's body behind like this, but knew there was no other option. Best-case scenario, it would be recovered when this was all squashed, and given a proper burial, like so many people deserved.

"We left Carrsville, just as things started to get bad. Wasn't in the plans, but neither were the cambions. Overhead Suffolk police chatter about "demons with fucking axes." *Centurions*. We realized that, unlike in

268

Carrsville, Suffolk was being hit with fallout from Norfolk. So we relocated, but didn't get far. Held up here for a breather, nothing more. Then found ourselves pummeled into a corner."

"Fuck's sake," John shook his head. He ran his right hand through his thick black hair. "I'm sorry about Trevor."

Laszlo nodded. "We appreciate it."

"The help, too," Bailey said, clearing her throat. "We'd have been absolutely *fucked* had you all not shown up."

"Sooner, we should've gotten here sooner," John mumbled."

"Suppress that shit," Price said, zipping a glance back at them. "Focus on the now."

John nodded.

It was advice he himself had given trainees about losses in the field. And yet, now he found it a struggle to follow himself.

"Where y'all headed?" Laszlo asked.

"Bit of a complicated story, but right now," John said, "the safe house down on Manning."

"Thought so," Bailey said. "We're running low on ammo, too. Imps are one thing, but Centurions take entire mags to even flinch."

"Let alone Barons," Nil said.

"Or a Duke," Jam mumbled.

Bailey's brow furrowed. She exchanged bewildered looks with Laszlo, who then addressed John.

"You've encountered Barons and Dukes already?"

John sighed. "Barons, rachnids even. And one

Duke. A Hawk gunner helped a whole lot."

"I bet. Shit."

They reached the gymnasium, but Price halted them halfway across the waxed hardwood. He looked down, and then slowly turned, revealing that he was studying his watch.

"Bold suggestion," he said.

"I know what you're going to say," John nodded. "And I want to object, but I can't."

Reva looked at him with uncertainty.

"I'm, uh, I'm lost," Bailey shrugged.

"You want to wait, don't you?" Laszlo said, looking at Price. "You want to wait until daybreak."

"Just before. It's 'bout eighty mikes."

"An hour and a half in here, especially if we can go undisturbed, would be ample rest." Nil made a great point, but he didn't hesitate to counter himself. "*But*, at the cost of relinquishing our help from others in need. Possibly even the integrity of that safe house."

"We're running on fumes as it is," John admitted, wanting to, but not mentioning Price's nap aboard the helo. "And, shortly, so will our gear. We'll do more harm than good, to ourselves no less, if we rush into the nigh now."

"There *is* some strategic benefit," Bailey said, initially hating the idea but now finding it difficult to contest. "If we go out there and keep pushing—Manning Road is what, a ten-minute drive?—in the dark, we'll hit every obstacle en route. Every cambion will flock to our position. And since we don't have NODs, our flashlights will be like invitations. To the ones that have eyes, anyway."

"Or, we *sneak* around the enemy," Nil said, seeing the clear merit to Bailey's point. "By then, unfortunately, the cambions will have occupied Suffolk. But if we stay undetected, we can creep right under their noses, and possibly even reach the safe house without ruffling a feather."

"Best-case scenario," John said, "they'll have moved on. Or at least dispersed. Unlikely, but possible."

"So either we move like a storm, or like a cat," Reva said, also not thrilled about the option but suddenly seeing too thin a defense for the other way.

"Essentially," Price said. "Other bad news we can avoid by advancing at daybreak…yeah, we have a car. But fitting five was a struggle as-is. So we ditch the wheels altogether, have as quiet a journey as possible. Five to ten-minute drive, we'll make good time taking back routes, yards, etcetera."

The operators either nodded in accord, or as a placeholder for their contemplation.

"We've got eighty mikes to work it over," Price assured them. "And we will."

And, over the course of an hour, they would.

Remaining quiet for nearly eighty minutes despite the audible mayhem in the distance was a challenge for them. But they did, and before the first hour was over, the turmoil had fallen silent. This was equally comforting as it was disconcerting. Once more, they had to internally debate which was more likely—

Dead or fled.

271

In this case, also practical, was hiding.

Not unlike the operators' present strategy. While providing maintenance for their weapons and gear, nibbling, drinking, even dispelling waste, nobody raised the question about their safety. Considering how imps had previously opened rifts in the sky just to pursue Serpent One, they wondered now that Norfolk was probably overrun, and it wasn't the only city to be, if the cambions were altering their focus.

Surely such an immense coup had some nucleus of intelligence behind it. Some strategy.

But so did mankind.

"When we do push for the safe house," Price said, about ten minutes into their waiting game, "it needs to be simple. Single column, staggered progression. John leads, so that first contact, if absolutely necessary, is subsonic. If he can neutralize without alarming others, win-win. If not, plan B—Laszlo, you achieve overwatch of some kind. I noticed the Galil. Seven-sixty-two, yeah?"

Laszlo nodded. He was presently cleaning his IWI Galil ACE Gen-2 with a cloth from his kit, and oiling the recoil spring. The AK-style rifle, complete with a banana mag, composite stock, vertical foregrip, and 1.5x optic, was presently their best long-range high-powered option, behind John's Marlin. Except that, unlike the Marlin, it had a better fire rate, even without going full-auto.

"Then that's you. Flank if you need to, but don't detach too much from the column," Price continued. "If nothing else, provide cover fire for the rest to advance to better cover. Then they'll do the same, John might switch to the Marlin for a better distraction, and you catch-up."

Laszlo nodded. "Got it."

"We be smart, keep it basic," Price said. "Use backyards, avoid the street, stay low and quiet. Ten to twenty feet intervals. John point, I'll shadow. Then the triplets—Reva, Bailey, Jam."

Reva and Bailey nodded unflappably. Jam's brow furrowed. He began to open his mouth but Price plowed forward, and he zipped up.

"Then Nil, and Laszlo on our six. Bang, bang, bang. Any questions?"

Head shakes.

"Good. I'm retiring for a few."

Nobody objected. In fact, Reva and Jam joined, individually of course. They chose separate bleachers, Jam squeezing between them for less a chance of rolling off.

"Old man is on top of his game, huh?" Laszlo said to John, trying to relieve some pressure on himself, and the grim weight of Brayton's death.

"Careful, he might hear you," John whispered back, even though they sat forty feet away, near one of the two exterior gym doors. "I'm convinced he doesn't really sleep, just rests his eyes."

John smirked weakly.

"But yeah. We're grateful."

"As Bailey and I for you. I'm sure that, uh…Brayton was, too. Is. For what you offered there at the end."

John shrugged. He glanced back, at Reva. She slept on her back, composedly, atop a bleacher step. A black rag over her eyes. John's broad chest heaved with a deep breath.

"I've been taught to be more compassionate," he

273

said.

"No point in hiding it now, huh?"

"At world's end, everything comes out. If anything can save us from damnation, why not love?"

"I can't believe I just heard that out of *the* John Aguirre," Bailey said, having unintentionally snuck up behind him.

John looked back and up at her. He and Laszlo were sitting, she had walked over to them.

"Yeah, well, keep it to yourself, will ya?"

"Sure thing, Romeo," she smirked.

John shook his head.

Bailey proceeded to give him heartfelt no-bullshit thanks for his team's assistance in the school, and what he "did" for Brayton. John tried to let this console him for not doing damn near enough, even if it had been out of his control.

He then looked over Bailey's kit and decided to distract himself with her gear. Especially when Laszlo confessed his own fatigue, and retreated to the bleachers for some shut-eye.

"Heckler & Koch," John said, clicking his tongue. "Nil won't admit it, but I know he's jealous seeing that in your hands."

"Yeah? I mean, he's got an EVO Nexus. Brayton had the same."

"No shit."

She sat opposite him, the MP5K crossing her lap. The stubby barrel and short vertical grip were almost iconic. What John least expected to see on the PDW was a drum mag. He pointed at it.

"Good touch. Especially against these demonic assholes."

"Demonic. Better watch your tongue, bud. I hear there's a guy that lectures against such terms back in Moyock."

"He can be a real stiff, huh?" John joked, holding a straight face.

"Sometimes."

John wanted to play more into the humor but felt the other circumstances making it difficult.

"Whatever the fuck they are," he said, "they're the worst. As despicable as vamps can be, they're not *all* monsters. Even full-mooners have a sense of animalistic pride. Cambions are just…"

"Evil?"

John sighed. "That word. I want to say *yes*, they are. But what *is* evil?"

"An undeniable absence of goodness," Bailey said blandly. It seemed to him that she was suddenly channeling all the rage and grief surrounding Brayton's death, if not everyone else's, as caused by the cambions. "Which they are. Sure, they have a caste, a hierarchy. But so does the Klan. So did the Nazis. No, John. Cambions *are* evil. And wherever they come from, I bet there are no peasants. No innocent imp wives and children. I bet they're born from some wretched slime and they look through the window, into our world, and they hate it, they hunger for it, they want to destroy. So they do, because it's all they know."

She had started to get heated up.

Bailey collected herself. And then, with awful simplicity, she spoke dismissively.

"And now it's all I do, too," she said. Her eyes briefly lifted up, and then returned to John. "I want to extinguish them from both planes. Maybe we'll get that chance."

"I fucking hope so," Reva said, having arrived behind John.

Bailey stood up, and hugged Reva in passing. She didn't seem to want to, but Reva insisted. Then she returned to the bleachers, possibly for some shuteye. When Reva sat down opposite John, in Bailey's place, it was much closer. Their weapons leaned off to the side, freeing their bodies of a little weight. Without being blatantly intimate, they held each other.

Their foreheads touched, hands on napes.

Over an hour passed since John first sat down. He and Reva had eventually leaned with their backs against a hamper containing basketballs, footballs, and the other gym equipment. Their fingers interlocked, Reva's head on his shoulder, her long braid coiled around John's other hand. Sleep had cradled them without fully engulfing.

Not woken by their need to leave, or daybreak if it had a sound, but a different tune. One that everyone except Laszlo and Bailey had come to recognize and cherish since Jersey. It was Price's satellite phone. The ringtone jarred those sleeping awake, and they shook themselves from any lingering shroud of fatigue as if sloughing a second skin.

Everyone assembled around Price.

He extended the antennae and hit speaker.

Calder's voice came through, amid a current of white noise. It subdued in waves, unwanted but better than a firm moat of static.

"...receiving, but listen, there's not...at any moment, something much bigger is ex...where exactly, unsure. Seismic readings be...conjunction with rift activity, East Coast and...even Cairo, Beijing, Syd..."

The operators were shaking their heads, kneading temples.

John attempted to get a word in.

"Breaking up a lot, Calder. You're coming in real fucking fuzzy. We are in *Suffolk*, do you read?"

A three-second pause.

"Copy, suggest you...house on Manning Ro...advised other units in...ust wait and resupply, further instructions to...omething bigger on the way...luck and Godspee—"

The call went dead as if the satellite had been ripped out of space.

Price's head bowed briefly and he ran a hand over his bald scalp. Then he stood with a sharp jolt, securing the phone back in its pouch, antennae retracted. He scooped up his cleaned and loaded SIG Spear, secured the strap, and shouldered the buttstock.

"We've been over this, stick to it. Nice and smooth, single column, staggered groups. Nobody is uncertain about where the safe house is?"

Zero shakes of the head. Zero nods. Stillness as individual game faces were pulled on, implicitly.

"We reach it, no matter what. Get separated? Stay

low, stay quiet, fire only when needed. Use blades if feasible. Everyone ready?"

"Bang hammers," Laszlo said in his deep yet smooth voice.

The others nodded austerely and stood, if they weren't already. Price beckoned them and Serpent One, now with Mamba Two, disseminated from the Lakeland High School gymnasium. It was ten, maybe fifteen minutes until dawn. The nascence of daybreak was already seeping into the sky, which, as they advanced down the *side* of the road on foot, they noticed was blemished by scattered pillars of smoke throughout the town.

Into a suburban sprawl they ventured, navigating backyards and avoiding the main road when possible. On foot, they were able to move significantly more quietly than in a car, almost imperceptibly by comparison. Except that they were far from invisible, especially with the creeping light of dawn over Suffolk.

Their ROE was simple. They were to prioritize movement over confrontation. If feasible to circumvent enemies, they would. Worst-case, John could make first contact and eliminate quietly. If his enemy required more firepower, Laszlo would move up to cover with his 7.62, while the rest advanced in intervals.

Their advantage of projectile weapons needed to be exploited here. Even if they were dangerously low on ammunition, they could still run faster and farther than a Centurion or Baron could swing a weapon.

This concept stayed true to heart, and for nearly ten minutes didn't present itself as either an experience or issue. But that was before their movement between cha-lets spurred the senses of a patrolling Baron. Its eyeless head turned, and its bulky head tilted back; its jaws made a strange chittering sound.

Then a pair of Centurions appeared around vehicu-lar debris in the road. Rising sunlight glinted off their armor. But something else gleamed, held in their arms.

"Bows," John whispered into his mic, leaning against the sturdy wooden leg of a veranda. "They've got fucking bows and arrows!"

Price's heart sank. "Of course they do."

13

Bone. Or something comparable. The arrowheads themselves might have been teeth from some cambion Forked Tongue wasn't familiar with, and the shafts of the arrows another material altogether. Possibly a calcified tendon, or more simply, whatever iron-like ore that composed a Duke's mace. The bows were of no startling technology or complex design. Their simplicity was effective, and the might behind each draw terrifying. When the first arrow whizzed by John, he swore under his breath and tucked behind the veranda.

He engaged the armored cambion sixty feet away, his DDM4 making virtually no sound as it slung round after round in its direction. Most of his shots were hits, but the armor proved them dissatisfying.

When he sighted the Centurion nock another arrow, and draw the string back, he withdrew behind the sturdy wooden leg of the veranda. But the arrowhead impaled it, missing his face by inches.

"Fuck, these things are no joke," he said into his mic. When he looked back, he saw Price and Nil close in. Twenty feet behind them, Bailey, Reva, and Jam moved as a trio.

Laszlo hung back, only to vanish between two houses, moving toward the street that the enemy occupied.

"Advance to cover in five seconds," Laszlo said in his mic.

The gap between the veranda and the next house was about twenty strides, but included a chain-link fence four and a half feet off the ground. They would have to vault it. Easy for all of them to do, physically, but with gear and weapons not necessarily.

Especially with the threat of cambions now with long-range capabilities.

The second wave of an invasion.

Reports from Laszlo's Galil sounded two houses down. John peered around the veranda. The single Baron appeared to be fleeing down the road, or possibly trying to flank them. But the two bow-wielding Centurions were receiving 7.62mm rounds to the torso and head. Enough to distract them from John, and fixate on Laszlo, who John hoped was behind ample cover.

"Move," Price said. He and John broke away from the veranda, vaulted the fence, reached the backyard of a neighboring home, and glanced back. The triplets, as Price had called them earlier, reached the fence. Bailey vaulted first, and then Jam. Reva kept her rifle aimed at the Centurions in the road, just in case they turned away from Laszlo's direction. When it was her time to vault the fence, with Nil waiting to move from the veranda, two imps crept into view.

One had used the house as passage.

It leapt through a back window, glass shattering in its wake. When it collided unexpectedly with Nil, the two tumbled across the grass. Reva pivoted and fired with such succinctness that Nil would later thank her with wide eyes. Her 5.56mm rounds cut gashes along the imp's gaunt shoulder blades, tearing it away from Nil. He sprang to a knee and fired a curt burst at its chest with his SMG. The imp went down, and he rose to his feet. He walked over to it, put two more 9mm rounds into its skull.

"Laszlo, move!" Price demanded. He whistled at John. "Covering fire."

But the second imp, in that time, had diverted its attention from Nil and Reva to John and Price. It bounded from the roof of the veranda to the roof of the neighboring house. Shingles shed beneath its bony, clawed digits and it tumbled off gracelessly.

Almost crashing into Price.

It missed by a few feet, sufficiently startling them as they had solely concentrated on the cambions in the road.

From inside the house, a family of civilians watched through slits in the curtains. Awe gripped them, but fear stole their voices, thankfully. They remained un-detected by the cambions while this unnamed military force fought tooth and nail.

While the imp tumbled across the grass and re-gained its balance, John engaged it. Price's aim hadn't wavered from the huge archers in the road. Their armor had been dented and disheveled by Laszlo's hits. Some of Price's own shots began to penetrate meat. The power of his 115-grain 6.8mm rounds dealt ample energy, eventually downing one of the Centurions. It made the other blunder, and there was a great window of relief for the operators.

Laszlo was the last to vault the fence, and big as he was, an intimidating force on the mat to boot, he struggled with the chain-link. It rattled beneath him and one of the posts wobbled in the soil. Just as he cleared it, a crooked link caught one of his pouches and he got hung up.

"Fuck's sake," he growled, reaching back to unhook himself.

The imp that was giving John's aim a run for his money suddenly wheeled around to pounce on Laszlo. John's marksmanship was ready to prove itself but now Laszlo was in his line-of-fire, and he restrained. Capable of defending himself, Laszlo surprised everyone present, including the imp, with a swift draw of his Glock 40. The gun battered round after round of ten-mil lead into the imp's upper chest, even its head, at less than twelve feet away.

Black blood spotted the air above and behind the creature. Then it hit the grass like a ragdoll.

Laszlo finally detached himself from the rattling fence. He regrouped with the others, Nil slapping his back.

"Close-ass call. Great shooting, though."

They advanced, at a greater pace than before. Jam

moved ahead of Reva and Bailey, breaking formation. At first it seemed in order to reach John and Price, although he could just as well use his mic. Instead he passed them, too, and navigated between two houses, attempting to spot a street sign. Relief came over him, and he glanced back as John and Price turned the corner.

"Close, we're like, two or three blocks away," Jam said. He pointed past them, toward a perpendicular road. "Suggest we cut down Locust, like five houses, then left on McKinney. There's a small plaza. Safe house can be accessed via the fire escape 'round back."

"Good looks," John said. "Now fall back into formation. We'll—"

Jam was smiling a little. There was a mix of relief, joy, and even deserved pride on his face when it happened. The Baron turned the corner and swung its axe. When it connected with Jam's neck, there was no debate he ever saw it coming, or felt a thing.

The others had to experience the sight of it.

How the massive axe sundered Jam's neck in the blink of an eye, lopping his head clean off. Only there was nothing clean about it. The spray of blood was more than just arterial; it was a grotesque fountain that the Baron seemed to revel in.

John shouted incoherently and fired his DDM4 with a fury that didn't translate audibly, given the subsonic ammo and Surefire suppressor. He had only six rounds of .300 Blackout before the mag went dry. He unflinchingly dropped it, sling catching the rifle, and drew his Smith & Wesson with both hands.

Price was firing at the Baron, too, and had got off

his first shot before Jam's decapitated body even hit the ground.

The Baron wasn't armored, but its dense plates of bone and sturdy musculature kept it upright for some time. Even as bullets volleyed its body.

When the damn thing finally collapsed, it did so, thankfully, backwards. Not on top of Jam, as if his body could be any more defiled in combat.

John began to rush toward Jam, but he stayed his footing. Price had not moved, and John immediately realized that not only was there nothing to do, but moving toward the road and out of formation could be the worst decision.

Slowly, angrily, he backpedaled.

Reva and Bailey had already caught up, and were still rattled by the sight. Bailey's face glistened in the fresh sunlight as tears muddied her cheeks, mixing with dust and sweat.

While backing up, John bumped into Reva.

She grabbed his big shoulder and pulled on it. Her eyes and grinding teeth spoke volumes.

Nothing you can do, could do, they insisted, implicitly.

"We move," John said out loud.

He gulped and looked up. Laszlo and Nil reached them. Upon seeing Jam's body, a catalytic brand of rage and grief hit them like a wave. There were a few brief missteps, then the men gathered themselves and advanced. Or proceeded to, awaiting Price's next move. His command. Anything to let themselves focus on a task rather than wallow in the mire of another brutal loss.

"Jam said, he said, down Locust, then—"

"Cross, uh, McKinney, and…" Reva said, following John's words the best her recollection of where the safe house was.

"Fire escape, third building in the Kilby Plaza," Nil said, panting. Not out of fatigue, but channeling his emotions. "Could go 'round front, but likely bolted shut."

Price nodded. His head already on a swivel, hating that they were stationary for so long.

"Nil, I need you up with me," he said, beckoning. Nil didn't hesitate. Price looked at John. "Keep the distance between us, and Reva and Bailey."

John nodded once.

"Let's hoof it. Almost there." Price led, Nil at his heels. Diagonally, they cut across the backyards of neighboring homes along Locust Street, which ran perpendicular to the road they had been parallel to for so long.

Upon reaching McKinney Avenue with no issue, they crossed in groups. Each advancing operator stopped midway, using a stalled Jeep as cover to ensure the others weren't in any line-of-fire. Adapting to archers in the field was not something they ever expected to do, against cambions no less.

The blessing of daylight suddenly felt like a curse.

They could see all the horrors that pursued them, and were inflicted, with grave clarity.

Reaching the back of the shopping strip of white-painted brick buildings issued some relief to their nervous systems. But they knew not to take advantage of it. If the wicked never rested, they couldn't either, not until they were within the comfort of four walls.

An aforementioned fire escape caught Nil and Price's attention, while John provided cover for Reva and Bailey to turn a residency's corner and reach the back alley behind the taller buildings.

The fire escape was about forty feet ahead.

The buildings themselves to their left, as they faced back, awaiting the others. Right of them ran a thin treeline between a creek run-off and some scant foliage. A natural perimeter that separated suburbia from the shopping plaza.

Somewhere disturbingly close by, a woman screamed in horror. There was a sickening crunch as axe split flesh, and the hearts of fortified men sank with a foul feeling.

Seconds later, the narrow trees and thin foliage to their right buckled in the wake of a plodding Baron. Its massive shoulders and elbows parted the trees, buckling them. A swing of its double-bladed axe cut down some.

Nil and Price turned to engage the creature.

John moved forward just as the snap of bowstrings sounded behind the underbrush. An arrow cut the air inches behind him. A second grazed his right shoulder, cutting his rifle strap and spilling blood onto his shirt.

The Marlin clattered at his feet.

He spun toward the trees, firing his DDM4. The rounds made no sound, only the action of the bolt snapping back and forth; but the others' engagement was loud enough. His exposed left ear rang, and he wouldn't have it any other way. He wanted to hear the downfall of evil, that beautiful, coarse symphony.

Reva and Bailey were maybe twenty feet from John when a volley of arrows emerged from the treeline in greater number than before. One tooth-like arrowhead penetrated John's left thigh. The shaft lodged in his femur. A terrible cry of pain vaulted from his lungs. He somehow didn't fall, but his posture became so rigid that he struggled to keep firing with any integrity of aim.

Several operators called out his name.

Price and Nil, twenty feet to his right. Reva, about the same distance to his left. She moved closer, laterally, while firing her rifle. More arrows from the trees, before Laszlo attempted to flank the hidden Centurions and get their attention. An arrowhead zipped by Reva's face so close that the air stung her eyes. She recoiled, pure instinct.

The bullet-battered Baron pressed forward, swinging its axe at Price and Nil. They backpedaled, Nil dropping to his knee to dump the remains of Brayton's fifty-round drum mag into the Baron's legs. A horde of 9mm rounds pumped its thighs and calves with lead, battering its knees.

The Baron toppled before reaching John.

Bailey moved past Reva, her compact SMG spitting fire. Bullets hosed out at the wounded Baron, eventually cracking one of its horns into small chunks, and then demolishing an eyeball. The Baron crumbled to the ground in a heap of black blood, embers already rising from its flesh.

Laszlo's rifle announced each of its shots as he engaged the Centurion archers behind the trees.

And then they paused, while Reva and John embraced. They would have kissed had they had the opportunity.

Laszlo's voice cut into their ears.

He was out of sight.

"Four Centurions, I put two down but the galil is almost dry. Fuck, there's a rachnid, too."

"Copy," Price said, shouldering his SIG. "Catch up. I'll cover."

"I've got it," John said, stepping out of Reva's arms to pick up his Marlin. Everyone was so disturbingly low on ammo that only Price covered John, his slightly bigger-bore rifle slinging rounds into the trees, uncertain of what he was hitting.

"To me, to me," Nil said, beckoning Bailey and Reva. The latter went reluctantly, but when more arrows started to cut through the trees and foliage, she turned back toward John. She watched him actually duck two arrows, shoulder his Marlin, and fire thunderously in that direction.

Bailey delayed her progression to return. She drew her pistol to fire into the trees, while reaching out for Reva. The arrows ceased firing, and John turned toward Reva and Bailey, grimacing from the projectile still lodged in his leg.

Laszlo appeared sixty feet away, shouting "rachnid!" Just then one of the six-limbed beasts emerged from the trees, snapping its elongated jaws and salivating, bucking its horned head. Bailey knocked Reva aside and fired at it, distracting the creature from John. Wounded, he was the ideal prey.

Price's aim adjusted.

His SIG walloped the rachnid in its left side, but it still grabbed a hold of Bailey. its teeth clamped around her knee, shattering the patella and puncturing her hamstring. She screamed and hit the pavement, pistol clattering. The rachnid snarled as it nimbly backpedaled toward the trees again, dragging her away.

Reva regained her footing and lunged out.

John managed to actually grab her hand, the Marlin falling. His boots skidded across pavement as the rachnid effectively dragged them both. An arrow flew over his head, narrowly missing Reva behind him. Price and Nil provided suppressive fire, despite their low reserves.

John drew his revolver in one hand, refusing to let go of Bailey. He fired down at the rachnid, and although his first two rounds seemed to only irritate it, the third .454 Casull split its skull like a cracked pumpkin. A rank stench poured out and Bailey was helped to her feet.

Reva reached them, grabbing Bailey to help her limp back toward the others. Laszlo neared, scooping in to assist.

"John, get John," Reva snapped at him.

Laszlo didn't hesitate.

He reached for John, and there was zero reluctance in the big man to accept help.

Two screams overlapped.

Price shouting "move" and Reva exclaiming "John," both voices grating to the point of pain. The trees behind John had divided around a charging Centurion, its armor clearly damaged by bullets, but its momentum unhindered. The axe in its hands—not a bow—swung overhead, coming down onto John. One curved blade cleaved his left shoulder, where it met his robust neck. The cambion blade sank to his topmost rib, after shattering his clavicle and grating his upper scapula.

The lining of a lung ripped beneath the tissue.

Blood sprayed from his mouth.

John's strong upper body parted like a wishbone.

Reva scream-cried in a horrendous sound. Laszlo staggered back, terror freezing his face. Price fired, thirty feet away. Nil joined, but his hands began to shake to the point that his aim couldn't be accounted for. Laszlo snapped to, and unloaded his Glock into the creature's armored head, focusing on the exposed mouth.

Even as bullets tore through its palate, the Centurion wrenched the blade farther down, into John's torso. A massive foot raised, planting against John's intact right shoulder. It kicked forward, nearly splitting John in half.

The slide of Laszlo's pistol locked back, empty. He had dumped the entire mag of 10mm rounds into the Centurion's mouth before its body took one step away from John and crumpled.

Laszlo reloaded, and stepped toward John, then his stomach knotted.

John Aguirre was barely intact. Were it not for his pelvis and intestines, the latter now steaming on the pavement, he might have been completely bisected by the massive axe.

Reva's vision of John would forever be marred by what the cambion had done to him. But as she broke away from a limping Bailey to run toward John's corpse, her eyes forced a mirage of her lover's healthy, smiling face. She was almost within arm's reach of the gruesomely halved body when Laszlo's big arms wrapped around her. Anyone else would not have been able to hold her.

She screamed bloody murder.

There was no "let me go" or the like. She simply screamed. Reva couldn't articulate words. Her face was a torrent of tears and phlegm.

Price reached them and helped Laszlo restrain Reva. He knew that, although half of cambions were blind, none were deaf. They desperately needed to ascend that fire escape. Getting Reva and Bailey to would be a challenge; Reva's wound was less physical than Bailey's, but somehow more crippling.

Nil mustered the strength to contain his own grief until they were by the barred window that the fire escape led to. Three stories off the ground. A massive two-pound padlock kept it secure. He dialed the combo in, or attempted to. Price noticed the shake in his hands and, compassionately as he could, took over.

Once the window was up, Price knelt aside while the others filed in. His rifle had maybe four rounds left in the mag, but he still swept his aim under the guardrail, down toward the trees and the end of McKinney Street. His optic briefly floated over John's corpse, and a pain resonated inside Price's chest.

With everybody else inside the safe house, Price followed. He secured the window behind himself, and looked around. The space was the size of a single-bedroom apartment, but was almost completely devoid of furniture. A few seats and card tables existed, one TV mounted to a brick wall, one bathroom, and two mattresses in what could be considered the bedroom. Lining the walls were chests, and in the bedroom a credenza; all were neatly filled with weapons and ammunition, from pre-loaded magazines to loose cartridges in Tupperware.

It was regularly maintained, per Forked Tongue SOP, once a month.

Reva and Nil embraced in the kitchen, both trying to stay quiet. Nil struggled less, but there was still an agony in him that refused to evacuate.

Price took over Laszlo's futile attempts to consoling Bailey. Had she not been snagged, John wouldn't have gone after her.

"That isn't on you, and in a way it isn't on him, either. It's on us, for being who we are, and what Forked Tongue demands." Price cleared his throat to keep himself as focused and even vacant as possible. "In the end, the lives ruined and lost today…are on the cambions. Nobody else."

"I'm not arguing that," Reva said, her voice low and dry. Startling Bailey. She stood behind her left shoulder. Nil was still in the kitchen. He was running the sink water, over his entire head.

"We need to stay put," Price said, slowly.

"Neither that," she said bluntly. "I'm going to take a shower."

She looked down and Bailey.

"Come get me if anything happens."

"You got it," Bailey said, her voice suddenly a thin croak.

293

Reva nodded, almost robotically, and turned around. En route to the bathroom, she discarded her gear and shed everything but her shirt, pants, and boots midstride.

Once inside the bathroom, her mind debated the possibility of shedding her skin also. But that would mean ridding herself of the haptic memory of John's touch, too.

A burial she refused to give.

14

Having fed and hydrated themselves, the remains of the team that could no longer be considered Serpent One, plus Bailey Evans, focused on their gear. They replenished ammunition, but had to swap weapons for the most part. Compatibility was not a privilege here. Nor was complete detachment; the occasional sputter of civilian gunfire, possibly police, too, could be heard in the distance. Suffolk was mostly quiet, but it was not completely devoid of human life.

Through the bathroom door and over the torrent of shower water, Reva had screamed. A wordless vocalization of her pain and anger. It was abrupt and jarring, casting chills down Bailey's spine. Even Laszlo shuddered from it.

Fresh tears welled in Nil's eyes, as he prepared a KRISS Vector in place of his EVO. It reminded him of Jam, and he began to mumble words that the others didn't fully catch. Nor did they inquire.

Unbeknownst to them, Nil *prayed*.

Not for anything pleasant, though.

He prayed for vengeance. He prayed for violence and bloodshed. For the annihilation of a world he had never stepped foot in.

The cambion dimension.

When Reva eventually emerged from the bathroom, she was wearing her same clothes, but this was unavoidable. The safe house was not tailored to anybody.

She got something to drink, and began to nibble but quickly became queasy. So she set the food aside and joined the others around a small card table.

"I, um…" Nil cleared his throat. Reva squeezed his arm briefly. Nil nodded and continued. "I loaded up with regular 12-gauge, they don't have any slugs here. Basic bitch shit."

Reva's mouth twitched toward a smile but to no avail.

"They have a few N4s lying around, though. Believe that?"

"Top-tier, makes sense," Reva said simply.

Suddenly the TV on the wall flickered on. A jarring beep sounded, something that everyone recognized but dreaded hearing. The operators turned toward the screen. Reva got up from her seat to walk closer.

Video feeds displayed first without any volume. They were clearly taken by brave helicopter pilots and film crews. An occasional line of distortion and static cut through the videos. They were coming in a few seconds at a time—stamped with different numbers and locations.

An anchorwoman's voice came on, but it was too warped to fully process.

"Mute it," Price said.

Reva ran her fingers along the side panel of the screen, and muted it. What they proceeded to watch in horrible silence was how bad this 'upheaval' was across the world. As copilot Richie Fields had explained, rachnids swarmed city streets by the dozens, crawling over cars and pursuing unarmed civilians down alleys, into structures. Bow-wielding Centurions withstood barrages of gunfire from police and military alike, while sending their own volleys.

Dukes waded through smaller towns, devastating everything in their wake. An occasional glimpse of hope could be seen as attack helicopters exerted aerial dominance and mowed down cambions of all sizes.

Until the video feed shifted to a view of Manhattan. From a flaming rift the size of a skyscraper emerged an equally massive tentacle, the color of burnt scarlet, dripping a viscous mauve ooze and arrayed with what could only be described as car-sized teeth. The gigantic, flexible muscle coiled around Central Park Tower, a 150-foot-wide and 1,550-foot-tall condominium.

Everyone in the safe house had a visible or audible reaction, Laszlo even standing and walking around.

Except for Reva.

Her mouth moved to form an expletive. Shock was not absent in her, but she processed it differently. As if her mind had become a converter. She feared less; she angered more.

The gargantuan tentacle flexed, squeezing. Central

Park Tower shattered, over twelve thousand glass panels screaming before raining massive shards below. The steel frame wrenched inward as if a wire trellis cone squeezed in a stronger hand. The carcass of the building likely housed only corpses now.

The video feed destabilized as another enormous rift opened fifty feet from the news helicopter.

However many millions were watching now, caught a glimpse of the cambion world on the other side. It was grotesque, in a way that no terrain should be. Structures of flesh and bone, cartilage warped to withstand a ravenous species and the might of a timeless void.

A colossal limb of foul composition reached out—

The video cut to static.

Air raid sirens resonated through Suffolk. The TV flickered off.

When Reva faced the others, their heads were buried in their hands. But Reva made a beeline to the nearest weapons chest, and began digging for equipment.

Bailey began to ask something that lingered heavily on all their minds. How long would they wait? And for what, exactly?

Then, that sound again.

Only this time the sat-phone ringtone only cycled once before ending. Price excavated it from his pouch, and was about to dial Calder when the phone chirped. The screen lit up and a series of periods, dashes, and backslashes rolled out. Price's weathered brow furrowed.

"Morse," he said.

Nil got up so fast that his chair toppled behind him. He barely noticed, and then stood over Price's shoulder. He pointed at the phone, his mouth moving but no words coming out.

"What are the slashes for?" Bailey asked.

"Separates the words," Price said. "My Morse isn't as great as it used to be, sadly. Don't keep us in the dark, Nilsson."

"It's a, uh…it's a long message."

"Have at it," Price said, handing Nil the phone and scooting away.

Reva entered the kitchen, tore a piece of paper off a pad on the counter, and returned to the card table. She slapped a pen down on top of it. Nil gulped, thanked her quietly, and put it to use. His brain, too.

"Something bigger," Bailey thought out loud. "That's what Calder said, on her last call. That *something bigger* was coming. They must have detected it somehow, or maybe that video was 'old.' UK-time, or something."

"Possibly," Price said, suddenly feeling devoid of answers and hating it.

"My voice is shit right now," Nil said, setting the pen down. He slid the paper toward Price, who sighed and accepted it.

His expression wasn't indifferent to what he read, before opening his mouth to dictate. And then he looked at Nil, tacitly asking if he was certain.

"Wish I was wrong," Nil said.

Price stood up, and paced as he spoke clearly.

"Calder of Moyock to all FT personnel on the East

Coast. The world will come to know what FT is, and stands for. They will be angry, but they will also need us. We'll receive support unlike ever before. Let us not squander it."

He rubbed his mouth with his knuckles before continuing.

"The heart of the enemy is heartless, but not lifeless. At 1200 hours a mass exfil is to be conducted outside of major cities, to lead the willing into their world. The cambion threat shall no longer be a mystery to us, but a relic of the past, severed from our world."

Reva was nodding slowly and firmly. Her hands were on the N4, tightening around it so assertively that her skin made a sound on the plastic and steel parts.

"At 1200 hours, we take humanity's biggest step toward war, and change, for the better. Meet me on the other side. Crush this evil together. As one. Over and out."

A few long seconds passed.

Reva looked at an analog clock on the wall. It was almost ten in the morning. She marched past Laszlo, into the kitchen again.

She began digging through cabinets, distracting the others just as Nil started to muster the wits to say something. And then she slammed a plastic cooking timer onto the counter, and cranked it to the necessary time.

"We have two hours," she said. "Make your decision in that time, do whatever you must. With or without you, I'm going. Say one word, one goddamn word about not doing it, about John, and I'll rip out your fucking heart."

Not a soul made a sound.

Until Nil stood. "I need a shower before this," he said. "And maybe puke a bit."

"Let me know when you're finished," Laszlo said. Then he gave Reva a silent, compassionate nod. When he reached Bailey, she was crying. She wanted to go, she pled the heavens to let her heal enough to stand with them. But knew she could not; the wound was too dire, and although they had since tended to it well, it wouldn't survive movement for at least another twenty hours.

Certainly not two.

"This is a *Forked Tongue* safe house," Price told her. "It will not stay this empty for long. We are few, but we are *not* alone. Nor will you be."

It was his best way of saying she would be left behind while he and the other three joined Reva in what was undeniably a suicide op.

If the odds were any greater in their favor, it somehow wouldn't make sense to go.

"My birth name means 'the light of my life' in Armenian," Reva announced. "Which I've always distanced myself from. Except with John. Now that he's gone, and I know he isn't gone completely, but now that he's been stolen from me, on this plane, anyway…"

She realized she was rambling. So much for an effective speech.

An awkward chuckle paved the way for progress. She liked to believe it was, in part, John's doing.

"There is no light," she said, her smile visibly wavering. "And there will be no light, until the cambions are vanquished from our home. Which renders my life

301

forfeit, and there's no better purpose I have than to serve the people of this planet, and *their* families."

Despite the compassion and sentiment in her statement, there was something else brewing directly beneath the surface. Something arguably omnipotent.

Arevalous Bakhara channeled anger that existed on a plane untapped by most humans. Only victims of grave tragedies knew of this rage. There was more, though. Pulsing in her veins, eager to be unleashed—a devotion that transcended Forked Tongue, even love.

Reva, Nil, Price, and Laszlo shall return in
Forked Tongue: Vile Realm